INSIGHT

SANTINO HASSELL

RIPTIDE
PUBLISHING

Riptide Publishing
PO Box 1537
Burnsville, NC 28714
www.riptidepublishing.com

Insight

Cover art: Kanaxa, kanaxa.com
Editor: Sarah Lyons
Layout: L.C. Chase, lcchase.com/design.htm

ISBN: 978-1-62649-506-7

First edition
March, 2017

Also available in ebook:
ISBN: 978-1-62649-505-0

INSIGHT

THE COMMUNITY: BOOK I

SANTINO HASSELL

RIPTIDE PUBLISHING

For everyone feeling like the underdog. We'll win. And we'll get our happily ever afters.

TABLE OF
CONTENTS

CHAPTER ONE

Two weeks ago, someone had stolen Nate's car. The yellow '89 Corrado had been his only prized possession, and one night it had vanished from the parking lot of his apartment complex.

Cops in Brookside had never liked him or his family, so he'd taken the blow in silence and started going by foot. It wouldn't have been so bad if his job wasn't five miles away, or if the walk didn't require him to travel deserted stretches of road that heightened his already overactive paranoia. But he had no choice.

His two options had been limited to quitting his job and finally being evicted from his apartment, or walking to the liquor store in the middle of a Texas summer.

He chose to walk.

The first time Nate had shown up late and stinking of sweat, his boss had asked why he didn't just buy another car. What a joke. That old beater had been one of the only things his mother had left behind, and he didn't exactly have the credit needed to waltz into a car dealership and obtain a loan.

So, he walked and hoped no one would notice him on the side of the road. It'd been a few years since anyone had kicked his ass just for the hell of it, but being the pariah of Brookside was something that stuck with a guy.

Nate shot paranoid glances over his shoulder when he wasn't keeping his head down and his strides long, and tried not to think about how hot it was. It was the kind of heat that made things hazy, the air shimmering as his tread kicked up explosions of dust. It had bleached his hair an even paler blond and baked his normally fair skin to farmer's tan brown after the burnt layers had peeled away.

Now, he'd wrapped a shirt around the top of his head, was squinting behind sunglasses, and tried to ignore the beads of sweat that rolled down his nose and salted his parted lips.

Shade would have been nice, but his walk took him through slowly developing strips of land with nothing around but fields and distant trees. Despite the heat, being surrounded by nothing was a welcome reprieve from the thoughts and feelings constantly flooding into his brain when he was near other people. Open space was a natural barrier when he could barely summon the mental shields needed to block out impressions.

Nate stopped walking and shifted his backpack to one shoulder to grab his remaining water bottle, but a red pickup pulled up alongside the edge of the field before he had the bottle in his hand.

Fear swept in with a predator's speed. Nate shut the bag, yanked it onto both shoulders, and began walking again. His long legs drew him away from the vehicle that sat idling only a couple of yards away.

"Nathaniel, what the hell are you doing out here?"

Nate's shoulders relaxed. He squinted into the blazing sunlight to get a better look at the driver. A familiar figure, towheaded and possessing the same lanky build as every male in the Black family, filled the passenger's window. His uncle, Dade, leaned out.

"The hell you doing out here, son?" Dade repeated. His hair was everywhere, nearly obscuring the large aviator glasses he wore.

"Walking," Nate said. He approached the truck and shoved the lingering traces of anxiety aside. "To work."

"Why?"

"My car got stolen."

Dade stared at him before pushing the door open with a creak. He slid back to the driver's seat. All of the windows were open, and classic rock floated gently from ancient speakers. It was as hot inside as it had been on the road, and Nate hissed when his bare legs pressed against the seat.

"No AC?"

Dade twisted the wheel with one hand, settling the other on a large plastic cup that was precariously wedged into the cupholder. The Buc-ee's logo on the cup had long since faded, and the lid was missing, although a chewed-up straw stuck out.

"It broke, and your old auntie ain't about to give me money to fix it."

Nate rolled his eyes and unwrapped the T-shirt from his head. His hair was a damp mess beneath, twisted into snarls and clumps. "Thanks for the ride."

Dade smiled, easy and slow, with the sun brightening his expression even more when golden swaths of light fell across his face. "It's nice to be able to help for a change. I thought you were going to run off at first."

"Ah . . . Well, you know how people in this part of town are about me."

"Unfortunately, I do." Dade's face hardened. "Where am I taking you, son?"

"The Liquor World a few minutes down the road from Broadway and Dixie Farm." Nate glanced at his uncle from the corner of his eye. "I know you know it. You used to take us there before church every Sunday after my mom died. Until Theo ratted you out and Aunt Eveline reamed you for letting me try your special holy water."

Peals of laughter filled the car, boisterous and delighted. Dade slammed a hand against Nate's shoulder, digging his fingers in for a squeeze before he pulled away. The brief moment of contact was more than enough for Nate to feel the vibes emanating from Dade—pure intoxicated joy. It made Nate want to reach out more, feel more, so his uncle's infectious good mood could influence him a little. Instead, he just smiled faintly.

"She said you made our family look like a bunch of degenerates."

"Our family is a bunch of fucking degenerates," Dade said through his quieting chuckles. "My big sister just needs to accept that." He jerked a thumb at his enormous cup. "Drunks and lunatics. That's what the Black family has always been known for."

"And suicide."

Dade's smile dried up. He grabbed the cup, and Nate got a good whiff of liquor when Dade brought the straw to his mouth. "That too."

Nate turned his attention to the window. Talking to people had never been his strong suit, but killing a good mood certainly was.

"So, Nate, how the hell are you?" Dade asked when the silence stretched between them, vast and awkward. "Since you and your brother left the estate, I barely see you. No one knows where the hell Theo is now, but you're still in Texas at least."

"I'm barely here." Nate thudded his head against the seat. "I haven't figured out if there's a point to my existence yet."

"Don't say that."

"Why not? It's true. What the hell am I doing besides walking two hours to go to a shit job and then watching porn on my off days instead of looking for a new apartment since I'm getting kicked out of mine? Nothing. It's worthless."

Nate knew he was being dramatic, but it was hard not to be when his days were as rote as a kindergartener practicing penmanship. He did the same things all the time, and he did them alone. No friends, no lovers, no men who were interested in him besides the guys he sometimes chatted with online and chickened out of meeting in person. Even the ones who were just as anxious and introverted as him. When it came down to it, touching other people was too stressful when he barely had a handle on his "gift." And the few times he'd tried to meet someone . . . had not ended well.

"Heh." Dade shoved his sunglasses up to perch on his forehead. There were dark circles lining his pale-gray eyes, and his once-handsome face was haggard. "Now you sound like a real grown-up member of the Black family. Gifted, powerful, and completely fucking disappointed with life. Welcome to the fold, son."

The drive should not have taken more than fifteen minutes, but traffic kept them stalled in a sea of cars. They were the only ones with the windows rolled down, and Dade cranked his music up in response, AC/DC and Pink Floyd threatening to blow the tinny speakers in his ancient truck. Once they pulled in to the parking lot, Nate told his uncle to wait. He jogged in, purchased a bottle of Wild Turkey, and returned to the truck.

The look of surprise on Dade's face threatened to turn the moment into something uncomfortably emotional. His eyes went round as if no one had ever done him such a kindness, but then he only gave a short nod and told Nate he was a champ.

It was a good start to the shift.

The job still sucked though.

He put on his name tag and traded spots with the other cashier. It was a small staff for a small store, so he was left alone once the old man—a retired roughneck who now worked the counter part-time—left for the day. As dull as the gig was, he preferred doing it alone.

Nate was almost certain that life would be easier if he gave up "honest work" for a life of crime. Or prostitution. Or followed the bad examples of a few Black family members, and did something corny like open a psychic stand or tarot shop in Houston—use his barely functioning gift to rip off hopeful strangers.

He'd briefly worked at a bong and fetish shop before accepting the clerk position at Liquor World. At the time, it had seemed like a step-up. Working in retail was bleak and mind-numbing, but at least he'd progressed from the land of bongs and adult novelties to kegs and economy-sized bottles of Jim Beam.

He'd convinced himself it would look better on his résumé, and he had to remind himself of that repeatedly. It had become a mantra by the time he'd reached the four-week mark at the liquor store and come to terms with the fact that all jobs were awful.

It wasn't because the stock room was a nightmare, or that his coworkers were Texas good ole boys who'd looked at him like he was from outer space the first time he'd walked in wearing a J-Rock T-shirt while carrying a six-hundred-page book. That was surprisingly tolerable.

The job was a nightmare because eighty percent of the clientele consisted of his former high school classmates.

The frequent reunions with his graduating class generally led to one of three things: awkward silence, uneasiness, or a resumption of the hostility that had not faded with time.

Faggot. White trash. Freak.

All true, especially the last.

With his good mood blown and no one in the store, Nate set up shop with a book. It was slower than usual, and he enjoyed a solid hour of losing himself in the words of a queer paranormal novel before the bell on the door jingled to indicate the entrance of an unwelcome customer.

His gaze was fixed on the book in front of him, and he didn't plan on giving anyone his attention until he'd finished the page. He kept one of his earbuds in, a decade-old X Japan song blaring loud enough to be heard clear across the store.

The bell jingled again to signal a second customer, and this one approached the counter after only a moment of walking the store. Nate sighed. He tried to make himself appear welcoming and not thoroughly disgruntled, but probably only managed a blank look of surprise when he found himself face-to-face with Eric Flynn, a former football player at Nate's old high school, and one of the people who'd spent years making his life hell.

Nate's mouth went dry.

Eric plopped his stuff on the counter—two bottles of Johnnie Walker. Nate grabbed the scanner and aimed it at the barcode on one of the bottles.

"How's life, finger cuff?"

Nate's grip tightened on the scanner. "That joke stopped being funny the moment I realized that you people stole it from a Kevin Smith movie."

Eric put his forearms on the counter and leaned forward. "It always gave me a laugh."

"Right." Nate clicked the scanner repeatedly but it failed to beep. "Do you mind?"

"Mind what?"

"Backing up." The scanner beeped.

Eric shifted closer. "What's up with you these days?"

Nate tilted the second bottle as he aimed the scanner at it. The repeated clicks got steadily more aggressive until it beeped again. "Nothing."

"Hmm." Eric's eyes flicked down to Nate's phone, then at the cover of the book he'd been reading, and returned to his face. They remained there for a moment, not shifting to the total that flashed on the register.

Nate nodded at the numbers pointedly, and Eric pulled a card from his wallet. He slid it across the pockmarked counter before resuming his slouch.

"How've you been?"

There was a silence as Nate waited for the next punch line. It didn't come. He glanced at the door, half expecting some of Eric's old friends to appear.

"Why do you ask?"

"Why wouldn't I ask?"

"Well . . ." Nate swiped the card. "I'm working here, so clearly I've gone far in life."

"Ha. I'm apprenticing at my dad's plumbing company, so I'm not over the moon about my status either."

"Guess those big NFL plans didn't pan out after you signed with Baylor."

"I got kicked out." Eric rested his chin against his fist without explaining why. Considering how protected football players were by universities, he must have done something awful. "You look good, Nathaniel. Not as scrawny as you used to be. Finally got your weight up?"

Nate glanced at the clock, the printer, the old guy loitering outside of the entrance. He looked anywhere but at Eric and the lack of distance between them. The last time they'd been this close it had led to a beatdown in an abandoned subdivision—an incident forever memorialized by a jagged scar that bisected Nate's left eyebrow.

"Some."

Eric was still leaning on the counter, looking like he belonged there—like a big, lazy, ginger cat. He reached out and pressed the pad of his index finger against Nate's biceps. "I didn't mind you skinny, though."

Nate took an automatic step back. He started shoving the bottles into a large paper bag. The only sound in the store was the crinkling of the bag, the clanking of the bottles, and the low hum of the air conditioner. The television was almost always on when the others were at work, but Nate was working this shift solo and couldn't stand the low warble of the news.

"I was just thinking about you the other day."

"Why's that?"

"C'mon, Nate. Don't pretend you don't ever think about that night."

"The night you and your friends beat the shit out of me in the field?" The memory came back to Nate like lightning striking. Being held down and punched over and over in the pouring rain until everything had gone dark. Waking up hours later on the side of the road. "Or the days I spent in the hospital after?"

"You're so fucking dramatic. But you know I'm sorry for that shit. It was childish."

"Childish . . ."

There was so much more to say. So many ways Nate could emasculate this big piece of shit now that he was older and smarter and knew how to use words as weapons. But he didn't—couldn't— because he'd never forgotten waking up on the side of the road covered in blood.

Nate nervously wet his lips, and Eric's gaze followed the motion.

"It's kinda stupid when I think back to high school," he continued. "How mad Kelvin was, saying you'd tricked him into fucking you the first time, and how we gave you so much shit for being gay, but then we both did you again as soon as you gave us a cue."

Words were nothing. Words were harmless. They didn't compare to fists and kicks. Nothing compared to physical pain. Nate had known that since high school, since being jumped multiple times, since bloodied noses and the clatter of lockers every time they'd slammed his face into one. But knowing that didn't stop the anger. Or the desire to tell the truth.

It wasn't Nate who'd given them a cue. It wasn't Nate they'd taken turns on.

"This is sort of a weird-ass convo for a liquor store, don't you think?"

Nate's stare jerked over Eric's shoulder to see a really hot dark-haired guy watching them. His warm blue eyes were cut sideways at Eric, and his mouth was twisted down. Nate had almost forgotten there was another customer in the store.

"Oh. Hi." Smooth, Black. "Sorry. My stalker was just leaving."

Eric glared. "Seriously, Nate?"

"Seriously, Eric. Get the fuck out and let me do my job."

Eric looked like he wanted to argue, but he glanced over his shoulder to take stock of the newcomer and seemed to think better of it. They were the same height, but while Eric was brawnier, the stranger seemed . . . tougher. Maybe the way he held himself, the curl of his lips as he stared Eric down, or the fact that he clearly wasn't intimidated. At all. Which usually meant a person could hold their own.

"Come on, bro. You're slowing me down."

Eric sneered but kept his mouth shut through the rest of the transaction. It was only when he grabbed his bag, and their fingertips brushed, did his animosity seep into Nate through the mental channel he couldn't close no matter how hard he tried. The vibes were so strong it roiled Nate's stomach. He jerked his hand away, shuddering and cursing himself for not knowing how to control his own gift.

"Bye now, Eric."

"Fuck you, fag."

Nate said nothing and watched his tormenter storm out of the store. The stranger approached the counter and thumped down two bottles of white wine. Usually Nate could peg people's drinking preferences based on their appearances, so he was surprised that this tall, broad man with the l33t-speak gamer T-shirt was planning to spend his Sunday night with two bottles of sauvignon blanc.

"Want me to kick his ass?"

A startled bark of a laugh escaped Nate. "No, that's okay."

"You sure? I like knocking around rednecks."

"You do it a lot?"

"Mmm." The guy made a seesaw motion with his hand. "I don't usually get the chance, but I enjoy it when it happens."

"You should get a new hobby."

"Like listening to Dir en Grey?"

Surprised, Nate looked down at his own T-shirt. "You know who Dir en Grey is?"

"Sure. I saw them play when they came to New York a few years ago."

"Oh."

So that explained the accent. Nate tried to think of something else to say, maybe something about the Big Apple, but failed. He didn't even know why he wanted to keep this conversation going. Maybe because the guy had pretty eyes and a cute smile, or maybe . . . because he was exuding vibes that felt like sunshine on a beach. Nate had never felt anything like it. Usually he had to touch someone to get an impression, but this guy was like a beacon of warmth.

Dropping his eyes, Nate grabbed the first bottle and scanned it. "That's a good book too."

"You read paranormal romance?"

"Uh-huh." He was starting to look amused. "Why are you so surprised?"

Because it was about gay psychics. He'd picked it out for purely narcissistic reasons, but it was well-written and kind of nice to read about people like him even if they were fake. And even if their powers were awesome and his was pathetically useless.

"It's not exactly mainstream," Nate said finally. "So most people don't know about it."

"Guess I'm cooler than most people."

"Maybe."

Nate finished scanning and bagging the bottles. He mumbled out a request for the guy's credit card and ID, and tried to ignore the increased warmth flooding into him when their fingers grazed while passing the cards. It was rare to get good vibes from strangers. Often they were annoyed, impatient, angry, or anxious. For whatever reason, customers rarely gave off feelings that were healthy to absorb. It was part of what made this job so inconvenient. But this guy? Trenton Castille according to his ID? Nate felt nothing from him but curiosity, humor, and the buoyancy of a good mood. It was addictive. It made Nate want to touch him again so he could absorb more. Suck it in and make it his own. The very idea caught him off guard.

"Have a nice day, Nate." Trenton grabbed the bag and flashed another cute smile. "If that dude's still in the parking lot, I'm totally kicking his ass."

If Eric was still in the parking lot, Nate was screwed.

"Thanks for trying to defend my honor."

"No prob."

Trenton looked at him a moment longer, then tapped his knuckles on the counter before walking out of the store. As soon as the bell rang to signal his exit, loss slammed into Nate. He didn't know anything about Trenton except for the fact that he'd completely overshadowed Eric's negative vibes. It was an oddity, and the first time Nate had ever benefitted from his empath talent. Normally he had more interest in shutting people out than inviting them in.

Flipping the counter up, he walked to the other side and hoped no other familiar faces showed up before the end of his shift. The idea of running into any one else from high school, or Eric coming back again with his overpowering feelings of loathing, made Nate want to vomit. Or break down and finally get someone in his family to teach him how to stop being a third-rate psychic.

Growing up, Nate's mother had kept him and his twin brother away from the rest of the Blacks. It wasn't until she'd vanished, and they'd been taken in by her brother and sister, had Nate realized the strange phenomena he and his twin shared—feeling emotions that didn't belong to them, and Theo's intuitiveness that went far beyond good instincts—weren't unique to them, but were hereditary. It should have been exciting to learn they not only shared these traits with their family, but that their family was special. For Theo, it had been. But Aunt Eveline had had little interest in Nate's piddly empath abilities, and her obsession with Theo becoming a powerful multitalented psychic had made Nate uncomfortable. Especially since that was what had started changing Theo into a manipulative asshole.

But now Nate was in his twenties and slowly being driven to reclusiveness by his inability to block the impressions he absorbed from others. Maybe it was time for things to change.

Maybe.

Nate popped in his second earbud and began facing the store. At the end of the first aisle, he reached for a toppled Captain Morgan display, but a wave of vertigo hit him. He threw out a hand to catch his balance and knocked over several bottles, sending them crashing to the floor. The sound of breaking glass filled the store and pain blazed up in an arc from his hand.

The spinning sensation intensified and the store swam around him as color drained from his vision. Time slowed, and his surroundings darkened further before winking out of existence entirely.

He knew he was blacking out, and he knew, somehow, that it wasn't natural.

Nate's knees weakened, and he felt himself falling. The darkness swallowed him, but only for a second. When it ended, and his eyes opened, his confusion and alarm turned into terror.

The liquor store was gone. Everything was gone.

He was outside and standing in the middle of a road. Above him was a night sky with no stars. Across the road, a murky body of water stretched out to distant, twinkling lights. To his left were concrete piers, and a mammoth gray ship was anchored further down. The air was cool, much cooler than the humid Texas climate would allow in June, and a sharp wind cut through his clothes.

He realized then that he wasn't just standing on a road—it was a wide highway. The lanes were split by a broad, granite divider and dozens of cars rushed past on the opposite side. The breeze gusted again, briny and damp, stinging his eyes. Narrowing them against the wind, Nate looked around in awe. When he half turned to see over his shoulder, he shouted in alarm.

Headlights assaulted his vision, and Nate leaped out of the way. The side of the vehicle brushed his side, and he fell, knees slamming against the blacktop and teeth clicking together from the impact. With his palms pressed flat against the ground and breath coming in violent bursts, Nate looked up and around.

What the hell was happening?

Across the highway and beyond the squat buildings were enormous high-rises. They shot up into the starless sky, towering sentinels that dominated a place that was nothing like Brookside or Houston; nowhere Nate had never been to. Even so, there was something familiar about it . . .

Forcing himself to his feet, Nate rubbed his stinging hands together. He wanted to wake himself from this dream, but he started walking, destination unknown, through the night. Each footstep echoed in the darkness. It drew his attention downward, and Nate saw that his shorts and Chuck Taylors had been replaced by combat boots and skinny, black pants.

Breath coming faster, Nate started to jog down the sidewalk. When traffic halted beside him, he glanced at the line of cars. The tinted windows of a Dodge Charger showed his reflection clearly, and Nate froze, unable to immediately process what he was seeing.

The customary Black family features—blond hair and steel-gray eyes—were there, but the face, as much as it looked like him, wasn't his. The jawline was identical to his, as were the broad shoulders and lanky build, but where Nate had built up muscle, his reflection was narrow and waifish. It also had much longer hair and lacked his tan and the scar.

It wasn't his face staring back at him. It was Theo's.

He reached out to touch his reflection just as a voice shouted in his head: *Run.*

Adrenaline jolted through his veins, but before Nate could move, the world blinked again.

CHAPTER TWO

I t took two days to learn that Theo was dead.

The official cause of death was listed as suicide by drowning.

It took another two days for Nate to emerge from the stunned shroud of his grief and realize he didn't buy it. During that time, Aunt Eveline had taken complete control of the funeral preparations. Nate didn't protest. He was too raw and on edge to make decisions about caskets or the burial. Sleepless nights were spent replaying the vision over and over again. Every time his eyes drifted shut, he heard that unfamiliar male voice in his head: *Run.*

And when he tried to function during the day, he was swamped by guilt because he'd alienated his own twin for years. Nate hadn't even known Theo had wound up in New York.

Well, he hadn't known before the vision.

Even now, as he sat in a pew with the priest droning on about Theo "going home to God," memory of the vision sent a chill down Nate's spine. His stomach roiled, and he shot to his feet. He'd never been good with churches, and now, the saturation of human emotion bleeding into him compounded with the reality of Theo's death. The situation magnified until Nate felt like the din of misery would choke him. The pain of nearly three dozen people crept up his throat and formed a lump, preventing him from swallowing. From breathing. Chest tight and his eyes wide, Nate tried to block everything out, but found that it was impossible when all he could do was visualize his twin's thin body beneath the sleek metal casket.

Nate lurched out of his pew, his battered, monochrome Chuck Taylors squeaking loudly against the floor, and staggered toward the bathroom.

"That kid is a goddamn disaster," someone muttered.

Nate ignored the comment, but he could feel his family staring. They'd been watching and waiting since the moment he'd walked numbly into the church and stood beside the coffin. The sick feeling had started as soon as he looked down to see the face identical to his own, slack with death and frozen in time.

The door to the bathroom slammed against the opposite wall when he burst inside, choking on the bile that surged up his throat. There was somebody washing their hands, but he only caught a glimpse of silver hair before he threw himself to the floor in front of a toilet. Not bothering to kick shut the door to the cubicle, he gagged violently, but only brought up stomach acids since he hadn't eaten in days.

Tears welled in his eyes, streaming down his face as the heaves rocked his entire body. By the time it was over, he was so worn out, he stumbled getting to his feet. Breathing hard, he turned and found Eveline standing by the sink.

"Sorry," Nate rasped, leaving the stall. "Wrong bathroom. Didn't notice."

He inched by her, careful not to touch, and twisted the faucet on with shaking hands. He scrubbed them clean before dipping his head down to rinse his mouth, gargling as she watched him with flinty eyes. Nate's gaze quickly shifted away, and he splashed water across his overheated skin. It didn't help. He was still feverish and half-delirious with lack of sleep.

"Are you on drugs?"

Nate's spine straightened, and he looked at her through the mirror. Eveline was wraithlike behind him, her iron eyes piercing and undoubtedly judging. She loomed over him, blond hair gone silver with time and hanging well past her shoulders to contrast with a black maxi dress.

"No," he said, voice still hoarse. "I haven't slept. Nightmares."

She said nothing, and the hard lines of her face did not soften. She was only a decade older than Dade, older than Nate's mother had been, but the severity of her expression made her seem far beyond her early fifties.

"Pull yourself together and get back inside. Your uncle is already drunk."

Nate just stared, nonplussed.

"Sit with him and keep him in line."

"I'm not—"

"You will."

The words bounced off the tile walls. Her gaze darkened like a coming storm, but when he didn't refuse, she nodded. As she turned away, the large cross she wore glinted beneath the flickering fluorescent lights as she left the bathroom.

Nate waited for a full two minutes before he did the same. He slipped into the pew next to Dade. He didn't pull away when the older man laid a hesitant hand on his arm. They sat together, and Nate closed his eyes, latching on to Dade's energy and focusing on an alien sentiment that he barely recognized as compassion. He tried not to puzzle out the underlying prickles of his uncle's own guilt.

When the service and burial were over, he rode in a black town car with Dade and Eveline. For most of the ride, nobody spoke. The reek of alcohol and cigarette smoke rolled off Dade, and Eveline regarded her younger brother with near palpable disgust. When her attention wasn't pinned on him, it shifted to Nate. He turned away and stared out the window, trying not to think about his twin's body being lowered into the ground.

The driver was leaving Houston, where Theo had been buried in the family plot, in order to return to the Black estate in Brookside Village. The urban sprawl of subdivisions and shopping centers gave way to ranch-style homes on large lots, narrow roads, and expanses of fields and trees that were no longer found in the nearby suburbs. Nate slumped in his seat, cheap suit jacket wrinkled and his forehead pressed against the window.

He'd lived in Brookside all his life, driven through this same area more times in the past few years than he could count, but had never been hit with the nostalgia that he had right then. He could remember the exact color of the linoleum in the kitchen of the little trailer he'd grown up in, the one their mother had moved into when she'd decided to cut herself off from the family. He and Theo had explored the fields that stretched around Brookside as kids, pretending to be adventurers, ghost hunters, or explorers. They'd discovered abandoned houses and discarded items that were only treasured by young children.

Everything had changed when their mother vanished. And everything got worse when they'd been forced to live in the large house with Eveline and Dade. If living on the Black estate had taught him anything, it was that his mother had been right to keep distance between them and the rest of the family. There was something off about them all, especially Eveline. And it had nothing to do with the mutant, psychic genes that ping-ponged through them all, causing varying shades of mental instability, suicidal tendencies, and addiction. Once upon a time, Eveline had possessed the ability to reduce him to tears with nothing more than a nasty look and a sharp tone.

"You coming back with us, Nate?"

Nate started at the sudden question and looked at Dade. He was wilting against the leather seat, his eyelids heavy and shirt partially unbuttoned.

"I should probably go home." Nate turned to Eveline. "I don't want to talk to a bunch of people."

"You mean you don't want to explain why you ignored your brother for the past five years," Eveline said. She lifted a pencil-thin eyebrow. "Right?"

"Eve—"

She cut Dade off with a look. "It's a little late for you to show concern for his welfare. And even so, he doesn't need a drunk to defend him. You've been pathetic since Lorelei died. I assume you'll be even less functional now that Theodore killed himself."

The car jolted on the road, and Nate dug his hands into the underside of the cushion. "Can you pretend to have a soul long enough for me to get out of this goddamn car?"

Dade dropped his eyes as if he didn't want to see the fallout from the comment. Nate glared at him, unable to understand why the family was so terrified of his aunt. Why did Dade, and why had his mother in her youth, allowed Eveline to control them?

"They allow it because I protected them when our own parents were taken—"

"Stay out of my head," Nate said sharply.

"—from the people who wanted to hurt us," Eveline continued. "God blessed this family with the gift of sight, whichever way it has manifested, but every single one of you is too weak to understand how grateful you should be. You're all a disgrace, and soon enough, you will regret it."

Nate wanted to tell her that she was batshit insane, but judging by the glitter of anger in her eyes, she'd already heard him think it. Silence stretched between them until Dade cleared his throat and put a hand on Nate's arm.

"Please come, Nate? The family would love to see you."

"Why?" Nate slumped in the seat again. "Nobody seems to miss me when I'm gone. You're the only one who seeks me out, and we're talking right now."

"That's not true. Jeremy would probably like it if you were there."

Unlikely. Dade's estranged son had identified the Black family as a whole big barrel of instability almost as soon as he'd met them, and had stayed away ever since. But Dade's eyes were so hopeful and pleading that Nate caved. But the repast was just as horrifying as he'd expected.

He rarely saw so much of his family at one time. Sometimes he forgot how many of them there were until they came together, usually for a funeral, and the house overflowed with pale-skinned, gray-eyed, blond psychics. There were only a handful of outsiders present. Most people who had the guts to tie themselves to the family typically did not stick around for long.

Instead of congregating in the great room with the rest, he wandered. Everything in the house was solid, mahogany, and shining, but the shadows were ever-present and made the rooms oppressively dark, even in the middle of the day. Heavy black and gray curtains blocked the windows entirely and forbade any stray ray of light from making its way into the gloom of the house.

He wound up in the bedroom that he and Theo had once shared, looking for the belongings Dade had collected from New York. Nate spotted a patch-covered backpack, but instead of going through it, he approached the window to tug back the heavy curtain and let fresh air into the stuffy room. A strong gust swept in, smelling richly of summer rain. The sky was darkening above trees covered in Spanish moss that drifted down to the ground on the several acres that surrounded the house. The property was filled with a tangle of greenery and a small, dark greenhouse that had been deserted for years. Theo had loved to play inside as a kid, pretending that something sinister was hiding behind the grimy, molded glass. He'd liked the idea of relics of the Black family's eerie history and would camp inside the greenhouse and make up stories about it all. Nate had never been as enthusiastic. It had just made him uneasy.

"Are you okay?"

Nate looked over his shoulder and saw that Dade had slipped into the room. He'd freshened up and changed clothes, although he still smelled faintly of booze. It was like a cologne that clung to his skin, never washing out no matter how he tried.

"I guess." Nate turned back to the window, staring down at the greenhouse.

"Don't let her get to you," Dade said at length. "She's not— She tries to blame us for things. You and me both, for not being there for Theo, but she never was either. She wasn't even there for your mom when things got bad . . ."

"So why the hell do you let her treat you like she does? Why is everyone so afraid of her? She treats us all like shit. That's why my mother hated her."

Dade winced. "It's complicated, son. She felt betrayed by your mom . . . They never got along. When your grandparents passed, we were real young and Eve took up all the slack. It made her a little . . ."

"Insane?" Nate scoffed quietly. "Yeah, I know the story. They died, she worked hard to raise y'all, and then my mom started acting a fool."

He knew all about his mother's teenage antics. When he'd been a kid, the older folks around town had made it a point to bring up her past, even when Nate and Theo had been with her. Apparently, she'd run away from home on more than one occasion. The only incident he really knew about was her disappearing to New York, then coming back to the inevitable bleakness of Brookside shrouded in a deep depression. She'd given birth to them a year later. No one had speculated about who the father was. No one had seemed to care anymore, including her. Then right after their twelfth birthday, she'd left one more time, in the middle of the night, but this time she never returned.

Dade ran his fingers along the chipped wooden windowsill. "When Lore disappeared, I was angry. Angry that she abandoned you guys, and I was angrier when we realized that she'd probably killed herself. And now I can't help thinking that maybe it's her fault. Maybe that's why Theo killed himself too."

"He didn't."

"Didn't what?"

"It—it wasn't suicide," Nate said, stumbling over the words.

"What are you talking about?"

Dade looked bemused, and Nate instantly regretted saying the words aloud. He didn't want to explain and couldn't have even if he wanted to; he still didn't understand why or how the vision had come to him. According to the death certificate, Theo had drowned the day before Nate had blacked out in the liquor store. He'd never had a vision before, and he had no idea how or why Theo's death had been projected to him.

"Yes, dear, what are you talking about?"

Stiffening, Nate saw that Eve had silently entered the bedroom.

"Never mind."

Eveline glanced at Dade. "Why don't you go find something useful to do?"

"Like what?" Dade queried, eyebrows drawing together and not appearing to catch the hint.

"Like go away so that I can speak to my nephew alone. He doesn't need you to play daddy now."

"Oh." Dade looked more like an uncertain teenager than a fortysomething-year-old man, and after a moment he muttered something and walked away with his face cast toward the floor.

Nate sighed. "Yes?"

"Is that how you speak to me?"

"I guess."

"You should show a little more respect for the person who pays every time someone in your family dies. I could have had him cremated."

"Why didn't you?"

Eveline's words rolled off her tongue as easily as if she were talking about the weather. "Even if he was a troublemaker, I didn't despise the boy. It's a shame he decided to follow his mother's example instead of making something of his talents."

Nate clenched his teeth and turned to the window. He glared at the steadily darkening sky.

"Oh, but I forget, you don't think your brother killed himself." Eve moved closer. "And why would that be, darling?"

"It doesn't really matter what I think. My theories don't change anything."

"They don't." When he didn't elaborate, her face lapsed into an expression of suspicion. Surprisingly, she dropped the topic and stood side by side with Nate, both of them watching as fat raindrops fell from the sky.

After a moment of tense silence, Nate started to turn and head for the door, but Eve grabbed his arms, pointy fingernails digging in.

"I didn't come in here just to antagonize you."

"Shocking."

Eve's thin lips lifted into an ugly smile. Dade always said she'd once been as lovely and spirited as Nate's mother had been. Now she was cruel and cragged, frown lines deepened with time and bitterness. Every smile and look was full of poison.

"Your living arrangements will be changing soon."

"What?"

"I've already spoken to the manager at your apartment complex. I wanted to check on your situation, to see if you truly couldn't help with the funeral arrangements. I found out that you are being evicted, and I've also come to learn that you were fired last week. I thought you were the responsible one."

Nate didn't deny her claims. He'd closed the store early, without cleaning up or asking permission, the night he'd had the vision. His boss had called repeatedly in the past week, but after learning of Theo's death, the desire to answer questions or make excuses for himself had vanished completely. "Can you just leave me alone? I don't have the energy to fight."

"There's nothing to fight about. Sadly, you are the only remnant of your immediate family. But fortunately, you are the most sensible one even if you're the least talented. So," she said, jabbing at him with one clawlike fingernail. "You will become a functioning member of this family, stop working dead-end jobs, and stop spending your days on the internet. And you'll move here. You have nowhere else to go, anyway."

If his insides hadn't felt like they were being ripped and turned inside out, Nate might have laughed. He didn't even want to know how she was aware of his pathetic attempts to find connections online. He didn't want to know how closely she'd kept track of him over the years. Or why.

"First, I'm not moving here. Second, you don't even like me, so why would you want me to?"

"I don't have to like you, child," she said. "You are part of this family, and right now, we need to do all we can to keep it together and become strong again."

They stared at each other, her intense, him stone-faced and unwilling to share the vision or any of his suspicions about Theo's death. He didn't know what she was trying to imply, and frankly, didn't want to figure it out. In the past, he and Theo had talked about Eveline's persistent fears, but neither of them had been able to figure out if their aunt was justifiably uneasy about the rash of disappearances and deaths that plagued their family, or if she was succumbing to paranoia. Whatever the case was, he remained silent. He was uneasy enough without her making it worse.

Eventually, when he didn't argue, she inclined her head and turned away. Her hair fell over one shoulder, the silvery mass reaching her hips. After she was gone, the tension bled out of his frame. He sank to the floor next to Theo's bag. It was a faded backpack covered with band logos and buttons, the same backpack that Theo had used in high school. He stared at it, at the tattered fabric, worn from years of abuse and travel, before finally reaching over to go through what remained of his twin.

Dade had not bothered to fold any of the clothing before stuffing them in the backpack. Wrinkled shirts with metal accents were stuffed inside along with balled-up jeans and too-big sweaters. Everything was shades of black and gray, and when Nate picked up a threadbare plaid shirt, he realized that some of the clothing still smelled like his brother.

He dropped the shirt as if it burned and began going through the other pockets. He felt around gingerly, almost afraid of what he would find, but the only item of note was a moleskin notebook tied shut with a leather thong.

Nate unwrapped it and gazed at the nearly illegible scrawl of Theo's handwriting and the more intricate drawings that danced along the inside cover and margins. He handled it gently, turning the pages as if they might crumble to dust in his hands.

Theo had kept the same journal since middle school, a detailed record of all the impossible things that had flashed behind his eyelids during the night. While Nate had been gifted only with empathy, Theo had been a talented empath and had also received premonitions via his dreams. He'd documented them dutifully over the years, hoping they'd someday make sense.

The journal was full of obscure lines and mere fragments of thoughts, as well as long pages of text that could have been full-length novellas or essays. None of it made sense without context, but Nate's heart skipped a beat when he reached the halfway point.

lore chase to new york

The page was torn so the rest of the words were cut off, but it had been written almost ten years ago. Had Theo seen himself going to New York, chasing whatever their mother had been chasing?

Nate sagged against the wall with both knees drawn up. When his eyes closed, he saw Theo's reflection in the window of that Charger. He saw the gaunt cheeks, the parted lips, and shadowed eyes. The image had haunted him for the past week, and Nate knew it would continue to haunt him until he found out what had happened to his brother.

The silence around him was unnatural. All he could hear was the thick soles of his own boots pounding against the ground, and a muffled rush of water slamming against the pier. Everything else was muted, still.

An invisible force propelled him forward, one foot in front of the other, long, steady strides as he grew closer to his destination.

He moved automatically, something slithery cold sweeping across his mind. It was foreign and frightening, but he had to keep going. He continued even when a phantom voice said in his mind: *Run!*

The room was dark when Nate opened his eyes. It took a minute to recognize the rug, the shape of the furniture, and the drapes that hung nearly to the floor. He'd fallen asleep in his old bedroom at the Black mansion, and judging by the darkness in the room, no one had come to wake him after the repast had ended.

Nate ran his tongue over too-dry lips and forced himself to stand. An ache intensified in his head, as well as the throbbing in his injured hand, which sent shocks of pain radiating up his arm. He pressed his good hand against it with a wince. The pain helped to pull him out of the vision. He'd spent the past week learning to differentiate between dream and vision and still grew confused sometimes. What he did know for certain was that he was somehow watching Theo's final moments.

His eyes adjusted to the darkness as he left the room. The hallway was much less stifling, and he inhaled shakily, glad for the cool air against his sweaty skin. He wiped a hand across his face and then through his hair, tired and hurting, and wanting nothing more than to be gone from the mansion. He would walk home if he had to.

A clatter drew his attention, and Nate tensed before realizing it had come from Dade's bedroom. Relieved that he wouldn't have to face Eveline, he moved down the hall. The door was ajar, the dim glow of a lamp casting a swath of light through the darkness. Inside, Dade was shirtless, outgrown blond hair hanging around his face. He was cross-legged on the hardwood floor with the bottle of Wild Turkey more than halfway empty sitting nearby. He had a photo album open on his lap, and he was hunched over it, expression etched with pain.

"Why'd you let me sleep so long?"

Dade jumped, nearly dropping the book. "What the hell are you doing here?"

"I'm leaving. I just wanted to tell you that I'm taking Theo's stuff."

"Oh." Dade looked slightly lost. He was glassy-eyed and his face was flushed. He shook his head as if trying to clear it. "Yeah. Yeah, of course. You need a ride?"

Nate didn't bother to point out that Dade was drunk. "I'll just walk."

"No." Dade stood unsteadily, and the book he'd been holding fell shut on the bed. "No, just stay here. It's dark out and these kids drag race at night."

"I'll be fine."

"No!" This time, the words came out stronger, and Dade's expression turned fierce. "Please, Nate. Just stay for me. I'll drive you back first thing."

Nate wanted to argue, but Dade looked so desperate that he swallowed the protests. "As soon as you sober up, I want to get out of here. Or as soon as it gets light. Whatever comes first."

"Of course. I don't blame you." Dade's words were slurred, but he wasn't totally out of it. He seemed more exhausted than anything else. "If I could get out of here, I would."

"Why can't you?"

Dade shrugged, a thin hand gesturing without real meaning. In that moment, more than any other, he seemed the most like a husk of the handsome young man Nate had only seen in pictures.

"If you moved out, you'd probably be less miserable. And drink less."

"Nah, kiddo. I don't drink 'cause of the misery. I drink 'cause I can't sleep. I've had insomnia since I was thirteen—after my first premonition. My body's way of fighting off the visions."

"You don't like having them?"

"Fuck no. Who wants to see shit like that?"

Dade didn't explain what *that* had been, and the haunted look on his face made it seem like a bad idea to ask. Especially if he'd been fighting sleep for three decades in response. But beyond that, it struck Nate that he wasn't the only one who didn't appreciate his talents. He wasn't the only freak among freaks.

"So, are you staying?"

Nate nodded and Dade's shoulders relaxed. He mumbled something about getting Nate some blankets for the other room and shuffled out, his shoulder brushing Nate's when he moved past. A pained ache blossomed in Nate's chest, and he picked up the book to distract himself, but the ache only worsened when he looked inside.

It was a photo album full of pictures of his mother—young and fair-haired, beautiful and smiling. She didn't look much older than fourteen in some of the pictures, and he could practically see the happiness draining from her face as he flipped pages and the pictures of her grew more recent. It wasn't until Nate had gotten through most of the book did he realize that something was off about it all.

He turned back, the plastic-covered Polaroids crinkling beneath his touch, and realized the entire album was dedicated to his mother. Not only that, but many of the more recent photos—when she couldn't have been more than thirty—were candid. Taken well after she'd cut off ties with both Dade and Eveline. In the pictures, she was sitting at a distance from the camera in the woods, sunbathing or sleeping.

Nate's gut clenched, and he didn't shut the book when Dade returned.

"What the hell is this?"

Dade froze.

"What are all these creepy pictures of my mother?"

Dade's mouth moved, but he didn't say anything. He didn't have to—the guilt on his face made it clear that the sinking feeling in Nate's stomach was much more than a suspicion. He dropped the photo album and stalked across the room. Before his uncle could react, Nate pressed his hands against Dade's face.

The blanket Dade'd been holding fell to the floor, and Nate reached out instinctively with a gift that he normally could barely control, driven by the need to know just how bad all of this was.

The images that he pulled from Dade's mind were as clear as Nate's own memories.

Lorelei, weeping bitterly into Dade's chest, and him stroking her hair and whispering in her ear. Nate could hear very few of his words other than, "She's right. We have to. It's just the way it is. Please don't cry."

Eveline, standing over Dade and Lorelei, her eyes blank, her mouth a grim line.

Dade and Lorelei, him still trying to soothe her as he guided her down to a bed.

Nate ripped his hands away and took a step back. "Dade, what the fuck?" His voice rose with each word and shook the way it had when he was young, when Eveline used to terrify him. "What did you do to her?"

Dade's face blanched and fear rolled off him. "I— I—"

"Were you— Did you do something to her? Did you hurt my mother?"

"Nate, I—"

"Tell me!"

"Please, stop, it's not—"

"Tell me, goddamn it!" Nate grabbed Dade again. Rage flared up inside him, licking white-hot, burning him from the inside out. All he could see was his mother's tearful face, Dade's stroking hands, the candid pictures, the empty look in his mother's eyes.

"I didn't hurt her." Dade tried to jerk his hands away, but Nate wouldn't release him no matter how violently the impressions slammed into him. The fear remained, but with it came self-loathing so strong it saturated Nate. "We had to. We had to do it."

"Do *what*?"

Dade shook his head, lips still parted and eyebrows knotted up. "Nate," he said, voice crumbling. He looked adrift in the sea of guilt that was buckling him. "Nate, for God's sake, please. We had to. You don't understand how we grew up. We had no fucking choice. With everything that happened, everything they did to our family, she made it seem like we had no choice. And after what happened to Lore in New York—"

"Who's *they*? What the fuck are you saying to me?"

Breath shuddered from Dade's mouth. "Don't make me say it, kiddo. Please. If you saw it, if you saw us, you know."

The words rang in Nate's ears, made real by Dade's memories and Eveline's earlier words: *"He doesn't need you playing daddy now."*

Anger overtook Nate's senses until his vision darkened at the sides and tunneled with only Dade at the end.

"We had to," he was still saying. "You don't understand what those people could do to us if we weren't strong. Why do you think I stay here?"

None of it made sense. None of it mattered. All Nate could think was that he and Theo were monsters.

"Nate, please—"

"Shut the fuck up!"

Nate bolted forward, fist cocked back, and swung it into Dade's jaw with as much force as he could muster. Dade fell backward, his head cracked against the dresser, and he crumpled in an unmoving heap. There were no more excuses. No more paranoid conspiracy theories and half-truths. There was nothing but silence.

CHAPTER THREE

What if he's my father?

The Wal-Mart loomed above him, made up of blurred lights and a sea of cars even though it was well past midnight on a Thursday night. Nate didn't remember making the decision to walk here, but it had been hours since he'd fled the house with his brother's belongings, and this was where he'd wound up.

Nate dragged the backpack over his shoulder, breath hissing out when his hand throbbed in response. He unsuccessfully tried to force the question out of his head just as he had for the past three hours, and moved one foot in front of the other, feeling sluggish and worn.

What if he's our father?

He stopped just inside the store, a blast of cold air barreling out of a vent and cooling his sweaty, dust-covered flesh. His eyes slid shut, tongue dragging over parched lips. It wasn't until the greeter, an old woman with dyed-black hair, cleared her throat quietly did Nate peel his eyelids up and move away.

After grabbing a bottle of water from one of the small refrigerators by the registers, Nate huddled in the electronics department and guzzled it down. Thudding the empty bottle on a shelf, Nate caught a glimpse of his reflection in the video game case and winced. He was a mess. It was surprising that no obnoxious Brookside cops had stopped him as he'd stumbled along the road. Not only was he sweaty and dirty, but he had a small smear of blood on his cheek from where the wound on his hand had reopened. He looked like a serial killer. Or the escaped victim of a serial killer.

Nate wiped at his face and glanced around self-consciously. His eyes met those of a guy standing in the same aisle. His brows were arched as he stared at Nate, a CD grasped between two of his fingers. Something was familiar about him, but Nate couldn't place what or why and at the moment, he didn't care. He backed out of the aisle, moving faster when the guy's eyes followed him, and made a beeline for the first aid section. Grabbing a pack of gauze and some tape, Nate headed to the family restroom and pressed his back against the door once he was locked inside.

He sucked in a long, deep breath and couldn't help but think about Dade. About their voices rising in the silent house, him shoving his uncle backwards, the crack of his head hitting the side of the wooden dresser, Dade splayed drunkenly on the floor. Dade had been knocked out cold, and although Nate had checked three times to ensure that the man was breathing, a niggling worry returned. What if he was a murderer?

Sucking in one last, shaky breath, Nate pushed himself away from the door. He hunched over the sink to clean and bandage his hand before attempting to make himself more presentable. Washing up was easy, but his clothing was a separate issue entirely. He wound up rifling through Theo's things and tugging out a T-shirt that still smelled of cigarette smoke. In the face of what had happened, the reminder of his twin was easier to take.

After arranging Theo's—no, now they were his—belongings, Nate's gaze caught on the notebook. As Dade's words replayed in his mind, about something happening to Lorelei in New York, Nate found himself thumbing to the page that had caught his attention previously.

lore chase to new york

Why did everything go back to New York? His mother, this premonition, Theo's death . . . It almost made Nate wonder if he should follow suit and go there himself. He understood very little about what had gone on in his mother's and brother's lives, but that city seemed to connect everything.

The door rattled, and Nate jumped, shutting the book and returning it to the backpack. The person knocked again as he shoved his arms through the straps and had begun to pound by the time he used a paper towel to wipe up the water that had splattered the counter. When he opened the door, a middle-aged woman was glaring at him. The toddler by her side had mimicked the expression.

"Sorry."

The straps of the backpack were worn from years of use, but they still hurt his aching shoulders as he walked through the store. He picked up several bottles of water and a box of granola bars. With a stop at the ATM to extract the last of his money, he was out of the store and once again walking alongside the road in ten minutes.

What had started as a freaked-out sprint from the house was transforming into something else. A desire to get away from the town where so much had happened to the people he'd loved, and the realization that his family's secrets were darker than he'd imagined.

He kept walking, and started thinking about Dade's rambling confession, and about the fragmented memories that had flashed through his own mind. Then there was the notebook and Theo's childish scrawl spelling out a premonition he'd had a decade ago.

Nate had to know more. At the moment, his mind was only full of questions. What had chased Theo and his mother out of Brookside? And why had they both been drawn to New York? One possibility was that someone in their own family had driven them away. Lorelei had likely wanted to escape Eveline and Dade, although Nate had no idea why she would have come back. But what about Theo? Why had he fled across the country? And who had killed him?

Nate stopped walking and stared at the flood of lights on the road. Each car was heading back to where he'd come from—Brookside and that house of horrors, but that wasn't where he needed to go.

There was nothing keeping him in the Houston area. Nothing keeping him in Texas. No job. An apartment that he'd soon be evicted from, and the broke-down furniture that had come with it. His thrift store clothing wasn't worth anything. And besides, he now had Theo's things. The only item of value Nate had was his phone.

The idea returned with a burst of adrenaline, and with a racing heart, Nate rerouted his steps toward the beltway leading to Houston. Walking turned to jogging, and then he did the most cliché thing he could think of—he stuck out his thumb.

After fifteen minutes, he felt silly. Maybe people didn't hitchhike in real life and the drivers who'd driven past him were chuckling at his supreme stupidity. Nate was about to put his arm down and weigh his options when a white Dodge Monaco pulled to the side of the road a few feet in front of him. Nate looked around and jogged forward, splashing through the muddy grass. He peered through the rolled-down window at the middle-aged man in the driver's seat. His face had been weathered with age and the sun, his skin leathery and deeply tanned.

"You lost?"

Nate opened his mouth, realized he hadn't prepared an explanation, and closed it again. "Not . . . precisely?"

"Well, where ya headed, kid?"

"Out of Houston," Nate answered without preamble. "East."

"Well, I'm headed east too, toward Port Arthur. You can climb in if ya want."

Nate forced a smile and grabbed the door handle. As soon as his fingers touched the metal, he froze with widened eyes. A sense of horror assaulted him with chest-tightening intensity. His vision went blurry, surroundings staining red, and a high-pitched shriek of agony echoed through his mind, ricocheting like a bullet that couldn't find a surface to break out of.

The scream went on and on, a howl of terror, of death, and it didn't stop until Nate released the door handle as though it had set his hand on fire. He stared through the half-opened window.

"I—"

"You all right, son?"

"I—" Oh fuck. What the fuck? "I'm sorry, but I need to make a stop before I can go. I forgot to, uh, buy a thing. Thanks anyway."

"I can give you a few min—"

Nate didn't wait to hear the rest before he strode toward the strip mall he'd been walking near. Horror scenarios and thoughts of the true-crime shows he'd watched on Investigation Discovery had him wanting to call the cops, and he cursed himself for not looking at the license plate. Nate was halfway through the parking lot when he realized he was being ridiculous. He didn't even know if the impression had been directly related to the driver. The Monaco was likely a good sixty years old and had probably exchanged owners several times. If it had been the scene of a horrible crime, the person who had perpetrated it was probably long dead.

But if he had taken the ride, his inability to block out impressions would have led to him being stuck in an extended nightmare for hours until the guy dropped him off near the Texas and Louisiana borders. Nate had never been trapped in an impression before, and he didn't want to know what kind of havoc such a thing could wreak on his brain.

Damn. He was a disaster.

Nate took a deep breath and turned back to the road. The white Monaco was no longer in view, so after a moment of steeling himself, he stuck out his thumb again. Barely a minute passed before a slightly battered matte-black Chevy Nova sidled up beside him. Muffled rock music drifted out from the interior. Dir en Grey. One of Nate's favorite of their newer songs. Maybe that was a sign? Nate tried to tell himself it was, but his self-assurance that murderers couldn't be that rampant in Houston suburbs faded in the face of another opportunity to get into a stranger's car.

The dome light flicked on inside, and the driver looked out. It was the dark-haired guy from Wal-Mart. He was pressing a button on the illuminated CD player, and the volume was decreasing rapidly. Nate took in his shaggy, chin-length hair, light-blue eyes, and what appeared to be a Star Wars T-shirt.

"Before I ask where you're going," the guy said with a narrow-eyed stare. He didn't sound like he was from Houston or the South in general, and his accent was oddly familiar. "I'm going to ask you some stuff."

"Well. I'm not a hooker. So if it's about prices . . ." Nate shrugged.

The guy gave him an unimpressed stare and scowled. "Even if I was looking for a hooker, I wouldn't pay for a raggedy-ass one. You look like you just crawled through a drainage ditch."

"Charming."

"Hey, you're the one with your thumb in the air just asking for some douche bag to pull over and murder you."

"Well, thank you for this stunning exchange of insults, but I'm going to go now."

"Wait."

"What?"

The guy sighed and drummed his fingers against the steering wheel as he studied Nate through the barrier of the metal door. "Why are you hitching?"

"Do you normally play twenty questions before picking up hitchhikers?"

"I don't normally pick up hitchhikers, so I guess so," he retorted. "I'd just feel like shit if I turned on the news in whatever crappy motel I stay in later and saw that some blond guy got murdered on the side of the road. That possibility is causing me to play good Samaritan and offer your ass a ride. I even drove by you before, then felt bad and came back. We keep running into each other, so I told myself it was really shitty fate."

Nate gave him a considering look and idly reached out to run a hand along the side of the door, half-afraid of what impressions he'd get from it. All he felt was the dull hum of a mixture of emotions with nothing in particular standing out. It didn't mean anything about the guy as a person, but at least his car hadn't been used for evil just yet.

"I'm running away," Nate said for lack of a better explanation. "From life. In a sense. I guess. I'm not underage or something."

"I know you're not. Teenagers aren't allowed to sell alcohol."

They stared at each other. A billion cars whizzed by, and the guy rolled his eyes.

"Never mind." He leaned across the center console and unlocked the passenger door. "You're too old to be running away. You're just a bum."

Nate climbed into the car, cramming the backpack between his knees as he yanked the door shut. "Thanks."

"Don't thank me yet. As soon as I find out that you're some kind of weirdo or crackhead, you're out."

Nate couldn't resist a half smile. "I'm not into drugs, but I can't promise anything about weirdness."

The guy just shook his head and put the car into drive, guiding the Nova back onto the road and taking off with a loud roar of the engine.

CHAPTER FOUR

"**S**o, what's your story, kid?"

Nate tilted his head against the window and crossed his arms over his chest. His body sank into the ripped leather of the passenger seat as a warm, damp breeze blew in through the window. It was tempting to lean back into the worn fabric, but relaxing wasn't going to happen anytime soon. Not with a stranger next to him.

"You can't be much older than me."

There was a brief pause, and Nate looked over as the guy turned up the music slightly. The Dir en Grey song had ended, and another J-Rock song was playing. Surprisingly, he didn't recognize it.

"What's your name again?"

"Nate."

"Okay, Nate," the guy said. "So what's your story?"

"Do I get to know your name or should I continue to internally refer to you as Driving Guy?"

The guy snorted softly. "Trent."

"Tre— Wait." Recognition hit like a bolt of lightning, and Nate's eyes opened wide in the gloom. "You're the guy from the liquor store!"

"You got it, Master of Observations. I've dropped like sixty hints in the past minute."

Nate twisted in his seat, ignoring the sarcasm and trying to get a better look at Trent's features. How could he have forgotten the man who'd given him a chubby with a mere graze of his fingers? The good vibes that had spread between them would have been the stuff of masturbatory fantasies had the shit-show of the Black family and Theo not followed shortly after. It was the first time, ever, that his body had reacted positively to another person. Not that he'd ever be able to act on it. Having sex wasn't something that had worked out very well for him when he couldn't block out the vibes of the rare guys who'd tried to get with him.

"No wonder you said we keep running into each other."

"Yup. In the liquor store, at Wal-Mart, and on the road." Trent snorted. "Fate."

"Or maybe you just have bad luck."

"You're admitting you're gonna bring me problems?"

"No. I'm just . . ." *Way to make yourself look like a freak right off the bat, Black.* "I dunno. I'm just being emo."

"Does your emo have anything to do with your scraggly appearance or is looking ragged as fuck how you unwind when not at work?"

Well, at least Nate wouldn't have to worry about this guy wanting to get horizontal with him. Apparently Nate's current appearance was horrifying enough to warrant a constant stream of Deadpool-esque insults.

"Okay, for real, what's your deal?" Trent pressed.

"What makes you think I have a deal?"

"Because you were trekking around in the mud on the side of the road after I'd just seen you all beat-up and sad looking in Wal-Mart. If it was something as simple as car trouble, you'd have said so by now."

"It's nothing that will cause problems for you. It was just time for me to leave."

Not looking at all convinced with this explanation, Trent pressed on. "And go where? You didn't ask where I'm headed."

"Ah . . ." Nate frowned, realizing he'd yet again failed to come up with an explanation or a destination. "It doesn't really matter, I guess. You seem to be heading east, and I'm heading east, so you can just let me out wherever you get sick of me taking up space in your car."

"I am going east, but I'm going pretty far." Trent looked at him again as he cruised toward I-45. "I'm leaving Texas, heading up north. I don't really know how this hitchhiker/hitchhikee thing works, but I'm pretty sure you should be giving me an idea about where to take you."

"Like I said, just let me out when you start to miss your solitude. I'm not much of a talker in any case."

Trent smirked. "Sounds like a blast."

"If my intentions were to amuse you, I would have had prices handy."

"Okay, then."

Nate exhaled slowly. "Sorry. Habit."

"Being a smart-ass?"

"Yeah. Pretty much."

The smirk curved up into a more genuine-looking smile, and Trent reached out to fiddle with the stereo again. "I called you a bum-ass prostitute crackhead, so it's cool. Besides it would probably annoy the shit out of me if you talked a lot. I don't really like random people."

"Doesn't seem that way."

Static exploded out of the speakers as Trent flipped from the CD player to the radio. As Trent fiddled with the tuner, Nate found himself subtly taking stock of the other man. In the gloom of the car with only the blue neon lights of the stereo illuminating them, Nate could just barely make out a tattoo on Trent's forearm.

"Yeah, well, when I feel like I have shit way more together than someone else, it makes me feel confident when dealing with them. Aka, you."

"Nice."

Trent left the radio alone just as an advertisement for a department store sale played. He frowned and shifted in the driver's seat, rolling his shoulders. After a moment, he noticed Nate watching and raised his eyebrows. Nate quickly averted his gaze. The ad ended and was replaced with the nasal voice of a DJ from Rock 101.

"I don't have a set destination," Nate said. "I just need to leave Houston. And I know that sounds really weird."

"I'm glad you realize that." There was a pause. "Are we sure that drugs aren't going to be a problem?"

"I'm not on drugs."

"Just dying to escape the mean streets of Houston?"

"Brookside, actually. I'm from Brookside."

"Whatever, kid. Seriously, what's your deal? You seem cool and all, but if you turn out to be trouble, you're history."

Lying on the spot was not Nate's forte. Coming up with lies in advance was apparently not his forte either because he still had not prepared an explanation for taking off with only a ragged backpack, or for the way he'd looked in Wal-Mart.

"It's just complicated." He combed his brain for a plausible story. "I got in a fight with my uncle, a pretty bad fight, and I'm bailing. I'm tired of being here and need to get the fuck out."

"Why did you get in a fight?"

"Because my family hates me."

"Why?"

"I don't fucking know. Why does anyone hate anybody?"

"Usually people do something wrong to get hated."

Nate looked at the other man incredulously. "Wow. That's the stupidest thing I've ever heard."

"Well—"

"What about racist people? Or homophobic people? Or, like, the Holocaust?"

Trent made a face. "Okay, simmer the fuck down. I'm just trying to make sure that you're not a killer. For all I know you have weapons in that bag."

"I have a bunch of band T-shirts, a jail-broken iPod, and a notebook. And water. Want to check?"

"Sure, open it up."

Nate scowled but jerked the backpack onto his lap and unzipped it. He opened it wide and turned in the seat, pushing it toward Trent. "Feel menaced?"

Trent glanced over, driving with one hand and holding the bag up with the other. Nate watched, half-exasperated and slightly amused. Now that he had reason to look, he saw Trent was bigger than him. The nerdy Star Wars T-shirt was fitted to his chest, and his arms were corded with muscle. The fact that he apparently thought Nate was potentially capable of taking him on was a definite boost to his almost nonexistent ego. The dedication to working out and shirking the fragile twink image that his brother had loved was apparently paying off.

"Should we pull over so you can frisk me?"

"Sure," Trent said, pushing the bag away and refocusing on the road. "I'll get my rubber gloves."

"That would be a cavity search."

"True. But you could be a drug mule so, you know. Gotta keep those bases covered."

Nate laughed and was almost startled by the sound, but he couldn't stop. His shoulders shook as he let the bag slide back down to the floorboard and the sound filled the car. Trent glanced over, still wearing his serious face, which only made Nate laugh more. After a moment, Nate wiped a hand across his face and sighed.

"Are you done?"

"Yes."

"I'm glad my paranoia is amusing for you."

"Look, I really appreciate you giving me a ride. And I'm not making fun of you. It was just funny. And I had a really bad day." A bad month was more like it. Nate dug his fingers into the seat again, amusement fading as he forced himself to continue. "My twin brother died recently. The funeral was today. And afterward I got into it with some family. That's all there is to it."

When Trent didn't immediately speak, Nate rubbed his hands against his thighs as anxiety crept up on him again. What were the odds that he would find someone else willing to drive him in the exact same direction he was going? Someone who was obviously high-strung but still willing to give him a chance? Someone who'd run into him three times now, and who'd so far failed to trigger paranoia and discomfort in Nate the way almost everyone he'd ever met had?

"We were fighting over me being gay, okay?" Nate added, upping the ante with another lie. "Nothing scary. Unless you think that's scary."

Trent made a face. "No."

"Okay."

They lapsed into silence again. The wind whipping by overpowered the low warbling of the radio, but he heard Trent clear his throat and say finally, "Sorry about your brother."

"Thanks."

Trent nodded, focused on the road again, and turned the radio up louder.

Nate didn't remember falling asleep.

He remembered his eyelids growing heavy as the vibration of the engine, the breeze hitting his face, and the low melody of classic rock had combined until the tension had eased out of his body.

At first, keeping an eye on the stranger next to him and the direction they were going in had been his priority. His gaze had flicked between Trent and the road continuously, never able to fully see Trent even during the rare occasion when lights from the road slanted in through the windows and highlighted a detail here and there. He had a face just as handsome as Nate had remembered it being in the liquor store, well-muscled build, denim jeans, scarred knuckles, and confident hands that held the steering wheel almost lazily. Nate had always been a nervous driver.

After a while, Nate had turned toward the window and watched as Trent got onto I-10E and left Houston behind. There was no fascinating scenery on the interstate, no cool sights or landmarks to mark the beginning of his escape, but it didn't matter.

He'd stared at the trees that pressed in on either side of the expressway, looming into the star-filled sky, and it hadn't mattered that he'd left everything behind. It hadn't mattered that he had no one. All that had mattered was the solid weight of the car as Trent pushed past 80 mph and the road stretched out wide before them in a black ribbon illuminated only by the glow of headlights. As his vision had blurred and they'd sped through the darkness and over bridges crossing the streams and wooded areas that led them out of east Texas, the sense of freedom had allowed sleep to engulf him.

Now, he woke disoriented and flinched when the dome light came on above him.

"What's the plan?"

Nate turned, stretching and blinking rapidly. His eyes were barely focused, so he squinted at Trent. He'd opened his door but was still sitting in the driver's seat.

"Sorry. How long was I out?"

"Maybe two hours." Trent pointed to the clock, which read 2:27 a.m. "I've been driving all day. I was about to stretch my legs, but I really need to stop for the night."

"Oh." The word came out heavier than Nate had intended. He grabbed his bag and looked out the window. "Where are we?"

"I dunno. Louisiana. We passed Lake Charles a little bit ago. But there's a Howard Johnson Express up the road, and we're in a McDonald's parking lot, so I'm ready to call it fucking quits. My eyes are going to start bleeding soon."

"Okay."

They stared at each other, and Trent frowned, reaching up to comb his fingers through his hair. Nate saw that there were dark circles under Trent's eyes.

"Thanks. For the ride and letting me sleep." Nate put his hand on the door.

"Well, just wait." Frowning, Trent looked out the windshield. Darkness surrounded the cluster of stores, although it seemed that there were more wide-open spaces than wooded areas in the vicinity. "What are you going to do?"

"No idea. Walk up to the service road and hitch a ride probably."

"That's really dangerous."

"I know."

Trent stared at him, still frowning, and Nate started to open the door. He felt awkward under the weight of Trent's gaze and was anxious to leave. It was getting late, and if Trent was getting off the road, it was likely that anyone else who was driving through would be too.

"Look, I could keep driving you tomorrow. You aren't really bothering me." Trent rubbed his temples as if saying the words hurt his head. "Just pay half for gas or something. I'm broke, so that would actually be helpful to me."

Nate's hand dropped. "Are you sure?"

"Yeah. I mean, you're not that bad so far. You can't sleep in my room with me or anything, though."

"No, of course not. I know."

"Okay." Trent nodded. "Good." He twisted the key and pulled it out of the ignition, shutting the car off completely. "So, McDonald's."

"Yeah. McDonald's."

Relieved that the awkward moment was over, Nate pushed the door open and stepped out. He stretched, back cracking and body unwinding after sleeping half-curled in the seat. It turned out that the restaurant was not open, and they got back into the car to move around to the drive-through. Nate stared at the brightly displayed menu for a full minute before any of the pictures and words made sense in his mind. He ordered two cheeseburgers and fries off the Dollar Menu.

"I really hate McDonald's," Trent said. They'd parked around the side and sat on the curb to eat, because Trent said eating in the Nova was a no-no.

"I never eat it."

"Burger King type of guy?"

"Whataburger, actually."

"I have no idea what that is."

Definitely not a Texan. Nate smiled. "Honestly, I don't eat fast food unless it's something that can leave leftovers. It's expensive."

"Makes sense."

Nate shrugged. He was aware of Trent watching him, and avoided meeting the other man's eyes. There was something off-putting about Trent's bluntness now that they were out of the dark confines of the car. Like he would figure out that there was more to Nate's story or change his mind about being nice.

"How old are you?" Trent asked around a mouthful of fries. "You look young."

"I'm twenty-one."

"Huh." Trent stretched his legs in front of him. "Aren't you curious as to where I'm going? You're way too serious and quiet to be some, like . . . free-spirited go-where-the-wind-takes-you type of guy."

"I don't want to pry, as long as we are going the same way. Also, I'm bad at socializing, so it's better for me to speak as little as possible, to be honest."

"It's actually weirder if you don't ask me anything." Trent pointed at him with a fry. "Maybe I'm the killer."

Nate snorted. As soon as they'd left the Houston city limits, he'd started actively trying to get impressions from the vehicle since he couldn't touch Trent himself. He hadn't been able to pick up anything. It wasn't proof that Trent was not a threat, but there was something about him that put Nate at ease. That same something made him feel he could trust Trent enough to fall asleep without fear of being filleted.

"Okay, where are you going, then?" Nate asked. "Your accent tells me somewhere on the East Coast."

"I don't have an accent."

"Yes, you do."

"Huh." Trent seemed to consider that as he opened the box that his burger was in. "I live in New York City. I'm driving home from school."

Nate froze midbite. "Seriously?"

"Yup. Why? Do you have something against New Yorkers like all of my other Texas friends?"

"No . . ." Nate cleared his throat and pulled a bottle of water out of his backpack. "Where are you driving from?"

"Cali. I stopped in Houston to visit some friends, but I go to Caltech for grad school."

"Wow. You must be smart."

"I'm okay."

"What's your major?"

"Aeronautical engineering."

"That's awesome."

Trent rolled his eyes. "Yeah, let's see if Lockheed Martin or SpaceX thinks so."

Nate didn't know much about higher education, but he did know that going to Caltech was pretty damn impressive.

"What about you? Were you in school or anything before you decided to become a traveling bum?"

Nate crumpled up the yellow wrapper to his cheeseburger. "I couldn't afford college, and I wasn't a good enough student to get scholarships. Also, I just didn't want to go."

Trent laughed. "What's your plan, then? Pick a random city and try to start over because your family is homophobic? You have to have some destination in mind."

Nate hesitated with the words on the tip of his tongue. He wanted to tell Trent, not have the other man looking at him like he was a dumb kid without the ability to think ahead. But it was the first night, and he didn't want to admit that he was going to New York. He didn't want to admit *why* he was going to New York. It was too early in this arrangement to make it obvious that he was a freak coming from a supremely fucked-up situation. And he highly doubted that an engineer was *really* going to think they were both going to New York because of fate.

"If you turn out to still be normal and cool tomorrow, I'll tell you more."

Trent lifted his soda. "Deal."

CHAPTER FIVE

Four bucks for a toothbrush seemed absurd, but the Love's Travel Stop near the motel had showers, so Nate didn't complain too much. He stood under the scalding water and let it wash the sweat and dirt away before scrubbing himself with a cheap bar of soap. By the time he finished, his skin was flushed and steam was billowing out of the tiny cubicle. After spending the night wedged between a wall and a grimy vending machine, he was thankful for the water even if it was boiling him alive.

He threw on a fresh pair of jeans from Theo's bag—which were too tight and skinny for his liking—and a plain, black T-shirt before heading out. There were no messages on his phone, so he switched it off, got a cup of coffee, and went back to the motel. He was ready to go and sitting on the curb next to the Nova by seven thirty. Distracting himself by organizing the bag once again, Nate tried not to keep glancing at Trent's door.

The man obviously hadn't left yet, but there was a fear niggling at the back of Nate's mind that Trent had changed his mind about the deal they'd struck the night before. Nate couldn't say that it wasn't something he'd do if he were in Trent's place. There had been several times in Nate's life when he'd acted spontaneously in the middle of the night with only the shadows and his own overworked thoughts to guide him, and had banished the notion in the light of day. For example, finding guys online, setting a time to meet, and then remembering that he and sex were not compatible due to his crappy psychic power.

Trent emerged from his own room at a quarter to eight. He nodded at Nate and yawned. He was clean-shaven, but his hair was still damply sticking out in some places. He didn't seem to notice when Nate's eyes lingered on his tight, white T-shirt.

"You checked out already?"

"Yep. I woke up early."

"Fucking morning people." Trent leaned against the hood of his car and yawned again, pushing a pair of aviators on his face. "Okay, I'm going to see what the free continental breakfast thing is all about, and we can be on the road in like twenty minutes if you're good to go. I lost mad time in Texas."

"With your friends?"

"Yeah. They work for NASA. Have a giant house near 288."

"Wow." The shame of Nate's previous admission about not having interest in college, and not having a real job, burned the back of his neck. "Cool."

"Yeah, they're great. Anyways, I'll be back in a few."

Nate nodded and watched Trent walk away, gaze automatically falling to Trent's ass. The two firm, rounded globes looked delicious encased in thin cotton. Literally the best ass Nate had ever laid eyes on. Nate was still thinking about the beauty of Trent's body when he returned a few minutes later, armed with a bagel and a large cup of coffee. He seemed more awake, and his strides were longer, flip-flops slapping against the concrete as he made his way back to the car.

"Did you eat there earlier? Their food is pretty good. Can make your own waffles. It was awesome. I felt very competent."

Nate got in the passenger's seat after Trent unlocked the car, biting back a smile. "No, I just got something from the truck stop."

"Well, that was stupid. Waffles were free. You make bad life choices."

"Don't mince words or anything."

"I never do." Trent winked and put on his seat belt after he unloaded his pockets and arranged his belongings. It took him a full minute to settle. Each item had a particular place. Wallet in center console, coffee in cupholder, random pieces of paper on top of the dash, rubber-banded stack of envelopes tucked next to his wallet. When he was done, Trent started the car and fiddled with the radio for a moment. "Radio sucks. I left all my music in California, so all I have is the one CD that was already in the car. And the radio is all pop or zydeco music."

"No auxiliary port?"

"Nope. Radio is old as shit, and I'm too cheap to switch it out just so I can kill my phone's battery faster."

There was something charming about Trent's clear-cut logic.

"I left all my CDs in my old apartment," Nate said. "Which sucks. Some of them were J-Rock I'd downloaded over the past decade. Dir en Grey visual kei albums and stuff. Now I have to find somewhere to buy it all."

"I bet we could stream it," Trent said. "If I had a fucking auxiliary port."

Nate grinned. "Maybe we can scour a Wal-Mart for J-Rock CDs."

"Ha. What do you think I was doing when we saw each other?"

"Good point," Nate said. "We'll just have to cycle through the one CD you have to get our fix."

Trent laughed, seemingly delighted that Nate shared his appreciation for Japanese rock music. "I like the way you think, Nate. We'll play it again later. And I expect you to know all the words." He left the radio on a generic rock station and guided the vehicle out of the parking lot.

They filled up the tank, and as decided, Nate chipped in half. As soon as they were back on the interstate, the tension that had built during the night faded. It felt normal to be sitting next to Trent, looking at him sidelong and idly commenting on the music. But he still had trouble thinking of other things to say. Considering they had similar taste in bands and Trent's banter was effortless, it should have been easy to spark up a conversation, but Nate was terrible at small talk . . . or any kind of talk, really.

Working in retail had been horrible for an introvert. Even before Liquor World, when he'd worked with people nearer to his age, he hadn't fit in. He always struggled with what to say to keep people interested in a conversation when no witty retorts automatically sprang to mind and when he genuinely had no interest in their lives. After a while people stopped trying to engage him about anything personal. He'd never been a work friend—he was always just a guy people worked with.

It hadn't bothered him before, but as Trent hummed quietly along to a song, Nate knew he wanted to make a connection. He was interested in the type of person who seemed, for all intents and purposes, normal but would still do something risky like give a random stranger a ride out of the kindness of their hearts. He also appreciated the fact that Trent didn't continuously interrupt what had become long, comfortable silences with bullshit chatter. Even if that was what Nate was trying to do now.

"So why do you drive?"

They'd been coasting along I-10 in silence for an hour. The surprise washing over Trent's face made it seem as though he'd almost forgotten Nate was in the car. "What do you mean?"

"Why not fly home if you're going back to Cali in a couple of months, anyway?"

"I didn't want to leave my car in California, and I can't be in California without a car. And I figured I'd make some stops this time around. Take I-10 to Jacksonville, then I-95 straight up."

"Oh."

They lapsed into silence again, and Nate failed to think of a follow-up question.

"Well, what about you?" Trent asked. "Why don't you have a car? You can't exactly commute in Texas, can you?"

"Houston has public transportation, but there's none in the suburbs. Anyway, someone stole my car recently."

This time it was Trent who frowned. "Seriously?"

"I'm not lying," Nate said. "I just have really bad luck. Shit snowballs on me."

"Hmm."

"Look, I know it sounds like bullshit, but why would I lie when I could have just said nothing at all? It's not like I'm dying to impress you with my stories of living in Loserville."

"Pathological liar?"

"I'm not lying about my brother dying." Nate hesitated, unsure, and then pressed on against his better judgment. "He's the reason . . . That's why I'm going to New York. He was found dead there a few weeks ago. By the West Side Highway. The cops said he killed himself, but I don't buy it. I want to check it out."

Trent was still focused on the road, but one eyebrow had risen high enough to disappear into his hair. "Wait, you're also going to New York?"

"Yes."

"To find your brother's . . . killer?"

"No, I didn't say that."

"But you think he died in a suspicious way and not suicide."

"Yes."

"So how did they say he died?"

"They said he threw himself off the pier and drowned."

Trent frowned deeper. "Was he fucked up or something? I mean, like drunk?"

"No."

"So why would he go jump in the river to kill himself? He didn't know how to swim?"

"Well, exactly. That's my point. He did know how to swim. And he wouldn't have jumped off the edge of a damn pier." Nate knew it didn't sound as convincing as he'd hoped, but there was no way to remedy the situation without going into the tale of visions and psychic powers.

"This is nuts. You better not be lying to me, man. I'm feeling compassion, and that doesn't happen a whole lot."

This was exactly why he'd hesitated to share any information. Trent was going to need proof, and all Nate had was an article he'd found online a couple of days after he'd received the phone call from the NYPD, and a Tumblr fan account for the band his brother had been in called the Dreadnoughts. There had been very little information on the actual band members, except for their names and a few pictures taken during performances. Theo had been in a couple of them.

He unclipped his seat belt and pressed the back of his shoulders against the seat so he could reach into his pocket. He nearly slammed into the door when Trent switched lanes suddenly.

"You should put your seat belt on."

Grunting, Nate sat up straight. "I was trying to get my evidence."

"Well then, you shouldn't wear such tight pants if it was that difficult to get something out of your pocket."

"Thanks for the tip." Nate withdrew his phone from Theo's unfortunate skinny jeans and powered it up. It only took a moment to navigate to the tiny article that had discussed Theo's death. "There was a story on it in the *New York Post*."

Trent glanced at the phone. "Here, take the wheel."

"What?"

"Live dangerously."

"Shit!"

Trent took his hands off the wheel just as Nate reached over and grabbed it, steadying them on the interstate when the car zigzagged toward the other lane. Someone honked behind them, and Nate scowled, awkwardly steering as he tried his best not to touch any part of Trent. It was difficult since one of his arms was trapped between Trent's as Trent scanned the article.

When he was done, they switched places on the wheel, and their bare arms briefly slid against each other. The impression wasn't strong, but just like the day in Liquor World, bursts of warmth exploded out of Trent. They were like little static shocks with the power of infusing fondness and pleasure into the glumness surrounding Nate. Never in his life had he felt vibes so intense.

He shuddered and yanked away.

Trent was unreadable, his eyes hidden by sunglasses. A shred of discomfort caused Nate to put his phone back into his pocket.

After a while, Trent shoved his sunglasses up on his forehead. "I'm sorry I was being such a douche about this. I really just am a skeptical bastard."

"You don't have to apologize. I only showed you so you don't think I'm a liar."

"Well, I don't anymore. Jesus."

Nate knew Trent was still watching him, but opted to focus on putting on his seat belt instead of returning the stare. The strap pressed uncomfortably against his sweaty shirt. "So that's why I'm going to New York. I don't think I'm going to pull off a whole CSI investigation, but something isn't right about it, and I want to know more. That doesn't mean I expect you to drive me the whole way or anything. Just let me out when you get sick of me."

At that, Trent didn't reply. He propped his elbow on the open window, slid his fingers through his hair, and continued to drive.

With silence spreading between them again, time ticked by. It was interspersed with Trent's complaints about the growing stickiness of the day and the radio station announcing it would top out at over a hundred degrees. Nate was used to the heat, but the humidity seemed to grow worse the farther they drove into Louisiana. The air was thick, damp, and the AC was no help. Trent apologetically told him it was on the fritz right before peeling off his T-shirt. It was impossible to not glance over and take stock of him. Broad shouldered, defined chest, tapered waist, and the V of his torso dipping down into the thin pants—Trent's body was as attractive as his face. With sunlight streaming into the car, Nate could see that the tattoo on Trent's arm said *RIP Angela Rose.*

Trent caught him staring for the second time that morning, but this time Nate didn't look away. Trent grinned.

They gave up on FM radio and switched to AM, settling on a station that played Zydeco. By the time they were in Baton Rouge, it was past ten o'clock and the twang of the music combined with the heat to lull Nate into a doze. He was slouched down, seat belt undone once again despite Trent's disapproving glares, and the ripped knees of his jeans were practically touching the glove compartment as his head lolled to the side.

A touch to his upper arm jolted him awake, and his hand clamped down on Trent's wrist, fingers tightening. With wide eyes and parted lips, he blindly stared at the other man and didn't yank back even when he felt the electricity spark between them.

There were no specific emotions. No specific thoughts. Just a steady hum of mostly positive energy. His hand lingered, and a faint throb of attraction came through.

Nate jerked away. Trent being into him was so unlikely that Nate didn't consider it as a possibility. He'd received positive impressions so infrequently that it was more likely he was confusing attraction with friendliness.

"You startled me."

"Clearly," Trent said with a short laugh. "You freaked out."

"Yeah . . ." What a way to make himself look like a weirdo. This was why he stayed away from people. "Awkward."

"Nah, it's okay. I shouldn't be grabbing at you when you're asleep, anyway. You might start thinking I'm a pervert."

Nate kept staring at the dash. Nothing good would come of him responding to that statement.

"Well, anyways, two things. Your phone has been vibrating excessively, and it's messing up my enjoyment of this bad-ass music. And no, that wasn't sarcasm. I'm digging the Cajun French. Second, I need you to make a quick life choice for both of us because I can't decide."

Nate sat up straight and pulled out his phone.

"Ten or twelve?" Trent asked.

"Huh?"

"Ten or twelve?"

"Uh. What? Ten, I guess." Nate looked down at his phone. He had four missed calls and a number of texts, all from Dade. He scowled, deleting each message without reading. Fuck them.

"Everything cool?"

"Yeah. So, what were you saying?"

"Well," Trent drawled, rolling the last consonant. "I'd planned to spend the day in New Orleans since I've never been there and this is my second time doing this drive. I'd changed my mind twice, but you just made it up for me."

"How'd I do that?"

"Ten or twelve, remember? I-10 goes down through New Orleans and I-12 doesn't."

Nate's first instinct was to say he didn't really want to make a pit stop, but it wasn't his car and finding another ride was . . . undesirable. He didn't want to put himself in the position of having to trust another stranger, and he also didn't want to lose the brief yet addictive connections he'd had with Trent. He was craving those tiny moments of warmth and fondness that resulted from a mere brush of their skin, but Nate was also enjoying Trent's company.

Getting another ride wasn't an option. Any answers regarding Theo's death would still be waiting in New York whether Nate got there in two days or four.

"You let me decide this?"

"Yeah, why not? I'm trying to be more impulsive."

"How's that working out for you?"

Trent shrugged. "I'll let you know when we get to New York."

Driving through Louisiana in the dead of summer with the windows down had been hot, but walking around New Orleans in the middle of the day resulted in them seeking refuge after two hours. They were unprepared and poorly dressed for the oppressive mugginess, and when they collapsed in Jackson Square after standing in line at Café Du Monde, the feeling intensified.

"How the fuck is this a park?" Trent's body was draped across one of the wrought iron benches. His eyes were blue slits, glaring fiercely at the shade that was doing nothing to lessen the heat.

"The fountain is making the humidity worse, I think."

"Well, that fountain is fucked."

Nate laughed, the sound lazy and low as he slid down and sprawled his legs in front of them. His arms hung over the back of the bench, fingers sticky with white powder from the bag of beignets they'd eaten. He sucked the powder off his fingers, eyes half-open as he squinted across the green space at the towering, white cathedral beyond.

The structure made him uneasy. There was something about the entire square that was disturbing the continuous and pleasant mélange of impressions that washed over him each time his arm brushed Trent's as they explored the French Quarter. He hadn't intended to keep reaching out with his gift, but Trent was so mellow that he found himself doing it every time the opportunity arose. Wanting to feel more, wanting to know more, about the other man and what he might be thinking. In general, and about Nate. It was a nice change from the past week of focusing solely on misery and guilt and the unceasing parade of questions marching across his brain.

But now there was something else just beyond the bubble that surrounded them—a sharp tinge of . . . something . . . that made Nate want to cover himself with a mental shield. Assuming the weird vibes he'd been getting from the church wouldn't overpower any weak shield he could conjure.

"I don't like churches," he said after a while.

When there was no immediate response, Nate saw that Trent was focused on his now-damp fingers. He curled them into a fist, and Trent's gaze swung away. A flush crept up Trent's neck.

"Why? You a vampire?"

"Yes."

Trent nodded seriously. "What kind?"

"Kind?"

"There's the Anne Rice kind, the Twilight kind, and the True Blood kind."

"Don't forget the Black Dagger Brotherhood kind." Nate thought for a moment. "And the Sergei Lukyanenko kind."

"Who?"

Nate shook his head, not seeing the need to go into his fondness for supernatural books. "Never mind."

Trent jerked his chin at Nate. "You can be the True Blood kind. You're tall and blond like Eric Northman."

"I'm not hot enough to be Eric Northman."

"True."

Nate flipped him off.

"Just kidding, blondie. You don't make for bad scenery at all." Trent grinned lazily. "So, why don't you like churches?"

"They make me uncomfortable. All of those people are always either guilty or unhappy. That church might just be full of tourists, but when I was younger I hated them. All the bad feelings made me feel . . . bad."

"Eloquent."

"Heh."

It was an understatement. It had been so awful for him to absorb all that negativity that he'd wept until he'd gotten sick, and had begged not to be sent, until Eveline had finally relented.

"I don't like churches either," Trent said. "They remind me of my mother's funeral. The priest saying she was in a better place and a bunch of phony relatives in the front row with crocodile tears streaming." His lips twisted. "If I sound bitter, it's because I am. I hate my family."

"I know how you feel."

"Yeah?"

"Yeah. Especially my aunt. At my brother's funeral, she made it clear she wasn't happy about having to pay for both his and my mother's services even though their deaths were nearly ten years apart. I don't know if she really meant it or if she just . . . likes making herself out to be the pettiest asshole ever." Nate curled his hands around the edge of the bench. "Anyway, my mom disappeared when I was younger. Everyone assumes she killed herself. It's why they think Theo did the same."

"Jesus."

Nate nodded. "No one knows exactly what happened, but she just disappeared one day."

Trent's lips parted as if he'd planned to say something, but was grappling with the words.

"Suicidal tendencies seem to be genetic. So many people in my family are unstable, or drunks, and my mom . . . well, she had problems too." Nate's gaze darkened. The images of his mother and Dade flashed through his mind unbidden. "My family is so fucked up, man. Just beyond repair. In the worst possible ways."

"No wonder you left."

"There's a lot more to it," Nate admitted. "But it's complicated. And hard to believe."

"You could tell me. I know we hardly know each other but . . ." Trent trailed off, staring at Nate with the same intensity he'd shown since they first met. An unabashed curiosity and honesty that Nate rarely saw in others. "But I like talking to you. I like you in general."

"I— Well, I like talking to you too. Maybe I'll tell you more someday."

"Good."

CHAPTER SIX

They'd planned to get moving and drive until they hit the Florida Panhandle.

That was still the plan at six in the evening when they went to get oysters at a tourist spot. It took over an hour to be seated, and by then, Trent was so irritated by the wait that he claimed he'd sit there all fucking night if he wanted to, and he'd be damned if anyone rushed him.

Nate didn't plan to eat. He didn't have money to eat. But Trent glared at him like it was an insult, griped about eating alone, and ordered so much food that he forced Nate to share it. Fresh oysters, chargrilled oysters, jambalaya, shrimp étouffé, and a roast beef po'boy debris style. After a couple of hours, beer bottles littered the table, and they sat picking at the food and people watching. As they did, Nate's mind continuously wandered to his brother.

Since middle school, Theo had been infatuated with New Orleans. He'd believed there was something magical about the city. The thought had been fueled by books and movies, but he'd become obsessed with the history, the culture, the music, and the tales of superstition.

Unlike Nate, Theo had been a huge believer in the supernatural—their gifts for starters, but he'd also believed in curses, spirits, and maybe even people with other gene mutations besides psychic abilities. He'd liked being part of a secret layer to the world. Liked being special. Even though neither of them had loved being part of the infamous Black family, he'd thought the darkness surrounding their family's legacy had been romantic. Theo had spent months researching their history—tracking how far back the insanity went and how far back their gifts could be traced, but he'd had little luck.

Nothing was written down and actual records were hard to come by even though they'd all lived in Brookside for decades. The only thing they could confirm was that in the past four generations, the mental illness had grown more common, suicide in their family had become the norm, and spouses or significant others did not stick around for long. The question of whether Dade was their father returned, and Nate's stomach churned.

"You look tense."

Nate glanced up from his sweating beer bottle. "Just thinking."

"About?"

"My brother. Trashy tourists aside, he would have loved to be here. In the city."

"Huh." Trent set his own beer bottle down on the table. Sitting back in his chair, he extended his legs and placed a hand on his stomach. "I put New Orleans-ophiles in the same book as Japanophiles."

"What book is that?"

"The book of things that make Trenton unimpressed."

"What's wrong with admiring a city and wanting to go there? You must have if you've been thinking about it."

"There's nothing wrong with it. I did want to come here, but I'm not obsessed over it." Trent's shoulders raised in a slow, rolling shrug. "It just bugs me when people mythologize a place because it has a different culture, and then treat it like it's just one big fucking voyeuristic playground. Just because something is different doesn't mean you have to point and gawk and talk about it like it can't be taken seriously." Trent shrugged. "Or whatever. Fuck it. I'm half-drunk and feel like being a philosopher."

Nate watched Trent rub slow circles along his stomach, smiling faintly. "I see what you're getting at, though. But my brother wasn't like that. He just felt connected to the superstition and legends surrounding this place for other reasons. He liked thinking there was some place that he belonged."

"Why would he belong here?"

"It doesn't matter. I was just wondering if he got to come."

Trent's hand paused in mid-rub. "Why don't you know? Weren't you close?"

"No."

Typically, conversations about Theo brought back memories that had the power to send Nate crawling into his bed until they retreated, but it didn't happen this time. He didn't know if it was the combination of beer, food, and the warmth of the day, or if he was being drugged by the golden waves he'd been absorbing from Trent, but he found himself talking.

"I had a lot of problems in high school. I wasn't a popular kid, and after a while I became a target. I guess I made myself a target. I was gay and not very many kids were out, so when I got involved with one of the closeted ones and people found out, I didn't get off the hook unscathed. There's a lot more to it, but . . . yeah. People started at the bottom of the pyramid of Nathaniel-hate and worked themselves up to extreme acts of violence. And my brother made it worse. He didn't want his name thrown into the drama. He wanted to be with the cool kids."

"He got in good with the guys who bullied you?"

"Yes. He did a lot more than that—he fucked the guy I liked while pretending to be me. It ruined our relationship. We just cut each other off. After graduation, he left town. So I don't know if he went straight to New York or if he stopped along the way like we did."

Trent nodded. It seemed like he would lean in to say something more, but he turned his attention to a loud, drunken couple who had just stumbled into the restaurant.

The rest of the meal was quiet. It was natural, comfortable, and necessary with Nate's mind wandering down avenues that all led to Theo.

Twins were not supposed to hate each other. His mother had always told him twins were special, but that he and Theo were more special than most since they were connected by an enigmatic, supernatural bond. It should have been impossible to hate each other. But they'd managed. They'd managed and excelled at it, and now they would never have the chance to make amends.

But there was always the vision. Nate couldn't explain why or how it had come to him, and not for the first time, he wished he had someone to ask about it.

They left the restaurant and spent time walking through the French Quarter. Bourbon Street was getting crowded, but Nate barely saw the people. He passed it all in a blur of lights, strip clubs, stumbling tourists clutching plastic cups of half-drunk alcohol or large, neon-green containers called hand grenades. After a while it all looked the same, and Nate began shutting down the parts of his brain that did not want to deal with the sensory overload of being surrounded by loud, happy people. It wasn't until Trent grabbed his arm and tugged him along that Nate snapped out of the cloud of cynicism that had descended around him.

"I'm going to have to crash here tonight," Trent said loud enough to be heard over the music blasting from open doorway after open doorway. He leaned closer to Nate, listing forward unsteadily and grinning. Nate had somehow failed to realize Trent was holding a hand grenade himself. "I'm pretty close to being drunk, and I kind of want to say fuck it and go all out since I'm here. C'est la vie or as the kids say, YOLO."

"YOLO?"

"You only live once. Fucking wise, I know."

They had stopped walking after Trent led them around the corner and off Bourbon Street. They were in front of an art gallery, the windows full of brightly hued paintings that depicted scenes of the city's jazz culture. It was all oranges and yellows, pale blues and brass.

"If you're in a rush to get up to New York real fast, go ahead. Do you."

Trent braced one of his hands against the door to the shop, his breath warm against Nate's face. His first instinct was to back away, but he didn't. Despite the proximity, there was no flash of panic. No leeriness at the idea of their skin touching or Trent doing something unwanted or unexpected. If anything, warmth flooded him yet again. They'd known each other for only a day but it felt like more.

Maybe it was because they'd been alone for hours with nothing but the black whip of the road spooling out before them, or maybe it was something else. That deliciously strange sensation that sparked whenever they were close.

"I—" Nate cleared his throat. "Do you want me to find someone else to hitch with?"

"No. I told you I'd drive you the whole way. We've been having fun. I like you."

Nate smiled slightly. "Okay. I can't afford a room though."

"It's okay, you can stay with me."

Nate looked at Trent more closely, wondering how drunk he was. "I'll just wander and sleep in the car tomorrow."

"That's stupid."

"No, it's not. You don't know me, and I don't want things to be weird tomorrow because you're making drunk-cisions now."

"Drunk-cisions," Trent repeated. He listed forward again, his chest bumping against Nate's before he took a step back. "What are you all worried about? That we're gonna have drunken sex?"

"Uh. No. You're straight. I'm more worried that you'll wake up tomorrow thinking I took the chance to score a free room."

"Who says I'm straight?"

Sighing, Nate stepped away from the door and grabbed Trent's forearm. A hot whip of lust sizzled Nate's skin. He nearly lost his balance, but held on. Trent was just drunk. Drunk and maybe curious. It meant nothing. Clearly Trent needed distractions. Maybe one of the strip clubs that lined a patch of Bourbon.

"I just assumed you are," Nate said.

"So maybe I'm not. Assuming usually causes people to make erroneous statements."

"Good job using three-dollar words when smashed, Mr. Caltech. But I'm pretty sure you are. Have you ever been with a guy?"

"Yes. It was very engineers gone wild."

Nate scoffed. "How wild?"

"I kissed this guy a few times when we were drunk."

"That's it?"

Trent shrugged. "He started dating some other dude, and it didn't happen again. I wasn't interested in any other guys until now."

Until now. Jesus Christ, what was even happening?

"Okay, buddy. Let's go see strippers."

Trent's hand slid down, and he twined his fingers with Nate's. His palm was sweaty, slightly sticky, and somehow it still sent another shot of heat straight to Nate's gut. He disentangled his fingers, ignoring both the mischievous grin on Trent's face and the urge to keep reaching out with his gift to find out if this was legit.

They wound up at a smaller, dingier strip club mostly because they were hauled in by the people who worked the door. Once inside, Nate had no idea what to do. The girls were friendly, charming, and more physical than Nate had expected.

Never having been in a strip club, he'd populated all kinds of notions in his mind about no touching rules and bouncers who hovered, but a long, lean girl with bronze hair and a dark tan had straddled Trent almost as soon as they'd walked in. She proceeded to grind against him in a mimicry of fucking that had Trent's fingers digging into the chair, and Nate keenly interested in the way his new friend's face flushed when he was turned on.

Nate watched while Trent was distracted, feeling safe in his ability to observe undetected. He focused on the way Trent's Adam's apple bobbed in his throat, the way his hips gave an aborted jerk when the girl ground down on him, like he was close to losing control and was forcing himself to keep a grip on it. The way his T-shirt clung to his arms, the cords of his neck when he tilted his head back, and the occasional low swear.

It all built up until Nate was frustrated, turned on, and agitated. Bitterness made him spend money on overpriced drinks, but he stopped caring and hung out by the bar. Thoughts of his family, of his uncle, kept infiltrating the small buzz he had, and he wanted to keep them out. They were gone. Brookside was in the past. It didn't matter anymore. He was free.

Three shots later, he found himself blindly following when the girl asked Trent to go into the VIP room with her. Nate had started to refuse but had caved immediately once Trent's heavy lidded eyes fell on him. Nate's dick went from half-mast to fully erect almost instantly.

It was a stupid reaction, and his body was a traitor. Trent was drunk, likely just open to experimenting, and Nate screwing up his ride to New York was a bad idea. He'd never made a friend this fast, and had definitely never felt this at ease with another person. Besides, he hadn't had sex in ages, so why fuck up his ride just to get laid now?

Nate's last attempt to mess with a guy he'd met online had been disastrous. Horrific vibes had pressed into him as soon as they'd touched. Experiences like that were the entire reason he spent most of his time nearly celibate, but rationale fled his mind once they were in the small, dark room.

The girl, Mandy, was beautiful and clad only in a metallic thong, but Trent kept staring at Nate instead of her. Nate kept his eyes on Mandy. She was no help.

"I think your friend could use a hand," she said, lips spreading in a wicked smile.

"Shut up," Nate muttered. He glanced over at Trent, and his balls tightened in response to the sight of Trent slumped in the chair, long legs sprawled and the unmistakable hardness in his jeans.

Mandy ground against the pole and did some kind of acrobatic move that should have gotten her into a better paying gig than stripping. "Why don't you sit a little closer?"

"Yeah," Trent said, voice low and nearly lost in the music pounding from the speakers. He tugged Nate closer on the couch, leaving one of his arms extended along the back. "Unless you don't want to sit closer . . ."

It was a little late for that since Nate was crushed against his side, one hand maddeningly close to Trent's denim-clad thigh. "Uh. I don't know."

Mandy laughed. "Eyes up here, sugar. Don't scare him."

Trent looked up at her, nodding, but now Nate couldn't turn away. He was so fucking hot. Everything, from the stubble that covered his jaw to the plush pink of his lower lip and the messy hair that reached the nape of his neck, was perfect.

The music changed, seemed louder, and Nate could see Mandy writhing against the pole in his peripheral vision but could only stare, openmouthed, at the way Trent was pressing his hand against his own dick. There was no mistaking the hard line of it through his jeans.

Trent tilted his head back, watching Mandy from beneath half-closed lids. Nate's breath caught when Trent turned and looked, once again, at him instead of the girl on the small stage.

"I'm really hard," Trent said, breath a wash of alcohol.

"Oh. I, uh, that seems normal."

"Yeah." Trent's eyes settled on the erection raging in Nate's skintight jeans. "I thought you were gay."

Nate shrugged helplessly. His fingers itched to brush against Trent, to get closer, especially when Trent palmed his own dick and squeezed.

"Fuck," Trent breathed.

"Take it out, sweetie. I won't tell."

Nate licked his lips anxiously, shooting Mandy a glare. "Stop. Please."

She was still grinning, dancing idly and more keen on watching them. "Get a clue, kid."

When Nate said nothing, she rolled her eyes and jumped off the small platform, sky-high heels clicking against the floor. She strode over to them and leaned forward, unzipping Trent's jeans with one decisive flick of her fingers. Trent shuddered and slid his hand inside, pulling his dick out and pumping it with no hesitation, as if permission had been given to get off right there.

Nate sat there, paralyzed, even as his body grew hot, demanding he touch his dick as he watched Trent fuck his own hand. But he couldn't move, couldn't stop watching, even as Mandy coaxed him to help Trent out.

"Nothing better than watching two pretty boys go at it," she purred.

Trent's arm descended from the back of the couch. His hand rested on one of Nate's shoulders and pulled him closer before pressing his face into the sweaty crook of Nate's neck. A hot rush of vibes coursed between them, and Trent's lust saturated Nate. He absorbed it hungrily, reaching out with his gift without hesitation. The buzz of alcohol and their combined desire was making him stupid, careless, and he sucked in Trent's emotions like a vacuum.

"Sorry," Trent whispered. "Just so fucking horny, and you look so good."

Panting, Nate fumbled with his own jeans. He couldn't get the fucking things open. A low, feminine chuckle penetrated the fog of mindless need that consumed him, and he got the button undone.

It took a matter of seconds to go from frustrated and trying to shove his jeans down to jerking himself off with fast, rough movements as Trent's lips brushed his neck.

A strangled sound escaped Nate's throat, and to his dismay, Trent pulled away. But the disappointment faded because this was better. Staring into the light blue of Trent's eyes as they got off was everything. Their faces were so close that he could practically taste the sweat on Trent's face, the cloying sweetness of mixed drinks on his lips, but when their foreheads pressed together, noses brushing, they didn't kiss. They just locked eyes, breathing against each other's face, until Trent released a low, ragged sound, eyebrows knotting up as he came. He went slack against the couch, sticky and covered in his own semen, and then watched Nate. Trent licked his lips, eyes rapt on the motion of Nate's hand, and reached out to rub the back of Nate's neck. Mandy, it seemed, was totally forgotten.

"I'd suck your dick if I didn't think it would freak you out," Trent said, the words clumsy and slurred. "I've always wanted to try."

The words set Nate off. He was coming hard within seconds, striping his chest and neck, mind whitewashed and eyes unseeing. Without the alcohol in his system, he'd have been mortified by the sounds coming out of his mouth—high-pitched and broken. Needy. But he was drunk, so they just got louder as a hot, wet tongue slid against his throat after he threw his head back against the couch.

"Oh God."

The sound of someone clapping interrupted the haze of lust. Nate looked up blearily, fumbling to cover himself when he realized Mandy was the one applauding.

"Nice show, boys. I almost feel bad for charging you."

"Whatta scam," Trent said. He casually pulled away from Nate, like he hadn't just licked jizz from his skin. Trent stood up, tall and muscular and so hot that Nate felt he must have imagined the past ten minutes. Trent zipped up and jerked his chin at Mandy. "But I guess I can't get mad."

"Nope. Something tells me you needed that push, booboo."

"True."

Nate got to his feet, mind spinning and feeling like he'd been transported to an alternate universe as they forked up nearly a hundred bucks and left the tiny room. They took turns washing up in the bathroom and left the strip club. Nate allowed Trent to lead him to yet another bar as he replayed the jerk-off session over and over in his mind. Had it been the stripper getting Trent so hot or had it really been him? Was it the booze or was the constant blaze of desire exuding from Trent real?

The questions circled until Trent got so drunk that Nate had to assist him in getting a hotel room. Nate shoved Trent on the bed, watching with a half smile as he curled up and fell instantly asleep. It was tempting to stay, but with doubt already gnawing at him and Trent totally incoherent, Nate forced himself to stagger back down to the street.

The throngs were getting wilder the later it got, and the stench of stale alcohol and vomit was enough to kill the mood. He wandered most of the night, bought more beignets and loitered in Café Du Monde as enormous roaches skittered underfoot. After a while, he found a bench outside Jackson Square and curled up on it. He turned on his phone so Trent could call him in the morning, and the voice mail notification loudly chimed.

Seeing Eveline's phone number was enough of a shock for him to play the message.

"I know where you're going, and it's a mistake. Whatever you think about me and your uncle, it isn't worse than what you'll find up there. Don't be an idiot, boy. Don't be like your mother. Come home."

He deleted it and closed his eyes, but sleep didn't arrive.

When the sun rose he returned to where the car had been parked and waited for Trent. The fear that Trent would leave him behind wasn't too far from his thoughts, especially if last night had been a colossal, drunken mistake that Trent now wanted to take back. It wouldn't be the first time a straight boy regretted experimenting in the heat of a moment. That was what had started everything back in high school.

Fear wormed its way into Nate until he paced the sidewalk in agitation, rubbing his hands together and obsessively looking at his phone to check the time. But Trent showed up an hour later. He was sleepy and hungover, but he was there and grumbling about Nate being a "flatleaver." He let Nate use the bathroom in his hotel room to wash up, insisted on breakfast before leaving the city, and neither of them mentioned what had happened in the strip club. Nate wondered if Trent even remembered.

The car was sweltering by the time they returned to it. It was already well into the eighties and humid when they left New Orleans at half past nine.

Nate dozed off more than once, his head tilted against the window and arms crossed loosely over his chest. He woke up twice to find Trent glancing at him, but his eyes skittered away quickly each time, and neither of them spoke for the next several hours.

CHAPTER SEVEN

T he world blinked as soon as the wave washed over Nate's head.

The sun disappeared, and the sound of seagulls, distant laughter, and the crash of gray-blue waves faded away. There were only shadows, a whisper of movement, and the sensation of sinking into nothingness. He thrashed in confusion but knew he had to keep swimming. The instinct to survive overpowered everything else, even when the darkness settled and vague, shadowy shapes formed around him.

A large avenue, the rank smell of a river, and further down—a large military ship. He was in New York again.

Run.

The vision was not as clear as it had been the first time, but Nate was still Theo.

Run.

The world blinked and time skipped, and he was on a pier, facing off with someone.

Run.

He could feel Theo's confusion, but there was no surprise—no feelings that would result from being confronted by a stranger.

Run.

Theo had obviously planned to meet someone on the pier that night. It was the voice telling him to run that was unexpected.

Run.

So he'd ignored it.

Nate was slammed by a wall of hostility from the murky figure in front of him. He started to turn away, but an invisible grasp suddenly held him in place. He tried to resist, to regain control, and he was hit with the sensation of his mind being ripped apart.

"*Nate!*"

The voice burst in, distorting the already cloudy vision and sending ripples gliding across it. His surroundings twisted, darkened. Impressions seeped in from the real world—a mix of concern and fear that made Nate want to disengage from the vision and see who was transmitting those emotions to him. But he didn't go back. He remained in his brother's body, in the vision, arguing with the faceless person on the pier while he slowly lost control of his mind and body.

"*You should have stopped when I warned you, Theo. You should have just left it alone!*"

The vision had distorted so much that the voice was garbled, genderless, but filled with frustration and anger. Then, without warning, hands violently pressed against him, and he was falling. The sensation of weightlessness lasted only a second before his body hit the water.

He broke the surface, but a sharp pain whited out his vision and crushed his mental barriers. He sank again. The water stank, and the salty-sourness filled his mouth as his limbs failed to cooperate. To swim. Stay afloat. Do something. Survive.

His head was too heavy, and his body wouldn't respond to his commands even when he strained against the force keeping his arms at his sides. Water filled his mouth and nose and panic set in. He screamed. Water poured into his mouth.

"*Nate!*"

Nate's eyes snapped open. Blue skies and the beginnings of a sunset stretched above him.

His lungs burned and his mouth was puckered and salty, but the darkness was gone.

New York was gone. The predator was gone. He was in Jacksonville again. He was with Trent.

Surging up, Nate doubled over and retched seawater into the sand. His eyes squeezed shut, damp hair hanging in his face as his lungs burned, rejecting his attempts to suck in air.

"Shit, man. What the hell happened?"

A palm pressed between his bare shoulder blades, and Nate tensed, shying away. The hand didn't move—if anything, it became more insistent. Another hand joined the first and then Trent was pulling Nate away from the foul puddle and helping him to sit upright.

Nate stared, wild-eyed, as one of Trent's hands cupped the side of his face and the other braced his neck. The gallop of Nate's heart steadied, and the warmth of Trent's concern flowed into him. He latched on to the feeling, wanting it to fill him and push the horror away.

Placing his hands over Trent's wrists, he took a deep breath and exhaled with a sigh as the connection strengthened.

Trent's eyebrows narrowed slightly. His gaze flicked down to where they were touching.

"What happened?" he eventually asked. "You just sank like a rock."

"I— I—"

Nate's teeth were chattering even though it was ninety degrees and the sand was scalding the bottoms of his bare legs. But he could still feel the chilly New York air. Could still smell and taste the water.

"Let's go," Trent said.

Nate let himself be hauled up, strong hands under his arms nearly dragging him. The heels of his feet dug into the sand, and Trent grunted, nearly tripping over a young woman who was sunbathing on a striped towel.

"Is he okay?" She pushed her sunglasses to her forehead. "Did he drown?"

"He's fine." Trent threw one of Nate's arms around his neck. "Just got a little cocky with the swimming trying to show off for the New Yorker. Right, babe?"

Nate coughed again, throat burning. He tried to pry Trent's arm off him. "What?"

"That sure got your attention." Trent steadied Nate. "Next time don't go out so far, man."

When the lady chimed up that he should listen to his boyfriend, Nate just stared at her and then at Trent. After a moment, Trent tugged him along again. This time, Nate independently moved his feet, but his mind was still disconnected from the motions. They left the beach after Trent grabbed their bundle of sand-covered clothes.

Before Nate could think to protest, his bare feet were kissing the sizzling concrete as Trent led him to his hotel.

"I'm fine," Nate croaked. "I can find my own place to stay."

"Yeah, okay." Trent stopped in front of a ground-floor room by the pool at the motel and pulled out his key card. After fumbling with it and swearing quietly at the magnetic strip, Trent unlocked the door.

"I really am," Nate insisted. He hovered in the doorway as Trent chucked their ball of clothing onto the floor.

"Nate, relax yourself. Come in and shut the door before the cold air goes out."

Nate gingerly closed the door and pressed his back against it. He wanted to sit down. The nausea and dizziness hadn't entirely faded, but he still hesitated to go deeper into the room.

"What the hell happened out there? You legit nearly drowned and started freaking out when I pulled your raggedy ass out."

"Freaking out how?"

"Like a freak."

Nate slid down to the floor, leaving a damp streak against the door. "Maybe I'm just dehydrated."

"Uh-huh."

"What do you want me to say? I'm sorry I got sick and blacked out? I'm sorry you had to drag me across the sand and apparently tell random people that we're a gay couple? What the hell was that about?"

"Don't change the subject. And don't give me that dehydrated bullshit. We've been traveling together for a couple of days now. You've fallen asleep I don't know how many fucking times in the car because I know for a fact that you're just wandering around at night when I get a room, and I know that's your plan tonight too."

"I—"

"No, no, don't lie. I'm not stupid."

Trent sat on the edge of the bed and ran a hand through his hair. He squeezed some of the water out, and it dripped down the sides of his face, droplets trailing to his clavicle and farther. Nate's eyes automatically followed them but he jerked them away and instead stared at the bright, turquoise wall next to the bed.

"Look, I'm sure you're doing it for money, and that's all good. But the point is, you sleep like shit, you barely eat, and you're always passing out in the car and mumbling wild shit, and you did it again just now. We don't know each other well, but we've been spending a ton of time together while crossing this country, and it's been fun. New Orleans was the best time I've had since I started grad school, but the sleep talking is starting to creep me out."

Nate sat up so fast his spine popped. "Sleep talking?"

Trent hesitated and stood up again. He grabbed the ball of clothes and began untangling them. His wet trunks clung to his thighs and ass, showing every line of rock-hard muscle. "It's not coherent. Sometimes you sound scared. Like you're being attacked. It makes me wonder."

"Wonder what?"

Trent draped a damp T-shirt across the back of one of the chairs in the room. "How much of what you said was the whole truth? I know it's none of my business, but I wonder. Did something bad happen to you?" When Nate didn't respond, Trent spread his palms. "I'm not judging you. I'm not saying I think you're a liar and I'm going to toss you out of the car. Even though we just met, I'm worried about you. That's all."

Nate rubbed his hands against the carpet, slumping against the door as weariness set in. The urge to unload some of the burden was hard to resist. Sharing secrets had never worked out so well for him in the past, but Trent was different. He had to be.

"You'll think I'm crazy if I tell you the full story."

"Remember what I said about it not mattering what I think in a couple of days?"

"Yeah, but you will literally think I'm disturbed. Like should be institutionalized."

When Trent just waited, Nate looked at his reflection in the full-length mirror lining one wall. He flinched at how much weight he'd lost in the past few weeks. It had taken him years to ditch the slight, frail build he and Theo had inherited from their mother, but lack of balanced meals and protein had caused some of the weight to slide off his already lean frame. The muscle was still there though, leaving his body sinewy and hard.

"I'm waiting."

Nate's eyes snapped to Trent. "Fine. You really want to know?"

"That's why I'm asking, man."

"Fine," Nate said again. He set his jaw, teeth grinding as his heart sped. "Before the police contacted me to tell me he was dead, I had a vision of my brother's death, and it keeps coming back. Just now in the water? I blacked out, and it happened again. I was him, and I felt it when he was shoved off the pier. I felt how helpless he was, how paralyzed. I felt it when he started to drown."

When Trent didn't immediately reply, Nate jumped to his feet. "That's why I didn't want to tell you. Everyone always thinks I'm a freak, and I knew you would too and kick me out of your car."

"What the hell? Why would I do that?"

"Because people getting weirded out and wanting to keep their distance from me is the story of my life. And I didn't want it to happen with you. I didn't want— I just wanted us to be friends."

"We are friends," Trent said quickly, taking a step forward. "And I didn't say I didn't believe you."

"So then say something. Don't stand there and give me that look!"

"What look? I don't even have an expression!"

"You don't have to. After forty-eight of hours of constantly being in your presence, I can read you pretty well."

Trent moved even closer, his hands pressed together in supplication. "Look, calm down. I'm not saying I think you're crazy. I didn't say anything."

"Do you believe me?"

"I don't think you're lying."

Nate scoffed. "Oh, I get it. You think I really believe it so it's not lying. But you still don't buy it."

"Well, the idea of you having a vision about your brother's death is a little hard to swallow, Nate. And I'm trying here. I want to believe you and be on your side. But there's nothing in my mental toolbox to explain how that's possible."

Now that it was out in the open, Nate was weighted down by the need to prove himself. He knew what Trent was thinking. That he was so traumatized by Theo's death, he was willing to grasp at straws as a coping mechanism. Or that he was trying to latch on to the idea of murder so he wouldn't have to justify a suicide—as if he were some über-religious Texan. And he couldn't fault Trent for having doubts. Those things made sense. This supernatural, extrasensory strange thing that Nate could do didn't make sense.

"I'll prove it."

Trent frowned. "Prove what? The vision?"

"No . . . I—" Proving one thing just required exposing another secret. "I'll prove that psychic powers exist. Give me something of yours that you have an emotional attachment to."

Trent was still frowning at him. "Why? What are you going to do?"

Nate sucked in a breath and elbowed past his fear and self-doubt. Maybe, for the first time, he could use his talent to gain someone's trust. Maybe this would work. If there was anyone he could trust, based on the influx of constant impressions during the dozens of hours they'd spent in each other's presence, it was Trent.

"I'm going to prove I'm not delusional. You're an engineer. Engineers like facts and evidence, right?" Maybe that was scientists. "I'll give you proof that the world *you* live in is only half of the story. There's more." Now Trent really was looking at him like he'd lost it, but Nate didn't back down. "Just give me something of yours that has a strong memory attached to it."

"Fine. You're creeping me out, but I can play along."

Trent rooted around in his bag and removed a small box. From the box, he gingerly pulled out a chain with a cross hanging from it, delicate and burnished gold. He held it out, the thin chain dangling from his fingers, and seemed reluctant to hand it over. After a second of trepidation, he did. And as soon as Nate touched it, there was a flash.

The same horror that had assaulted him when he'd touched that white Dodge Monaco a few days ago assaulted his senses again. The world washed over with red, and a jumble of pain and terror. Panic flooded his senses. Nate dropped the necklace.

"What?" Trent bent to retrieve it. "What's wrong?"

"What is that?" Nate asked, shuddering. "Why do you have it?"

Trent closed his fist around the chain. "It was my mother's. Why? What did you . . . sense?"

Nate sucked in a breath and looked at the necklace again. How could he explain? He hadn't expected Trent to trust him with an object that could trigger something like this.

"I'd rather not say."

"Just tell me. Please." There was a hint of desperation in Trent's voice, an urgency that pitched it low. He grabbed Nate's arm, and the impressions of his feelings joined the others. Before Nate could orient himself, he was stumbling to the bathroom to throw up. It was too much to digest, to figure out, and he didn't know why the fuck he was playing Professor X with someone else's memories when he barely had a handle on his talent. He retched again, eyes squeezed shut and tearing, and crouched on the floor for several minutes before standing up to wash his mouth out.

When he left the bathroom, Trent was sitting on the edge of the bed. The necklace was nowhere in sight.

"Are you okay?" he asked.

"Yes."

"Okay."

Nate sat down on the bed next to him. "Did someone hurt her?"

Trent looked up, his jaw clenched and eyes full of pain. "Yes."

"That's all I could feel," Nate admitted. "Sometimes when there's a strong feeling attached to an object or a place, I can feel it too. Like bad energy. When it's really powerful, I get sick. But I didn't see anything specific. I just . . . knew something awful had happened, but not exactly what. I'm sorry."

"Don't be sorry." Trent turned to face Nate. "They found who killed her. I didn't mean for it to seem like I wanted you to go all . . . psychic CSI. It was just a surprise that you could . . ." He swallowed hard, his fingers clenching. "That you could feel what she felt."

"I'm sorry," Nate said again. "I'm sorry to dredge this up."

"No. I'm sorry," Trent said quietly. "You told me you could pick up on memories, and I gave you the necklace she wore when she died. That's fucking awful, and I feel like a bastard." After a brief hesitation, he touched the side of Nate's face. "I didn't mean to hurt you. I didn't think anything would happen."

They looked at each other as Trent dragged his fingers along the curve of Nate's cheekbone. When his hand fell away, Nate missed the sensation. Two days of knowing Trent, and he was addicted to his touch. Slivers of the vibes Trent almost always exuded were sliding into Nate and swarming inside of him until the cold slithery sensation was pushed out. Nate didn't understand how it was that just a slight graze of Trent's sun-warmed skin could wash away so much negativity. What would it be like if they got even closer? If they kissed? Or fucked.

Nate looked away. "Do you believe me now?"

"Yes." Trent cleared his throat. "So, can you pick up on what other people are feeling or just objects?"

"I can do both."

There was another stretch of them looking at each other, considering each other, before Trent left the bed and began pacing the room.

"Is it effortless or do you have to try?"

"It depends," Nate said vaguely. "But it's not always a good talent to have. Sometimes I don't know if there *is* a good talent to have."

Trent stopped pacing. "So you know other psychics."

"Yes . . ." They were entering into territory even more treacherous than admitting his own talents. It was everything Eveline had always sworn him not to do, but he was doing it anyway. "It's hereditary. My entire family has psychic talents." The astonishment on Trent's face prompted Nate to fumble into an explanation. "My brother was an empath, but he was also a precog—he got premonitions. So does our uncle." *Father.* "I've never had visions before, so I don't really understand why it's happening now."

"Well, how does it work?" Trent asked. "Can't you just . . . get one? Like that chick in *Twilight*?"

Nate looked at him sideways. "I've never read *Twilight*, so I don't know. But you have to be either a precog or a postcog, and I'm not either. I started wondering if maybe . . . someone was sending them to me. Someone who saw what happened."

Trent's brows rose. "Like who?"

"I don't know." Nate wiped a hand over his face and exhaled slowly. "I just know it's not me. I'm not a very strong empath, let alone suddenly having other psychic powers. And in my family, we seem to inherit gifts. My mother never talked about her talent, but I think she was probably an empath since both me and Theo are, but I guess she could have had multiple gifts. My aunt is a telepath—she could hear my thoughts and sometimes send messages to me. Usually to tell me how useless I am."

"Holy fucking shit." Trent combed both hands through his hair. "Is everything real? The whole X-Men crew?"

The question startled a laugh out of Nate. Some of the tension eased from his body, and he relaxed against the bed—the first time he'd been on one in days. "I don't know. I'm not close to a lot of my extended family, but I've heard stories about people with rarer talents. Telepathy I think is pretty rare. Then there's postcogs—people who can see the past. Allegedly there are actual people with telekinesis out there, but I've personally never seen someone control objects with their mind."

"Damn. What I could do with some psychic powers . . ." Trent shook his head. "It sounds incredible."

"It's not always a good thing," he repeated. "Sometimes it's hurtful. Or sometimes it just causes trouble."

"For example?"

"For example . . . in high school it led to my life being miserable," Nate admitted. "And my brother and I not speaking to each other anymore."

"How?"

Nate looked out the window, the light streaming in through the pale curtains and blinds. It was nearly eight and the sun was just starting to dip downward.

"There was this football player. Kelvin. He always seemed like an asshole, and one day he was teasing me not only because I was the only out gay kid in our school but because my whole family has a reputation in Brookside for being . . . a group of odd drunken messes."

Trent returned to the edge of the bed.

"Anyway, during the summer before my senior year, we ran into each other in this wooded area by the park. I used to go there to be alone, and I guess he was running along the trail. He started the usual crap . . . like shoving me around and being a dick. It wasn't anything different than what happened at school, but this time we were alone. He pinned me to a tree, and I reached out with . . . my talent." Nate swiped a sweaty hand through his hair. "I reached out and could feel that he was attracted to me. That he wanted me. It was the first time I'd ever felt that, so I was stupid and acted on it."

"What happened?"

"We kissed. And then fooled around in his car. After that, we spent the whole summer secretly meeting and fucking around. He was the first guy I was with. Before that . . . I didn't know how to meet anyone. I didn't try." After all this time, the memories still made him feel sick. "But then my brother found out about it. Theo was too afraid of being alienated to come out and make a move on any guys at school, so he was annoyed that I was hooking up with Kelvin. He was jealous, and when Theo got jealous, he got spiteful. When we got back to school, he intercepted a message Kelvin had left in my locker to come to a party. I wouldn't have gone, anyway. The football and cheer kids didn't like me, and I'd have known it was trouble. So Theo went, pretending to be me. He wound up letting Kelvin and a couple other guys take turns on him. Apparently Kelvin didn't like me as much as I'd thought."

Trent's nostrils flared. The anger in his face was unlike anything Nate had seen so far on their journey. No half smile or dancing mischievous eyes. Just pure rage and protectiveness for a guy he barely knew.

"Was that dude from the liquor store in on it?"

"Yep. That was his friend. The bullshit I got after that was nonstop. I hated my brother, Kelvin, everyone. I was pissed that I'm supposed to be some psychic, and yet I hadn't known Kelvin hadn't really cared about me."

"Did you tell him he'd fucked your damn brother?"

"No. Even though I was angry at Theo, I didn't think we both needed to be fucked up and bullied every day, you know? Not that it mattered. He never even said sorry."

Trent shook his head, jaw clenched. "You never confronted Kelvin?"

"I did, and . . . it was just weird. The whole thing was weird. We went from constantly spending time together during the summer to me avoiding him for weeks after the Theo thing when we were back in school, and when I finally did try to speak to him, everything had changed. He acted like . . . I'd bewitched him and he'd finally snapped out of it. Like he'd fooled around with me against his will. Total fucking bullshit. It all just sucked."

Trent squeezed Nate's arm again. "I'm sorry. If I could go back and beat the shit out of all of them, I would. It sucks you had no one to have your back. And no offense to your brother, but he was a fucking dick."

"Tell me about it." Nate released a slow breath, and let Trent's touch anchor him. "So, you see what I'm saying. Sometimes using my gift isn't a good idea. Kelvin was the biggest thing that's ever happened, but . . . hooking up with other guys hasn't been great either. The last guy I met had all these awful feelings of animosity and self-hatred. It was violent and ugly, and I freaked out. We'd gotten a hotel room and—" God, why was he unloading all of this?

"Fucking Jesus, Nate. He didn't—"

"No! No. I left before anything happened, but . . . the idea that something *could* have is still traumatizing. I was naked with someone who had a serious desire to hurt me because he couldn't stand the fact that he wanted me, and— I don't know. It's been hard for me to trust meeting anyone online since then. It's hard to trust anyone sometimes." Nate covered his face with his hands and groaned. "I'm sorry I'm oversharing, but there is so much bad shit associated with my gift that it's all word vomiting out of me. I've literally never spoken about it with anyone else before. I didn't know it would feel this good to unload."

And just like that, Trent was pulling him close without a second thought. Rubbing his back and enveloping him in all of that warm goodness. God, it was addictive. The touch and feel of him. His smell. Nate melted against him before he could stop himself, and this time he deliberately tapped further into Trent's emotions. There was attraction there, yes. But there was also compassion. And sorrow.

"Thank you."

"For what?"

"Listening."

"Heh. It's all I can do, but I'm glad it helps." Trent brushed a hand over Nate's hair. His fingertips brushed the back of his neck. "This thing you can do—it means you're an empath?"

"Yes. A channel opens between me and whoever is projecting emotions. Or if it's an object, I can feel whatever emotions were attached to it. Sometimes it's stronger, sometimes I can hear things or I see a glimpse of something, but it's never clear."

"If I'm angry, do you get angry?"

"If I let it affect me that way. If I'm not fully in control. I mean, I'm not that good at it. I can bring up a mental shield, but it's weak."

Trent nodded slowly, his face still half-buried in Nate's damp hair. "Then how did you see a vision of your brother dying? Isn't that a postcog thing since it happened in the past?"

"It is, but . . . it felt like someone had planted the vision in my head. Like they sent it to me."

"Who?"

"I don't know," Nate said. "That's what I want to find out."

"Christ." Trent finally pulled away. "This is intense. How are you so normal?"

Nate could have laughed. "I'm not."

"You are, Nate. You're fucking strong. I couldn't handle hearing the details of my mother's death when I sat through the trial. If I had to *watch* it happen, I would lose it."

"Sometimes I feel like I'm on my way to losing it."

Trent looked troubled and several times he started to speak before stopping himself. After a while he said, "Stay here tonight."

"No. I'm fine."

"Don't be so fucking hardheaded." Trent brushed his thumb over Nate's arm. "Come on. You need to sleep."

It was tempting. So tempting that Nate didn't refuse when Trent suggested he at least take a shower and a nap. It was more reasonable than staying all night, but in the end that was exactly what happened. A nap turned into a coma-like sleep, and when Nate's eyes snapped open hours later, it was with a pounding heart and to the sight of drawn curtains and complete darkness in the room.

He shifted on the bed, and his fingers brushed against someone's hand. Trent. They were both in the queen bed.

Confusion eased, but his heart was racing and his body was taut with tension. Nothing seemed exactly real, like he was still caught in the nightmare he knew he'd been having but couldn't remember.

The dreamlike feeling didn't fade, even when Trent rolled onto his side and asked, "You okay?"

Nate didn't respond. He felt Trent move closer, and then warm breath brushed his cheek.

"Nate?"

"Yeah," he said hoarsely.

"You were talking in your sleep again."

Nate closed his eyes. "Sorry I woke you up. Sorry I'm still here."

"Stop." Trent touched his face. "I wish I could help you."

"Me too."

Trent's touch turned into a caress. The tips of his fingers smoothed along Nate's cheek, then down to his jaw and up again. "Can you feel what I'm feeling right now?"

Hints of warmth were soothing enough to chase away the remnants of Nate's nightmare, but it also felt good enough to stir his arousal. Nate took a deep breath. "Kind of."

Trent slid closer, bracing his forearm against the mattress so he could look at Nate's profile in the darkness. After a beat, cool lips brushed Nate's cheek, then trailed down to his mouth, following the same path as his fingers. Nate inhaled sharply.

"How about now?"

"I . . ."

Another kiss. This one was openmouthed, and the dampness against his skin sent fire coursing through Nate's body. He opened the channel between them, and let Trent's vibes flood into him. He instantly felt yearning. It was so strong and real for them only having met a few days ago, and yet . . . everything Trent felt was mirrored in Nate's chest.

Was this what happened when you spent so much time with another person? When there was nothing between you but the center console of the car as you spent every hour of the day getting to know everything about each other?

Was this what Nate had been missing all along?

He inhaled deeply and turned to face Trent.

"I can feel you."

"And is that a good or bad thing?"

"It's good," Nate whispered. "Like this fucking flood of ... of light and warmth. It's almost powerful enough to wash everything else away."

Trent ran his hands through the silky strands of Nate's hair and then cupped the back of his head.

"If I kiss you, will it make it stronger?"

"I don't know."

"Can I try?"

Nate didn't speak. He couldn't. His heart pounded and his breath came in sharp bursts, but he slanted his head and leaned in as Trent did the same. There was a deep inhalation, and then their tongues were tangling. Nate drowned in the feel of this strange man who'd come into his life as if by a force stronger than coincidence.

Nate couldn't bring himself to end it when the kiss grew frantic. He couldn't do more than groan when Trent rolled him on his back and pinned him to the bed. Trent's hand slid down from his face to his chest and dragged over Nate's nipple.

"Oh shit."

"This okay?" Trent asked between increasingly sloppy kisses. "I can stop."

"Don't."

Nate's body was alight with sensation. His desire combined with Trent's in a fireball of both their lust until he couldn't handle it anymore. It was like overload, and after several minutes of breathlessly tonguing each other, Nate reached down to grab his cock. He'd fallen asleep in the cheap board shorts he'd worn to the beach, and it was easy to shove them down to pull his dick out. He stroked it while their lips moved together, panting loud and moaning louder once Trent followed suit and began jerking himself off.

Their bodies were touching at every critical point—mouths, chests, thighs, and the slick heads of both their dicks as they grazed together on each upward stroke. But it still wasn't enough. Every slight brush of skin on skin was a tease, and Nate knew there was more.

"Let me touch it," Trent said hoarsely. "Swap."

Nate made a desperately grateful sound and grabbed Trent's dick. His eyes rolled back once Trent's fingers closed around his own.

Everything intensified until nothing existed but him and Trent in this hazy bubble of lust and want and affection.

"Better?" Trent's voice was lower, thicker, and he was speaking directly against Nate's lips. His hand flew over Nate's length. "Tell me how it feels."

"So fucking good," Nate breathed.

"Tell me more," Trent insisted.

"I just feel your hand, and your mouth, and your dick, but also everything you're *feeling*. Like flares of pleasure every time I squeeze you tight, and how close you are to coming. How bad you want to fuck." Nate arched into Trent's hand. "And everything else is gone. It's just you."

Trent moaned, a faint, ragged sound that was muffled against Nate's face. They kissed again, clashing tongues and clicking teeth that lost rhythm when Trent came hard enough for his shout to fill the room. The sensation of his orgasm rocketed through Nate's body, and he cried out as well, riding Trent's pleasure before releasing his own.

The room grew silent except for guttered breathing and the click of Nate's throat when he swallowed. His ears were full of white noise and balls of light danced before his eyes. He couldn't get it together enough to help Trent mop up the dampness that had spilled on them both.

After several moments of inhaling and exhaling, Nate came back down to earth. Trent had settled beside him again.

"Feel better?"

"Uh. Yeah." Nate licked his lips. "I feel great." Understatement. He felt incredible. He hadn't been touched by another person in so long that he was having a hard time calming down. His heart steadily raced no matter how many deep breaths he took.

"Good."

They lay in silence, but Nate remained on a high that he hoped would coast for the rest of the night until he fell into a blissed-out sleep. There was part of him that wanted to roll over and kiss Trent. Cover him in grateful kisses because this was the second time they'd gotten off together, and it was even better than the last. Two jerk-off sessions had somehow blown Nate's mind more than any other sexual experience he'd had in his life. He didn't know how or why, but something about Trent was special. The connection between them was just so goddamn strong.

Maybe there was such a thing as fate.

"Nate."

"Yeah?"

Trent was on his back, face turned toward the ceiling. "Do you remember what happened in New Orleans?"

"Yes," he said. "I worried you didn't, or that you did and regretted it."

Trent snorted. "No. We're good."

Two words Nate hadn't even realized he'd been waiting for set him at ease. "Good," he echoed, voice drifting off.

Trent patted his thigh and sighed. "We should sleep. We have to get up early tomorrow."

Nate's eyes slid open again, and he turned his face to see Trent's shadowy profile. If they spent the next day making pit stops, they'd have another night together after this one, but it was still too soon.

The very idea of once again venturing forth alone brought Nate almost as much trepidation as the idea of confronting the reality of whatever had happened to Theo in New York.

CHAPTER EIGHT

"**W**here do you want me to take you?"

Nate had been expecting the question the moment they'd turned onto the New Jersey Turnpike. The closer they'd gotten to New York, the more his anxiety had heightened. Now that they were actually in the city, he was completely on edge about whatever he would find, and panicking about never seeing Trent again.

"I don't know. Just drop me on the way to wherever you're going."

"Well, what if where I'm going is not where you're going?" Trent asked, hunched forward in the driver's seat with his eyes hidden by sunglasses.

"It doesn't matter, Trent. I have no idea where I'm going. Somewhere on the west side of Midtown Manhattan."

Trent exhaled through his nose. "You're just going to wander aimlessly around Midtown until you figure out where to go?"

"Maybe? I figured I'd go check out the area where he died."

"It's already getting late. Are you going to fucking sleep in Central Park or something?"

"If that's a good place to sleep, then sure."

"Wow. You're annoying me."

Nate pressed his head back against the seat. Trent's attitude had soured as they'd gotten closer to New York. He seemed impatient and irritated by Nate's lack of a plan and direction. Although their entire trip had been filled with one spontaneous moment after another, getting closer to reality apparently meant that Trent's patience for such things was gone. Or maybe he was as upset about the idea of parting ways as Nate was, and this was how he dealt with it. Especially since they'd spent the previous day in Virginia Beach playing tourist and kissing each other while trying to ignore the fact that their time together was running out. It was hard to believe that the best week of his life was already coming to an abrupt end.

"Seriously, what are you going to do?"

"I told you I have no idea," Nate said, sharper this time. "I don't have it all planned out."

"Fine." Trent took a deep breath. "Do you want me to drop you by the West Side Highway somewhere?"

"Yes, but not directly by the pier. I want to walk around the area and see if . . ." Nate gestured. "I don't even know. See if I get a feel for anything. Then maybe I'll see where his old band used to play."

"Fine."

Trent tapped his finger against the side of the steering wheel. A *tap, tap, tap* that increased in speed as his swears became more frequent and the traffic got thicker. Nate looked out the window again. The roads were a maze to him, branching off in different directions with so many signs that he had no idea where Trent was headed. Harlem River Drive one way, Amsterdam Avenue another. It meant nothing to Nate.

"Are we already in Manhattan?"

"Yes," Trent said curtly.

Nate sighed again and ran a hand over his face. "I guess just let me out whenever we aren't on a freaking highway."

The comment earned him a third "Fine."

Shooting Trent an irritated look, Nate glanced at the clock. It was almost eight o'clock, and he was tired and hungry. He'd wasted so much money over the past few days that he was down to under a hundred bucks and had no idea about what he was going to do for the night. As if reading his thoughts, Trent glanced over again.

"Look, if I wasn't subletting a friend's apartment, I'd tell you to stay with me. I have to talk to her first. It didn't even occur to me before now."

"I'll be okay, Trent. I get it. I'm not expecting you to do any more for me than you already have."

Trent didn't look satisfied with that response, and he clammed up again. They drove in silence for another twenty minutes and, before Nate was entirely prepared, they were pulling over on a busy avenue.

With the engine running as they double-parked, Nate looked at Trent in alarm. Saying a quick good-bye as a cop glared at them from the sidewalk wasn't what he'd had in mind for their farewell. But he didn't know what he'd had in mind. Something . . . more.

"Where are we?"

"Columbus Circle. I don't know why I brought you here, but it's on the west side and it's well lit. There are a lot of different subways and cops and shit." Trent raked a hand through his hair, causing it to tumble everywhere. "Don't sleep in Central Park, I swear to God."

"Is that near here?"

"Nate, don't fucking sleep in the park!"

"I'm not," Nate protested. "I'm just trying to get my bearings. I don't know anything about this city."

Trent's phone started ringing. He ignored it, focused on Nate. "I could stay and show you around for a while. Hang out until you have a plan. Or walk you to the pier."

"No."

"But—"

"No! I'll be fine. I need to do this on my own." Nate unclipped his seat belt. "Stop worrying about me. People do this all the time. No one's going to fuck with me. I can hold my own in a fight. Getting bullied for years made that necessary."

Trent didn't look convinced, but he turned, reaching into the backseat to fumble for Nate's bag. Rustling sounds emanated from the back, and his T-shirt rode up and exposed the long, lean length of his tanned back. There were a couple of scattered freckles near Trent's hip. Nate averted his gaze and tried not to think about how he'd run his mouth all over that body the previous day. They hadn't had sex, but they'd done a lot of touching and making out. Trent had teased him that they'd been living the awesome boy-on-boy action neither of them had gotten in their teenage years.

"Do you have my number?"

"Yes."

"Your phone charger?"

Nate fought a smile. "Yes. I'll be fine. Relax."

"I can't relax. I'll be worried about you. You—" Trent sighed in frustration, met Nate's eyes, and then grabbed hold of his hand.

The connection opened between them, but all of that warm affection and desire was dampened by worry and fear. It would have been nice to reach out longer, to drown himself in Trent's vibes, but the worry was all-consuming. Nate pulled back.

"I never connect with people," he said quietly. "But I connected with you. And I wish we weren't saying good-bye."

Trent's expression was fierce again. "Look, you're not going into the military. We'll both be in the city. We have phones. You can call me. We can hang out. And like I said, I'll ask my friend if you can stay with me until you have things sorted out." He searched Nate's face. "Okay?"

"Okay."

"Promise me."

"I promise."

"Good." Trent leaned in to brush a kiss to Nate's mouth. It was over so quickly that Nate didn't have the chance to respond. "And don't tell anyone else what you told me. About what you saw."

"I won't."

Within a moment, Nate was out of the car and Trent was gone. Nate stood on the sidewalk with his bag hefted over one shoulder. He watched the Nova's retreating headlights until they were lost and mixed in with the hundreds of others.

Steeling himself and pushing the sense of loss aside, Nate turned in a slow circle and tried to adjust to the city that sprawled around him. Lights, people, and enormous glass towers shooting up into the sky. They curved around him in a strangely disorienting circular pattern.

He was standing next to what appeared to be a large, metallic globe and across the street there was a seemingly random cluster of trees. The sidewalk expanded from a large park in a wide arc and was lined with food carts and stands selling items that he was too far away to discern. At the edge of the park was a large monument with gold inlay.

Nate looked up at the signs. At first, the numbers meant nothing, but then he thought about the few landmarks he did know of the city and realized he must not be far from the famous Forty-second Street, Times Square area. Tagged onto that thought was another—he was walking distance from where his brother had drowned.

Nate started his trek and lost his direction twice. It was difficult to figure out which way to turn to go up the avenues or down the streets, and he refused to ask a random person for help. It took him nearly ten minutes to get oriented and walk in the right direction.

The further up he went in avenues, the more the crowds dissipated, but even as the number of people thinned, the presence of concrete, buildings, taxis, schools, and stores did not. There was no reprieve in activity. Structures, businesses, and green spaces were clustered together in such close proximity that it was startling.

Nate didn't take much in. He kept his hands shoved in his pockets, his duffel bag slung over one shoulder, and made his way to the West Side Highway. The wind picked up as he got closer to the Hudson River, whipping his hair back as he approached the waterfront. It was as close to being deserted as Manhattan could probably get. With the exception of cars rushing along the highway, it seemed that Nate was alone for blocks in either direction.

Déjà vu hit as he crossed the wide, multilane road and walked alongside the piers. Everything registered without surprise because it was all exactly as it had been in the vision. The distant skyline, the sour smell of the river, and the dark stretch of water reaching out to what he now knew to be New Jersey—he recognized it all and it was easy to overlay the image of the scenery bobbing around him as he, in Theo's body, ran.

He bypassed Pier 90, then the *Intrepid*, and it wasn't until he approached a long concrete pier with a chunk of green space in the middle did something cause him to pause. Dread twisted his guts, and his feet moved of their own accord, taking him to the edge of the pier.

Nate could feel it all so clearly: the water rushing up to meet his—Theo's—face, then filling his mouth. Then he heard that voice again.

"You should have just left it alone!"

How had no one heard those shouted words? Seen Theo's attacker?

In a city that breathed life into the night, how could his brother's murder have gone unnoticed? Someone had stood on this pier, exposed and surrounded by open space with nowhere to hide, pushed his brother off the pier, then stayed long enough to hold him below the water with psychic force, all without a single witness.

Nate backed away from the edge. The impressions were so strong they practically assaulted him through the soles of his shoes. The sense of helplessness. The feeling of suffocation.

Nate turned to flee, but a glitter caught his eye.

There was a small memorial at the end of the pier. Flowers were taped to the side of the pier along with glass candle holders, pictures, and handwritten notes. Nate fumbled in the darkness for his keys and clicked on a tiny penlight that dangled from the ring.

The flowers were fresh, and the pictures were of Theo and the Dreadnoughts. It was one of the pictures he'd found on Tumblr, but there was also a more candid shot of his brother laying on the floor, a guitar at his side and his lips twisted in a sleepy smile. He was painfully thin and his hair was much longer than Nate kept his own, but the picture looked recent.

Nate's first instinct was to keep it for himself, but he didn't disturb the memorial except to extract a small card tucked between the candle holders. It said, *You will always be missed*, and was signed by *Holden and the rest of the staff at Evolution*.

A quick Google Maps search showed Evolution was a club in Hell's Kitchen, and it was only blocks away.

Evolution didn't look like much from the outside.

The club was on the bottom floor of a brick tenement-style building. It had tinted glass doors and an awning made from burnished metal that shone in the darkness. There was no name above the door, no numbers, and other than the line winding down the street, it had no distinguishing characteristics. Nate had passed it twice before realizing it was the right place.

Hanging out across the street, he tried to see inside but failed. There were two employees—a tall woman with red hair and a man who seemed almost entirely covered in tattoos—blocking the door. The space behind them was dark.

He had no other choice but to go in, even if the idea of getting in the line made him want to backtrack in the opposite direction. The waiting crowd was diverse in terms of age, gender, and ethnicity.

The only common factor in the nearly two dozen people was that they were all far more stylish and sophisticated than Nate. Days of wearing Theo's clothing had given him a slight leg-up in appearance since his own wardrobe had consisted of old jeans and T-shirts, but he was still looking rumpled after over ten hours of sitting in the car.

But he wasn't there for fashion, and he wasn't there to fit in. He was there for information.

Pulling at the collar of his shirt, Nate loped across the street and slipped to the back of the line. The two women ahead of him turned and stared. They were outrageously attractive. One had a short haircut with a hard part and was wearing a sharp black suit, while the other wore a dress and heels so high she stood eye level with Nate.

When they kept staring, he looked over his shoulder in confusion. "What?"

"Nothing," the woman in the suit said quickly.

"Wait—" the other began.

"No, no. We're good!"

The one in the suit grabbed her friend's hand and forced her to turn. They whispered to each other, but the traffic, the muffled beat of music, and the crowd drowned out their conversation. Nate realized belatedly their hands had stayed intertwined. He stepped to the side, observing the rest of the line. Many people stood alone, but most of the couples appeared, at first glance, to be same-gender. Leave it to Theo to be a regular at an upscale queer club.

It took almost an hour to get to the front of the line, and by then, Nate was sweating and shifting from foot to foot. Enough people had stared him down, both subtly and blatantly, for him to have realized that this was a potentially catastrophic idea. The suspicion was confirmed when he reached the front and was confronted with the red-haired woman and the tattooed man with the radio. The woman's eyes went round before her face returned to neutrality, but the man sneered. He looked much younger than the woman, who appeared to be in her forties, but the combination of his chalky skin, closely shorn platinum hair, and a body made up entirely of lean, sharp edges, tattoos, and piercings, gave him an aggressive look made more intense by flinty eyes.

"What are you, fucking stupid?"

Nate gaped. "What?"

"Not too bright, are you?"

The woman's stare shifted from Nate to the tattooed man. "You knew he had a twin?"

He gave a cavalier shrug. "It mighta come up."

"I see."

Despite her nonexpression, Nate could tell she was more put out with the asshole guy for knowing this information, than with Nate being there in the first place. He wiped his hands on his shirt and said, "Look, I wasn't intending to pop up and shock anyone. I just wanted to talk to someone who knew Theo."

The woman quit glaring at the tatted punk and inclined her head. "It makes sense. I'm sorry for your loss. That should have been the first thing out of my mouth but . . . you caught me off guard."

"I know. Sorry." Nate glanced at the guy again but found only a steady glare. "I wasn't sure how well-known he was."

"His band performed here regularly," she said. "But he may as well have been a part of the staff considering how much he was here."

"That's good to know." Nate tried to force confidence into his voice, but the hostile man at his side caused nerves to crawl over him. "I'm Nate."

"I'm Beck and our insolent bouncer is Chase."

"'Our,'" Chase repeated with another sneer. "This isn't your club, babe."

She ignored him. "Let us know what you need, and we'd be happy to try to give it to you."

Relief flooded Nate. At least one person was being forthcoming and helpful. "Would it be possible to talk? I'm trying to figure out why . . . I guess I just want to know what his life was like before he died."

"Yes, of course. We can go to—"

"You weren't close to Theo," Chase cut in. "So why the fuck would he go with you?"

Sweat beaded at Nate's brow as he watched the two employees stare each other down, Beck coldly and the man with outright animosity. Had he walked into some sort of work-related power struggle or did this have anything to do with Theo?

After a beat, Beck backed off. "You have a point, Chase. Escort him yourself."

"You're not my supervisor."

"And that's where you're wrong, charmer." For the first time, a hint of a smile touched her lips. "I'm overseeing all of you. Not just Holden. So take him upstairs."

Holden. That was who'd left the card on the pier, or at least who'd signed his name. Close friend, or just the boss man?

Chase's jaw clenched, and for a moment, it seemed like he would argue. In the end, he just jerked his head to the door and shot Nate a glare. "Get your ass inside."

Nate hesitated, and Chase grabbed his shoulder with one surprisingly strong hand and forced him through the door. Nate waited for crackles of animosity to filter through their connection, but nothing happened. Chase gave off absolutely no vibes. From the perspective of mental energy, it was like being touched by a corpse. Nate recoiled and stumbled into the darkness of the club.

"Keep it steady, jackass," Chase snarled over the music. "I need to find you a babysitter before you fuck up even more."

"How have I fucked up? You don't even know me."

"I know enough to have expected you to be the smart one." Chase grabbed hold of him again and dragged him through the crowd. "Let's go to the back."

The interior of the club had the same metallic theme as the outside. The walls looked like sheets of metal complete with exposed studs, and the light bounced off it in dizzying, neon rays as the room shook from the bass. It was difficult to tell which part of the club was considered the back, but instead of trying to figure it out, Nate tugged away from Chase's creepy non-emoting hand and shoved his own away through the crowd.

It was so packed on the dance floor that several people brushed against him along the way. The feel of damp, overheated flesh and sweaty, grasping fingers triggered a desire to bring down a mental wall, but Nate was so overloaded that he couldn't focus enough to create even a weak one.

It was a far cry from the past several days of music and sunlight in the peace of Trent's car. The sense of loss, and his yearning for Trent, was almost staggering.

Fighting growing nausea, Nate was relieved when Chase shoved him toward the bar and out of the crowd. The reprieve was brief because Nate nearly collided with another person—a slight young man with reddish-brown skin and bronze hair shot through with gold highlights. Nate edged away, but recognition sparked in the man's face immediately.

"What the fuck?"

"Twin," Chase said shortly. "Babysit him while I go warn the man."

"What—" He took off before the guy could finish his sentence. "How—"

"I'm sorry," Nate said. "I wasn't going for shock value. I had no idea everyone knew my brother and would instantly fucking recognize me."

"I— No, it's fine. I just didn't know, and fuck, you're the spitting image of Theo." The guy took a calming breath. "I'm Elijah Estrella. I'm the drummer of the Dreadnoughts. The band Theo was in."

Nate nodded, vaguely remembering Elijah's face from pictures on the Tumblr page. The pictures hadn't prepared Nate for a slight frame several inches shorter than him, wrapped in skintight booty shorts and a deep-cut tank top, though.

After a beat of open staring, Elijah put a hand on Nate's hand. Nate jerked away. What was with these people?

"Who's he going to warn?" Nate asked warily. "Holden?"

"Yup. Holden Payne—he owns the club."

"I hope he doesn't make it seem like I'm here to start shit. I'm not here to question anybody. I just—"

"Holden also knew your brother," Elijah added quickly. "He'll want to meet you. Trust me."

"Okay. All I want is to talk to someone who was close to Theo."

"Holden was close to him. He helped Theo a lot when he first got here."

"Helped him, how?"

"You can ask him yourself."

Elijah clasped his hand and pulled him in the direction Chase had gone. Nate tried to extract himself, but the kid was like a lamprey. By the time they reached a spiraling metal staircase, his head was spinning and Elijah was nearly vibrating with pent-up questions.

"I can't believe I never knew he had a twin." Elijah shook his head. "Were you two not close?"

"You could say that."

Elijah gave another resentful head shake. "And you're identical. Except for Theo being cocaine-chic skinny."

Nate had no idea if that meant Theo had really been on drugs or not, so he ignored it. Especially when it was possibly only an attempt to get a rise out of him. "How long was he in your band?"

"About a year."

In Nate's opinion, that wasn't long enough for them to feel entitled to every bit of Theo's past. "Chase didn't look surprised to see me."

Elijah scowled. "That's weird. I don't think Lia or Taína knew either, and they spent almost as much time with Theo as I did after he joined the band."

"He didn't spend time with Chase?"

The upper floor was darker and mostly illuminated by flickers from candle clusters sitting on small tables wedged between sleek purple sofas. The entire area was sectioned off by a rope and sign that said, *Private Parties Only.*

"No. Not at all." Elijah stepped over the rope, encouraging Nate to do the same. "And it's not like Chase is his type, so I doubt they ever fooled around."

"Was Theo fooling around with anyone?"

"He had a boyfriend," Elijah said after a pause. "Jericho is all big and jacked up like a UFC fighter. One thousand percent Theo's type."

Nate filed that tidbit of information away, and remembered that the Dreadnoughts' bass player's name was Jericho. "So, why would Chase know about me when Theo's own band didn't?"

"Who knows. Chase is like practically fucking omniscient though, so maybe that's why."

Startled, Nate looked down into Elijah's dark eyes. Was he being literal or joking? Chase's strong mental walls had been weird, but that didn't mean he was a psychic.

They stopped walking in the middle of the large room. Toward the back and near a door marked *Staff*, Nate saw Chase talking to a tall man in a sharp suit with light-brown hair.

"Let me see if it's okay to bring you over." Elijah started to dart off but paused. "What's your name, anyway?"

"Nathaniel. But everyone calls me Nate."

When Elijah hurried over, Nate stared after him. He'd been at a loss since walking away from Trent earlier in the evening, but now he was overwhelmed to the point of drowning in it. This was moving much faster than he could contend with, especially considering he still hadn't come up with a story other than *I wanted to meet Theo's friends.* Not that it was a complete lie. Nate did want to know the people who'd surrounded his brother, but his motivation was a lot different than they'd expect.

After a moment of waiting, Holden looked in his direction. Nate took it as his cue to approach. Beck ascended the winding staircase and joined them. She stood next to Nate and patted his arm, as if sensing how out of his element he was.

Elijah looked up. "I was just telling them to be nice because you seem really nervous and want to figure out what happened with Theo."

"Uh. Thanks, I guess."

Holden held out a hand. "It's a pleasure to meet you, Nate. I'm Holden Payne."

Nate hesitantly shook Holden's hand, and for the second time that night, he was confronted with a complete block after attempting to use his gift. Nate frowned. It deepened when Holden's mouth curled up into a slight knowing smile. Beside Holden, Beck and Chase were watching closely, Beck with a head tilt and Chase with narrowed eyes.

"You met Chase," Holden said. "He told me he's already exposed his entire ass to you. Sorry about that. My brother was never taught manners, so you'll have to excuse him."

"Half brother," Chase said pointedly.

Elijah very obviously bit back a smile. Beck hovered nearby, looking on edge and worried.

What the hell was going on with these people?

"I appreciate you all introducing yourselves, but I feel like I'm missing something."

"What a shocker," Chase muttered.

"Be nice." Elijah swatted Chase's arm. "He's new. He knows nothing about any of us. I mean . . . like, nothing!"

Chase's narrow shoulders rose. "Sounds like a personal problem to me."

"Chase." Holden's polite smile turned sharp, and he reached down, closing his hand around Chase's shoulder. The two of them scowled at each other, and then Holden leaned down to speak in Chase's ear. Elijah looked on, fixated on Holden's profile, even as Chase's arm wound around his waist.

The three of them made quite the spectacle, and Nate had no idea what to say to regain their attention so he could demand some clarity. And goddamn, he needed some. The mysterious crap was getting under his skin, and their secret smirks and condescending tones made him miss Trent like nothing else.

This was why he typically stayed alone.

"Where are you from, Nate?" Beck asked when the others continued conferring with each other.

"Texas. From the Houston area."

"Did you fly out?" she asked.

"No. I, uh . . . I hitched."

Beck looked startled, but Elijah grinned. "Hey, that's how I got here a few years ago!"

"That's cool?" Nate shifted his gaze to Holden and Beck. This needed to get back on topic. Now. "Like I told them, I wanted to speak to someone who'd been close to Theo. He had a lot of problems, but I'd never known him to be suicidal. I . . . want to know what had been happening in his life before he died."

Beck nodded. "I'm not sure how much insight I have about his mind-set, but I'm willing to offer assistance in other ways. Whether you need a place to stay or a meal."

Holden's expression soured. "Getting your hooks in already?"

Food and a roof over his head were secondary to the missing details of Theo's life, but something told him to hold back on asking her anything until they were alone.

"If that's what you call small talk." Beck's smile withered. "I'll manage the floor while you speak with Nate."

She walked away without another word, and Nate was already over Holden's pompous attitude. He crossed his arms over his chest, struggling to compose himself with them all scrutinizing him. After a moment he said, "Is one of you going to tell me why I needed a special introduction? It's been a long day, I'm tired, and I'm really not up to this cool, suspenseful sequence that's playing out right now."

Holden looked surprised even as a laugh popped out of his mouth. "We can talk alone, and I'll explain some things. I know you and your brother hadn't spoken in a long time—"

"Wow! So everyone knew about this but me?" Elijah demanded. "Since when am I the designated asshole?"

"Shut up and let's go."

"Go do what?"

"Go join the Peace Corps. What do you think, moron?" Chase's face was stone cold as he grabbed Elijah's upper arm. "Let's go put that ass of yours to work for the rest of your break."

"Ugh. This isn't my break."

"Well, it is now."

Chase gave Elijah a little shove and smacked his ass as Elijah started walking away. Together they headed deeper into the VIP area.

"I employ quite a few characters," Holden said. "Let's go into the office and talk."

"What do you have to say that needs to be talked about in private?"

"Elijah said you seemed clueless about what Theo was involved in, and I wanted to be the one to tell you."

"Just tell me now. This is private enough."

"There's a party due up here in the next several minutes." When Nate continued to stare stubbornly, Holden sighed. "Listen, Nate, your brother had a lot of messy things going on before he died, and he was a regular at this club. If you don't hear from me, you'll have to deal with someone else. He developed a reputation in the Community, and not everyone will be as kind as I'm being."

Nate held up a hand to thwart the words. "Wait, just pause for a minute. What community? What are you talking about?"

"If you don't know that, then we really do need to talk."

CHAPTER NINE

Nate flinched when Holden flicked on the florescent light. The office was small and cluttered. There were boxes shoved in a corner, a wall full of screens connected to surveillance cameras, and a desk cluttered with paperwork. It was also too bright in comparison to the rest of the club.

Looking like a king holding court, Holden sat on the desk with one foot braced against the chair. Now that they weren't in the gloom of the lower levels, Nate saw the full extent of Holden's effortless sophistication and good looks. He might as well have wandered off the set of a modeling shoot.

"How can you not know what the Community is?"

"The . . . LGBT community?"

"No." Holden's hazel eyes were intent on Nate. After a moment of silence, he beckoned Nate closer and lightly touched his hand. "Do you wonder why you can't read me right now?"

Nate's mouth went dry. "What are you talking about?"

"Don't play stupid. I'm not some redneck from Texas who's going to judge you or say you're a demon for being a psychic."

Nate pulled his hand away. "And I'm not some sassy fucking queer from New York. Maybe you should speak plainly so I don't have to figure out your riddles."

Holden's eyes did a slow circuit of Nate again before settling on his face. "Did you think the psychic genes only ran in the Black family?"

Nate forced his face to remain neutral. *Give nothing away, say nothing to anyone, never tell anyone what you are*—the words Eveline had raised them to live by. The words Nate had regretted not listening to whenever he'd used his talent on someone in the past. But Holden's eyes were knowing, so the denial caught in Nate's throat.

"So you're a psychic, then?" he asked, instead of playing the rhetorical question game.

"Yes. There's more of us than you think."

"I see." Nate's heart pounded. All this time he really had thought the Blacks were the only ones. The idea of there being more like them, of not being alone, was exciting and terrifying at the same time. "How do you know how many there are?"

"We don't. Not entirely. But we try to track psychics who aren't attached to the Community, and hook them up with us as soon as we can."

"A psychic community," Nate said slowly. "What is it, like a Facebook group?"

Holden's mouth twitched. He either found Nate's naïve questions amusing or thought Nate was an idiot. "No, but word of mouth does spread via social media. That's originally how the founders met. Lone psychics, looking to find connections, who stumbled upon each other decades ago on ancient IRC chatrooms."

"What connections were they looking to find?" Nate asked incredulously. "I had no idea there were other psychics outside my family. Or if there were, I figured it was rare."

"Most people think that, which is why so many of us end up isolated or lonely or . . . hospitalized because there's no one there to tell young psys that they're gifted and not insane." Holden searched Nate's face, his smile becoming encouraging. "I know it sounds hard to believe to an outsider, but I grew up in the Community. There are way more of us than you think, and now we're a support system for each other."

It sounded good, but it also seemed like Holden had given this speech several times before. He had the verbiage down pat.

"And this . . . Community provides support."

Holden nodded. "Exactly. Over time, the Community has grown from a small group in New York to a nationwide organization that helps unconnected psychics reach their full potential. My role at Evolution is to take in new LGBT psychics. Being queer is alienating enough without the added stress of not understanding why you sometimes hear voices or can predict the future."

Nate rocked on his heels, trying to digest the influx of information. An entire network of psychics who helped one another. It sounded too good to be true.

"That's why you opened this club?" Nate asked. "To help queer psychics."

"Yes. Don't believe me?"

"I don't believe anyone's that altruistic."

"And they say New Yorkers are cynical," Holden drawled. "I guess altruism runs in the Payne family. My father, Richard Payne, was one of the original founders of the Community. So, I have a vested interest in helping to guide unconnected psychics like you and Theo in the right direction."

"And what's the 'right direction'? Toward your Community and your club?"

"Not just toward the Community—toward reaching your full potential, which you can do *through* the Community." Holden was no longer hiding his indulgent smile. "You're skeptical."

"I'm skeptical of most things," Nate countered. "But considering I grew up terrified of anyone finding out about my gift, it's hard to believe there was this miracle community waiting around the corner all along."

"But we were here all along, and it's not too late for you to connect with us." Holden touched Nate again, hand sliding up his arm to his shoulder. "The world in its current state is a dangerous place for psychics, Nate. We would be completely vulnerable without the Community to not only help us find purpose in our lives, but to keep us safe. Do you have any idea what would happen if the world found out there were so many of us?"

"People would want to use us," Nate said finally.

"Yes. And experiment on us. It's happened before—especially in times of war."

The idea of someone mentally poking and prodding him to gauge reactions was horrific. If people could unintentionally send Nate into a tailspin by transmitting their vibes, someone doing it on purpose would be more than he could take.

But all the times Eveline had warned him and Theo to be discreet, and he'd asked why it was such a big secret, her concerns had been specific to the Black family. As if someone was out to get *them*. Not psychics in general.

"Listen," Nate started. "I can see why this . . . Community would be helpful for some people, but I'm not one of them. You don't have to sell it to me. I'm only here because of Theo."

Holden's eyebrow flew up. "Are you sure? Judging by the fact that you hitched across the country, it looks like you need some assistance. We can provide you shelter and even a job if you plan to stay in the city. I can hook you up with Community Watch—our flagship. They do everything from job placement to educational services and housing."

"Thanks, but no thanks. I can make it on my own."

A glimmer of frustration caught Holden's expression. He crossed his arms over his chest and tossed an errant hair out of his face. "This is my job, Nate. This is how I met your brother. He sought me out after learning about the Community, and I helped him find a job with the band, a place to stay, and I even tried to have his back when everything started falling apart. It's why the Community put me in this position."

It was starting to sound a lot like Holden had some psy induction quota to fill, and Nate was right here to help him check off a box. Conveniently, this entire spiel had also allowed Holden to steer them away from discussing Theo.

"Forget the Community stuff for now," Nate said. "If you want me to hear you out, you'll tell me whatever you know about my brother. You said everything had started falling apart, but how? Help me understand why he would throw himself off that pier."

Holden's earnest nod and serious gaze gave the impression of him being attentive to Nate's questions, but something about him rubbed Nate the wrong way—a slickness that made it unlikely Nate would ever trust him.

"Your brother had trouble from the moment he bragged about his surname."

Now that took Nate off guard. "Why would he think anyone cared about that?"

"Because once he found out that people in the Community tend to . . . revere psys with special talents, he thought his connection to an entire psychic clan would put him on a pedestal." One of Holden's eyebrows arched, and his tone took on a sarcastic edge. "And I see that look you're giving me—suspicious and leery, just like Theo. He always seemed torn between wanting attention and hating that people knew the baggage that came along with it. In this case, the baggage was dealing with the fact that not everyone gave a damn about his name and that some people already knew that your infamous family can be . . . messy."

"Wait, back up. How does anyone here know about my family? We live in a tiny town in Texas."

Holden rolled his shoulders in an elegant shrug. "I assumed there was a point when one of the early Community founders crossed paths with a member of your family. It's not exactly something a person forgets—an entire family of psychics."

There were definitely enough of them for that story to be plausible, but if so . . . Nate suspected that meeting had involved Eveline. Or his mother. Eveline had been paranoid about people knowing their secrets for decades, but it had been Lorelei who'd gone up to New York to escape and had come back a shadow of her former self.

Unless he was overthinking this and making connections where there were none.

Fuck.

What if he was losing it too? What if Nate was a ticking time bomb—a mix of Dade and his mother. A cold sweat broke out on his forehead, and he struggled to keep his voice even. "Would our infamy be the reason you're so intent on bringing me into your Community?" Nate watched Holden but saw no flicker or twitch to indicate his motives had been revealed. "If families like ours are so rare, it must make you look good to be collecting us."

"You're a very suspicious person," Holden said. "And much more direct than your brother."

To that, Nate said nothing. He turned away from the gaze scanning him, dismantling him, and paced the office. "So, you're saying people disliked Theo from the start because he bragged about his name. Did they not believe him?"

Holden slid off the desk and approached Nate, forcing him to stop moving around the narrow space.

"I can't speak for everyone, Nate. He was an outsider, and he associated with the Community while refusing to officially become a member."

Nate narrowed his eyes. "Why did he refuse?"

"I couldn't say. But why would your brother pay the dues and do the work if he could get the benefits merely by spending time with the right people? Or sleeping with them." Now it was Holden who was being cynical, but his sardonic smirk made it clear he didn't care about trying to hide it. "The point is, people didn't take to him the way he wanted, so he lashed out. As for why people didn't like him? Well, as I said, the boasting about belonging to a family who has enough psychics to form an army sometimes backfired. Some found it unlikely he was telling the truth and some found the idea . . . concerning."

Concerning? These folks clearly had never seen the Black family all together, towheaded and slight and flighty and drunk, or they'd know there was nothing to fear. But when put in Holden's words . . . it *did* sound dangerous. But not any more dangerous than an entire *community* of psychics. At the end of the day, people were people. And a large group of people, all with various forms of psychic powers, were bound to turn up a few bad apples.

"If Theo told you anything about us, you'd know that suicide before thirty is common, and that alcoholism and mental illness run in the family. We're not a threat."

"Maybe so. And maybe the instability you speak of is why he was so frustrated. If growing up a Black wasn't all fun and games, and he wasn't able to get the upward mobility he'd hoped for by dropping your name, it must have seemed like he had been born into all that dysfunction for nothing. Either way, he responded the wrong way and tried to force himself on others, making enemies of people who didn't accept him." Holden glanced at the wall of cameras, his mouth drawing down. "I tried to help the situation, to introduce him to people, but nothing worked. He instantly burned each connection I made for him. Everything he touched, no offense, went to shit."

Nate tried to think of a response to that—something that didn't show how much it hit him in the gut to know that Theo's tendency to wreck relationships had followed him across the country. But he couldn't. All he could find to say was, "Was he lonely? Because that more than anything else . . ."

"I don't know." They were the first words to leave Holden's mouth that were heavy enough to sound regretful. Compassionate. "He expected fast acceptance, and honestly he *should* have had it. He was right to think people in the Comm valued powerful psychics, and he was multitalented, which is rare. But he wasn't easy to like because of his arrogance and spiteful behavior. Things got worse because . . . again, no offense, but your brother was the type of person to destroy something if he couldn't be part of it. His reputation suffered, and instead of coming to me or his band, he killed himself."

Nate could believe that Theo had attracted negative attention, maybe even manipulated and pressed buttons until someone snapped, but he knew Theo hadn't killed himself. The lie was like poison, seeping into Nate's pores. He wanted to scream it from the rooftops, or at least into Holden's smug face, but he looked down and took a deep breath. It probably seemed like he was collecting himself due to the grief, and while that was true, he felt numb to it. Now, his concern was digging up the facts. And sticking to Trent's advice not to reveal what he knew. Especially to someone like Holden.

"Listen," Nate said. "I buy that Theo pissed people off. Believe me, I more than anyone know what he was capable of if he felt . . . left out." That was an understatement. "But *how* did he fuck this up so bad? What did he do to make the Community that is allegedly so supportive completely turn its back on him?"

The troubled look returned to Holden's face, but his tone was defensive. "The Community didn't just turn on him. Your brother had friends. He had the band. There was so much potential for him to fit in here, but he wanted *everyone's* love and attention. And he was angry and despairing when he didn't get it. It was the worst possible mind-set for an empath, because he could tell when someone didn't like him or trust him, and it drove him to extremes in order to cope. He started partying hard, doing drugs, cheating on his boyfriend with everyone under the sun—"

Nate wasn't surprised, but he tucked that information away for later.

"And as, I don't know, *revenge*, he started to spread negativity about the club and the Comm." Holden's jaw clenched, and a muscle in his cheek ticked. "It was the final straw for a lot of people. Comm members are loyal, and they will turn their backs on anyone who tries to tear it apart."

"Why would he speak negatively about you and the Community if you helped him so much?"

"Bitterness?" Holden suggested. "Resentment that he didn't find himself higher up on the social ladder? Like I said, he had an entitlement that was difficult to contend with, and he showed it during a time when there was already turmoil."

"What kind of turmoil?"

Holden cut his hand through the air, an indication that he was done with the discussion. "That part has nothing to do with your brother, and it's not something I'm prepared to discuss with a stranger." The more questions Nate asked, the more tidbits of information Holden gave up. Nate wondered if that was why Holden was going from smooth to frustrated, since he was likely giving up information he hadn't planned to delve into. "There's still enough gossip for you to find out about it soon enough anyway, unless Beck has managed to shut it all down." His smile was mocking. "It'd be nice if she was that useful."

There were most definitely power struggles in the club, and they weren't just between Chase and Beck. "Does she work here?"

"Yes, but I didn't hire her. My father did. They're . . . close." Holden's mocking smile went down several degrees. "I guess that's one way to move up in the Community since she's essentially a void."

"What the hell is a void?"

"Someone without psychic abilities. In her case, she's a psychic with such limited ability that she's basically ungifted. Not the nicest term, but it's apt." Holden smoothed his hands along his suit. "She's resentful because I'm a powerful empath, and she's basically nothing."

Wow. What an indictment. If Nate hadn't been sold on Holden's altruism before, he definitely wasn't now.

"Does the value in inducting a new psychic—"

"Don't say *inducting*. That makes the Community sound like a cult."

"—depend on how powerful that psychic is?" Nate went on, ignoring Holden's protests. "Like, does bringing in someone like Theo—an empath *and* a precog who also had the last name Black— make you look good to your dad?"

"To be honest? Yes."

"Okay. Well, then I'm sorry to inform you that I am also 'basically a void.' I won't do you any good, so don't go out of your way to induct me."

Instead of the irritation that Nate had expected from Holden, his eyes actually crinkled at the sides. He was more attractive when he wasn't snarking and smirking, which was dangerous since he was already ridiculously handsome.

"You're blunt. I like it."

"I'm not usually."

"How are you usually?"

"Nervous around strangers." But then . . . that was because he tended to be waiting in anticipation of absorbing negative impressions, and he couldn't glean anything from Holden. Was this what it was like to have a conversation with someone without that concern at the back of his mind? If so, Nate would take being a void any day. "I'm a total fail at conversing."

"Huh." Holden did another slow scan of Nate. "Doesn't seem that way to me."

Nate's hands curled into fists. Any other time the attention would have been flattering, but as far as he was concerned Holden wasn't trustworthy. It was even possible that he was a person of interest if Theo had gone around slandering him and his precious Comm.

"Is everyone here a psychic?" Nate asked after an awkward moment of sweating under Holden's eye-fuck. "Or just the staff?"

"All of the staff are psy," Holden confirmed. "Not all of them are strong. Elijah is a low-skilled precog, and I already told you Beck is as good as a void. Chase, on the other hand, is the most powerful psychic I've ever met."

"What can he do?"

"The question is, what can't he do?" Once again, Holden's expression was chilly. Was there some resentment there? "Many of the patrons are psy as well. We obviously don't turn away voids at the door, but the Community is tight-knit and Evolution has become known as the place for queer Comm members to go."

"Sounds like a perfect little oasis. It's a shame that Theo couldn't find a place here."

"He could have had one if he hadn't broken the rules."

"And what are those?"

"It's a very simple code we live by—we never turn our backs on the Community, and we never betray the Community. He did both. In spades."

And yet Holden refused to say exactly how Theo had done those things.

The crackle of a radio interrupted, and a tinny voice emanated from Holden's back pocket.

"Mr. Payne, that lady is here again putting up those missing-person flyers outs—"

Holden yanked his radio from his belt and lowered the volume. "That's clear. I'll be right down."

Nate had already redirected his attention to their surroundings, pretending he hadn't heard the exchange.

"I'll be right back. I have to deal with a customer."

Nate nodded, not calling him out on the lie. "That's fine. I have nowhere to go, anyway."

"And like I said, I can help you with that."

"And like *I* said—I'll figure it out. A little rain on my back won't hurt me. I've been through hard times before."

Again, Holden's face warmed. And again, he touched Nate's arm without asking if it was okay. "I like you."

"Why's that?"

"I'm used to sycophants, drama queens, and desperation. And you don't want to impress me. It turns me on."

"Okay . . ."

Holden's laugh filled the office. "You're so unlike your brother. He would have taken that as an invitation."

"Would it have been?"

"Maybe. But he was too much of a handful. You're different. I can tell."

Holden seemed like the kind of guy who would tell you what you wanted to hear just so he could get you where he wanted you, and then flip the script until he got you to do what he wanted. But even knowing that, the compliment sat in Nate's chest instead of rolling off his back.

"Anyway," Holden said. "We'll discuss your living arrangements when I return. You sleeping on the street is unacceptable. We'll take care of you."

Nate watched Holden slip out of the room and was immediately relieved to be alone. The last thing he wanted was to become indebted to any of these people. For all that Holden claimed the Community was this amazing network of support, Nate wasn't impressed so far. If anything, he could see why Theo would have felt out of place since he'd so desperately wanted to fit in. And apparently his quest to fit in, or rather him lashing out after he didn't, had led to him pissing a number of people off. Holden included.

Nate looked at the wall of monitors to track Holden's movements and saw that he was jogging down the stairs leading to the lower floor. The monitor next to it showed Elijah and Chase standing pressed against a wall and having what appeared to be an intense conversation, even though Chase had his hand down the back of Elijah's pants. On a third monitor, Nate saw a woman clutching several flyers right outside the club door. She was arguing with Beck.

Unfortunately, the cameras had no sound. Instead of attempting to lipread, he went into snoop mode. He moved to the opposite side of the desk and jerked the mouse connected to the desktop. The monitor came to life without need for a password, but there were dozens of icons and open documents on the desktop. There were spreadsheets with product names and numbers, invoices, and a few browser tabs open to band websites. Nate clicked on the Outlook icon, and watched the program boot up. After giving the row of new emails a cursory glance, Nate saw one with a subject line simply reading *Dreadnoughts*.

A thrill of excitement went through Nate, but the email was from a fan asking when the band would be playing at the club again.

Looking up at the monitors again, he saw Holden had already dismissed the woman from the front of the club.

"Fuck."

With shaking fingers, Nate opened the search box on Outlook and typed in *Dreadnoughts*. The only relevant email that popped up was from Holden to his father.

Father—

New guitarist for the Dreadnoughts claims to be from the Black family. Skinny guy with white-blond hair. Beautiful singing voice. Is it possible?

Richard's response simply said, *Call me.*

The focus on their family was unnerving.

By the time Nate finished searching the computer for *anything* relating to his brother or family, adrenaline was soaring through him. Realistically, this could all be nothing but a bunch of people who'd mythologized his family after coming into contact with one of them years ago, and Theo's death had been a spontaneous attack or some crime of passion, but the sinking feeling in Nate's gut spelled something else.

Nate put the computer into sleep mode again and was doing his best to make the desk seem undisturbed when he spied a sticky note with the name *Taína* scrawled on it along with a phone number. Elijah had said someone named Taína was also in the band.

He pocketed the note and returned to his position on the opposite side of the desk just as Holden reentered the office.

"Sorry," Holden said. "Overzealous activists wanting to cover the walls with their flyers."

Nate nodded without comment.

"And then I stumbled on Chase and Elijah fucking in VIP." Holden pointed at the cameras. "Look."

On one of the screens, Elijah was shimmying back into his shorts while Chase watched. Again, Chase smacked his ass. This time, Elijah backhanded him. They were both disheveled and damp with sweat, and Nate's thoughts immediately went back to Trent. What would have happened between them if he'd ended up crashing at his place? He wished he could have. Things had been so much simpler in that car with Trent and the interstate unspooling ahead of them. Everything was less frightening and overwhelming with Trent nearby to have his back.

"I knew you were gay."

Nate's gaze snapped to Holden and away from the spectacle of Elijah and Chase. "Why does my sexuality matter to you?"

"Because I find you attractive."

Nate sighed. The conversation felt like an attempt at a deliberate distraction.

"I should get going."

"That's another thing." Holden pointed to the camera again. "About your living situation—you could stay with Elijah and Chase. They're roommates, but there's space in their apartment."

Everything about the notion of being in close quarters with Chase repelled Nate, but having unchecked access to Elijah? Who seemed gossipy and willing to overshare? That could work for a night or two.

"Wouldn't they think it's weird? They just met me."

"It doesn't matter. You could be part of the Comm. Like I said, we support each other."

Nate fought the urge to point out that they hadn't supported his brother once he'd broken their rules. Despite everything that had happened between them in the past, he wanted to defend Theo. It was just that the tools to do so were completely out of his grasp. He *could* see Theo lashing out after failing to get his way. It was exactly what he'd done to Nate in high school—he'd felt entitled to be the one sleeping with a popular football player. Felt that he was the one deserving of such attention.

But on the other hand, he could also see Holden's speech being nothing more than a defensive reaction from a person who'd not only failed to help acclimate this new psychic to the Community, but who'd failed to stop a member of the allegedly mythical Black family from turning on the Community before killing himself.

Judging by the knitting of Holden's brow and the tension knifing through his posture, it was clear this had all had an effect on him. But was it guilt and frustration over his failure to help the new Community inductee or guilt over having killed Theo in a moment of rage and panic?

Or was Nate jumping the gun by suspecting the first person he had access to?

A sounding board would have been nice, and in that moment, Nate missed Trent even more.

CHAPTER TEN

The voice was deep and gravelly—too low to be heard clearly even though the tone conveyed urgency.

"—not safe to keep pushing this. You're going to get us all fucked over."

"How?" Another voice. This one familiar. Like an echo. "I'm taking all the abuse out there, J. Y'all sit up here and stay hidden while I'm asking the questions about what happened to her. Everyone *hates* me now."

"Theo—"

"No, this is bullshit." A slam, feet stomping, and a grunt of pain. "You can't fuck me silent like you usually do. I'm not even part of Ex-Comm, and yet—" the voice grew lower "—you people are using me to find out information. Is that all this is? Do you people even like me, or are you just using me for my clairvoya—"

"Don't be stupid."

"Don't treat me like I'm stupid!"

The conversation dropped lower until J spoke up again. "Lay off for a while. They're catching on, and when it comes down to it, even if you think someone is on your side, they're all too brainwashed to ever really have your back."

Nate's eyes opened to sunlight slanting across his face. For a moment, he couldn't orient himself to his surroundings.

Above him was the highest ceiling he'd ever seen. Beneath him was a too-soft bed with springs stabbing his ass cheeks. Around him were bookshelves.

He was not in Brookside. He wasn't in the car with Trent, or in a cheap motel. He wasn't in that weird dream—where he'd been in someone else's body, lingering in a dark corridor with random points of patterned sunlight stretching across the wall as voices drifted toward him in alternating cadences.

He was at Elijah and Chase's apartment, which meant the events of the previous evening had really happened. He'd really stormed into Evolution with no plan or direction, and had really taken a room in the home of strangers who'd potentially been involved in his brother's death to get information? Nate had no idea what Chase and Elijah were to each other, but he did know that both Chase and his half brother, Holden, weren't people he could trust.

Groaning softly, Nate wiped a hand over his face. The heat in the room was unbelievable. It had to be pretty early in the morning, and yet the sun was burning through the curtains and pinning him to the bed like a giant blazing spotlight. He rolled on his side and out of the damp sheets beneath him. The position felt slightly less like he was melting, but his brain was still sluggishly shifting out of that weird fucking dream.

Had he dreamed of Theo in the past? Nate couldn't remember this happening before Theo's death, but it was now becoming a repeat occurrence. He was torn between wondering if it had been a dream or another vision, but the latter made no sense. He had no idea how these visions were being projected to him. In his entire life, he'd never had an inkling of a notion about being multitalented. There was no way he was a postcog.

"When it comes down to it, even if you think someone is on your side, they're all too brainwashed to ever really have your back."

Nate didn't know what any of it meant, but those were words to live by in this new reality. Was the person—J—talking about the Community?

And more importantly, why was Nate analyzing it like it'd definitely been a vision? In the past, he'd either dreamed of nonsense or nothing at all. This dream—vision?—had been so clear. So specific. He felt the chill of an air conditioner blowing on his back and heard the faint jingle of a wallet chain as he moved closer to the room the voices had emanated from. But he could still be reading too much into it.

Another perspective was needed. An objective one. Which was when he remembered that he'd never called Trent the night before.

"Shit."

Nate threw his legs over the side of the bed. He grabbed his phone from the mottled desk and swore softly. It was dead. Scowling, he pawed through his backpack for the charger and found a wad of bills. A quick count told him it was $160, and the desire to get in touch with Trent tripled. He'd stashed the money in the backpack before Nate had gotten out of the car. It had to have been him.

Nate plugged the phone in, quickly dressed, and slipped out of the room. The bathroom was right across the hall, so he washed up before exploring further. A short corridor with bright-yellow walls led to the kitchen. It was long and narrow, and crowded with mismatched barstools and various antique figurines. Elijah, in a dark-blue robe, was perched on one of the stools with one leg swinging over the other. He looked at Nate while smearing cream cheese on a bagel.

"Are you going to wear that outfit for your entire life?"

"No. But I'm conserving clothing."

"Poor baby." Elijah looked more judgmental than compassionate. "I guess Chase didn't give you the grand tour."

"Uh. No." More like Chase had jerked a thumb in the direction of the den. "He just told me to stay the fuck out of the way."

"Well, he's useless. We totally have a combo washer and dryer in here. You don't have to keep looking like a skank."

"Good to know."

Elijah wrinkled his nose. "Ugh. You need to work on being better at conversation."

"I've heard that before."

"I was just joking! Sheesh. Just . . . go take a shower and put on something awesome. If we're going to be friends, you have to be on top of your appearance. I can't have you detracting from the flyness that is me."

Nate couldn't suppress a slight smile. Despite his diva attitude, Elijah was charming. "Where's Chase?"

"Asleep. Now, go. Shoo!"

Elijah went back to his bagel, and Nate showered. He pawed through Theo's bags and found a faded-red baseball T-shirt and another pair of jeans far too skinny for his liking. He doubted it would pass Elijah's awesome meter, but it was better than the wrinkled and grimy shirt that he'd worn all day yesterday. After searching in vain for pants that were less constricting, he sat on the edge of the bed to call Trent. It rang three times before Trent picked up.

"Hey."

"Nate?"

"Yeah. It's me."

"I take it you're not dead," Trent said, sarcasm thick in his voice. "I tried to call you all night but it went straight to voice mail. I was worried."

"Yeah, I'm sorry. I found a place to crash and forgot to charge my phone."

"Oh." A pause. "So everything's okay?"

Nate leaned forward to press his forearms against his knees. "A lot happened. But maybe I can tell you when I see you?" He'd made this phone call hoping to hash things out with Trent, but now that the words were leaving his mouth . . . Nate couldn't help wondering if dragging Trent into a homicide investigation was a good idea. "Or whatever, you know. We don't have to do that."

"No, tell me when you see me."

"Okay." Nate closed his eyes and beat back the dueling urges to iron out an actual time when he could see Trent's handsome face again, and to stop encouraging the horrific idea of involving Trent in this mess. "So . . . when would we see each other?"

"When do you want to?"

"I don't know. Whenever you want to."

"Just tell me when you want to hang out, dude. Stop being such a tween."

"Shut up. It's just—" Nate wished he'd been born with Theo's ease at self-expression rather than useless empathy and lack of social skills. "Like, this situation is really heavy, and I don't want to cause trouble for you."

There was a stretch of silence, followed by a "Wow."

"Wow, what?"

"Nothing. I just thought you trusted me to have your back."

"I do trust you. It's not about that. It's about—" Nate glanced up and jerked back. Elijah was posted up against the doorframe like a thumbtack, not even making an attempt to pretend he wasn't eavesdropping. Nate's initial response was to tell him to piss off, but he bit his tongue given he was shacked up in the guy's apartment. "We can talk about it later. When do you want to meet up?"

"Are you sure you want to?" Again with the sarcasm. "All of a sudden you seem pretty hesitant."

"I'm not."

"Did you find someone more interesting to hang out with?"

Now Trent sounded jealous, and there was something incredibly hot about how little he cared about hiding it. Nate went from wanting to see Trent to needing to see him. And on the other side of that token, he regretted everything that had happened between them.

From the start, their connection had sparked powerfully, and it had grown with each secret shared and each intimate touch. How the hell could he keep his distance—and Trent out of trouble—when Trent kept reminding Nate of why he found the other man so goddamn irresistible?

"That's not possible," he muttered, avoiding Elijah's curious stare. "And you know it."

"Good. Let's meet tonight, then. After I see my fam."

"Where?"

"Fort Tryon Park in Washington Heights. Take the A train to 190th, then get on the elevator to go upstairs. I'll meet you there around six."

"Got it."

"Are you okay until then? With whoever you're staying with?"

Nate shrugged and cast another evil eye at Elijah. "I think so. I'll call you if anything changes."

"Okay." Another pause. "You can call me anyway. For whatever."

"Cool."

"Awesome."

Trent hung up, and Nate glared at Elijah harder. "Can I help you?"

"No. I was just eavesdropping."

"Usually people do that with stealth."

"Why bother?" Elijah flashed his dimples. "You're so awkward. I'm dying of secondhand embarrassment. Are you a virgin?"

"No."

"I bet you've had like one boyfriend in your entire life." Elijah's grin widened. He tried to grab the phone, but Nate held it out of reach. Elijah tsked. "So secretive after all we've been through together. You should be nicer. I could help you."

"Help me do what?" Nate plugged the phone into the charger again. "You're already helping me."

"Help you not be so embarrassing when talking to boys. Obviously. Who was that? Is he hot? Does he live in New York? When did you get here, anyway?"

"I got here last night."

"And you already met some guy you're into?"

"How do you know I'm into him? Why are you eavesdropping, anyway?"

Elijah rolled his eyes. "Relax, Kojak. I'm just curious about Theo's twin, plus I'm the nosiest person on this side of Manhattan. And you were so obviously into that person that I'm not going to dignify your first question with an answer."

Nate flushed. "What was so obvious about it? We were just making a plan to meet up."

"Uh-huh. Right. It doesn't take supernatural powers to see you stammering while trying to set a date."

"It's not even a date."

"Right." Elijah winked and gave Nate a quick once-over. "You look way better, by the way. Not exactly going to be gracing any New York street–style blogs, but you're hot so it's okay."

"I'm sorry I'm not as stylish as you and your retro-punk boyfriend."

"Oh god, don't let him hear you say *retro*. Ever since retro became equated with hipster, that is totally banned from the vocab. And he's not my boyfriend." Elijah flicked his fingers. "We just play around sometimes. What's the point of having a bunch of hot queer friends if we can't fuck each other?"

"Because fucking your friends usually leads to trouble."

"One—I grew up in Wisconsin where my fabulous gayness was wasted due to a drought of available men. I'm making up for it now. Two—if that's your attitude, no wonder your game is so weak." As soon as the words left his mouth, Elijah held up his hands. "Shit, I'm sorry I'm being so annoying. You just lost your twin, and I'm heckling you over your awkward social skills and bad fashion. I'm the worst."

Coming from someone else, it might have been irritating, but Nate just found himself smiling faintly at Elijah. "It's not that big of a deal. I appreciate your honesty."

"No, it is. Seriously. I'm lucky to keep friends with all of the grumpy bastards I hang out with." Elijah plopped down on the bed. The sash of his robe loosened, exposing his leanly muscled chest. "I'm also super touchy-feely so you're going to have to get used to that. Me and your brother together were like two spider monkeys hanging all over each other. Annoyed the shit out of Chase and Jericho."

Jericho. The bass player. Nate wondered if he was the J from the dream.

He really needed to stop acting like every random dream was a vision. He was starting to be paranoid like Eveline. Refocusing, Nate took in the range of emotions dancing across Elijah's face. There was no need to reach out and get an impression—the guy's open curiosity and eagerness to talk was easily read in his expression.

"I assume you and Theo were close?"

"Yeah. We were before he got weird. We sort of . . . drifted apart, which is maybe why he never told me about you." Elijah toyed with the sash of his robe. "We had a couple of falling outs and sort of stopped being as friendly as we once were, but . . . we were in the same band so it's not like we could avoid each other. No offense, but he wasn't the easiest person to be around."

That seemed to be the story of Theo's short life, and the simple words tugged at Nate's heart. He looked away, at the sunlight streaming through the gauzy curtains instead of the darkness wanting to shroud him at the thought of his brother having spent his entire life yearning for love while managing to push everyone away.

"What was the falling out about?" When Elijah hesitated, Nate beefed it up with a lie. "Holden referenced something, but he didn't go into detail."

"It's like this . . ." Elijah smoothed his fingers over the satin strip. "After he figured out that empaths can influence people, Theo could get anyone to do anything."

Nate jerked back. "What?"

Elijah sighed in exasperation. "Nate—you should know this stuff! Your brother certainly did, which was why he expected everyone to be all on his jock thinking he was hot shit. Do you know how rare a precog and empath combo is?" He waved off an answer to the question. "And he got cockier the more he honed his gift."

"Look . . . I know my brother could be manipulative, but him using his gift as some form of mind control is a little far-fetched."

"Not if you *really* think about, like, okay—con men or politicians—how do they get people to follow them?" Elijah raised his eyebrows. "I wouldn't be surprised if people like that are all empaths. It's a common talent."

"You're right," Nate said. "It is common. I'm an empath and have never been able to influence anyone. How do you explain that?"

"Maybe you're not as strong as Theo was," Elijah said bluntly. "Either way, the point is, Theo was so thirsty for attention he started influencing people with his damn talent to get it. And . . . this is total gay drama, but he knew I have a thing for Holden, and he *still* tried to mind-fuck him into, well, fucking. I was pissed."

"You're saying my brother tried to psychically influence Holden to fuck him?"

Elijah's big brown eyes rolled again. "Okay, so maybe I don't know that for a *fact*, but I think he did. I found them all over each other in Holden's office one day and flipped the fuck out. At first, Holden seemed annoyed that I interrupted but then . . . he just looked confused. And never wanted to be alone with Theo again." Elijah met Nate's gaze again, chin lifted. "It's like this—when Theo realized he wasn't fitting in the way he wanted, he became super attention seeking. I wouldn't put it past him to try to influence someone as socially powerful as Holden to be on his side. And by on his side, I mean speared on his dick. Which sucks because Theo was my friend, and I trusted him."

There was so much to unpack that Nate didn't know where to start. A laundry list of accusations was being thrown at his brother's name with every new person he spoke to. Drugs, cheating, betraying friends, breaking the Community rules, and now . . . influencing a man into bed? Was it even possible? Nate didn't want to believe you could transmit your own vibes as easily as you could absorb someone else's, but . . . but he'd always wondered why Kelvin's friends had gone for Theo at that party back in high school. Even if he and Eric had had a taste for guys, he'd always been weirded out that a couple of others had gone for it too.

And he'd wondered why those same football players had turned on him so viciously after it had happened. Part of Nate had expected them to demand a round two at some point. Instead they'd tormented him, and Kelvin had launched straight into accusations about Nate having tricked him into it. What if it was true, and only Eric of all people had ever been the queer one?

Could Theo have influenced Kelvin and the others into wanting him? And more importantly—was Nate powerful enough to have unintentionally done the same to Kelvin that first time they'd kissed?

Fear washed over him, cold and unstoppable, and left him shaken. Had he done it . . . to Trent? There were similarities in the situations for sure. Him finding his own attraction mirrored in Kelvin and then Trent. One time of fooling around leading to more because he'd constantly been spending time with both of them. Not to mention Kelvin having identified as straight, and Trent not having any experience with guys in the past.

What if this was all a product of his gift, and Trent flipped on him the way Kelvin had in the past?

Manipulating Trent's emotions was as good as stripping him of the ability to give consent. It was nauseating.

Nate exhaled slowly. Refocus. He needed to refocus. This wasn't about high school. It wasn't about Trent. It was about who had killed his brother. And how he was going to sharpen his shitty social skills enough to pry information out of Elijah.

"After that lady with the missing-person signs came in, Holden mentioned Theo had been badmouthing the Community." Nate paused, grasping at vague straws to try to prompt a real answer. "Maybe Theo thought if he started sleeping with Holden, it would undo whatever damage he'd done by running his mouth so much."

"Probably." Elijah propped himself up on his elbows, and the robe slid down his shoulder. Nate didn't know if he was trying to be alluring, or if he was just the most immodest person Nate had ever met. "After Carrie went missing, her girlfriend went buck wild with conspiracy theories, and Theo totally let himself get sucked into that drama. I couldn't believe he was feeding into her shit after everything Holden and the rest of the Comm had done for him."

At this rate, Nate was going to have to keep a psychic scorecard to remember who everyone was. He had no idea who Carrie was, but the lady who'd shown up at Evolution the night before was apparently her girlfriend. And they'd both known Theo.

As soon as Nate thought he had a handle on the potential motives of his brother's killer, new pieces of the puzzle were thrown on the table.

"What happened there, anyway?" he asked, keeping his voice even. "Holden didn't seem to want to go into detail."

Elijah bounded upright to launch into the story, and Nate knew he'd made the right choice by targeting the drummer for questioning. He might be as brainwashed by the Community as the "J" from the dream had claimed Comm members were, but he was a fount of knowledge.

"Carrie was a Dreadnoughts fan. She was a really smart, adorable punk rocker who hard-core dug our sound. She'd heard our stuff online and gravitated to the club that way. She was a psychic, but no one had vetted her, you know?"

"And . . . it's super important that psychics get vetted . . ."

"Yeah, especially when they're as talented as Carrie! Multitalented as hell, and a shiny new toy for all the other psys at Evolution. She stood out, and she and Theo bonded. They partied together, did coke together, and then one day . . . she was just gone." Elijah's voice lowered with each word. "It was really awful. Her girlfriend still isn't over it. She wants to plaster those posters all over the club."

"And Holden won't let her?"

"Nope. Neither will Beck. The whole reason Beck is even here is because Holden's father wanted some Community brass keeping an eye on all this drama. It's not a good look for the club or Holden, especially since your brother was running around perpetuating the rumor that the Comm had something to do with her disappearing. Honestly?" Elijah's voice dropped even lower. Who was he trying to hide this conversation from? Chase? "That was what got under my skin more than anything else. If it weren't for the Community, after I got to this city I'd have been another gay kid going to the Brambles to give blowjobs for ten bucks. You know? But they vetted me and got me connected. Holden gave me a job at the club before introducing me to the peeps in Dreadnoughts. The Community is *good*, and Theo was trying to take away from that."

Nate slowly nodded. He wondered if this rabid defensiveness of the Community was why Theo hadn't confided in Elijah about their family. It didn't explain how Holden or Chase had known, but if Chase was "practically omniscient" that was enough of an explanation. Unless Theo had actually trusted Holden, and this whole Theo-influencing-him thing was just a figment of Elijah's paranoia and jealousy . . .

"Okay, this—this is my question. If the Community was so great to him, why are you jumping to the conclusion that he deliberately turned his back on all of this—this majestic generosity that he was shown? Maybe he just had his own questions about whatever happened to Carrie."

"It's fine to have questions," Elijah said. "Questioning is what makes us all intelligent humans, right?"

"Yeah. Humans who can think for themselves and not repeat lines fed to us by organizations."

Elijah's lips pursed. "Listen, I'm sorry if you feel like I'm attacking your brother. And I'm not. I swear I'm not. But Holden did *everything* for him. And then as soon as Carrie's girlfriend claimed she disappeared at the club, and that the staff was stonewalling her, Theo bought it."

If Theo had returned Holden's generosity by slandering his club, it was entirely possible Holden had been angry enough to push him into the water that night.

"You should have stopped when I warned you, Theo. You should have just left it alone!"

The killer's words rang in Nate's ears. He wondered which of the people he'd met in the past twenty-four hours had been the one to say them.

"But why would he buy it if the Community, and Holden, had been nothing but kind to him?"

Elijah got to his feet, huffing out a breath. "You don't understand."

"What don't I understand?" Nate asked. "If you think I'm missing something, then help me see it."

Elijah looked around the room, apparently searching for an explanation, and threw out his arms. "Look—no one in the Community or at Evo is going around targeting other psys. That's stupid, Nate."

"But you don't know every psy, even *in* the Community, so how could you know?"

"Because!" Elijah huffed the more Nate challenged him. "Because most talented psys are like Holden. If you're powerful, or have the right connections, it's a magic ticket to success in the Community. Just look at what being tied to the Comm did for Chase! Even though he's only Holden's half brother, that connection meant a *fuck-ton*. His mother ditched him when he was a baby, and people love to speculate about whether or not he's really Richard Payne's kid since he's, like, super talented while Richard is basically a psychic dud like me. But it doesn't matter. He has the Payne family backing him up and the Community helping him along every step of the way."

If Richard Payne wasn't very talented, Chase's mother must have been amazing. But more interestingly, Nate was now wondering if Elijah's relationships with both Chase and Holden had more to do with him trying to get a step up in the Community than real loyalty.

"If he's Holden's half brother, and he's younger than Holden . . ."

"Um. Yeah. Richard definitely cheated on Holden's mom. She didn't leave him, but she mostly stays upstate at the Farm." Elijah glanced at the door and lowered his voice further. "Like this whole thing with Beck? Dude, they're so obviously fucking and no one has seen Holden's mom literally in years. Richard's shadiness could block the sun, but he's like top dog at the Community so we all just make zero comments."

"This sounds more like a psychic soap opera than real life."

"Heh. Tell me about it." Elijah cringed. "Anyways, I get it. You're playing devil's advocate because you don't want to think your brother was an asshole. I don't mean to talk so much shit, but there was a lot of negativity before he died. That's probably why Holden wants to help you. He feels responsible because he'd taken Theo under his wing."

"So, what you're saying is, it's entirely possible that Holden and Theo were actually lovers, and Theo didn't have to use psychic manipulation powers to make it happen?"

Elijah crossed his arms over his chest and gave a dramatic eye roll. "Yeah, whatever. Either way, Holden is the nicest person I've ever met. I fucking love that guy, and he's totally not getting caught in any of my thirst traps because I've banged his brother so many times."

"Jesus Christ," said a voice from the hall. "Are you talking about fucking this early?"

Elijah sighed. "Good morning, Chase."

Chase appeared in the doorway and braced against the frame of the door. He was wearing a loose white tank and jeans that sat so low on his narrow hips, Nate could see his pubes—just as pale blond as his hair. "You bitches been gossiping all morning? I can hear your fucking mouths in my sleep."

"I bet you think about my mouth in your sleep," Elijah said with a sweet smile.

Chase grunted and raked his eyes over Elijah before turning them to Nate. "How long are you staying here? I'll let you know right now, I pay most of the rent. This little twink gets paid chump change from gigs."

"Shut up, Chase," Elijah said, swatting him with the sash.

Chase ignored him and cocked an eyebrow at Nate. "Well?"

A good night's sleep had clearly not made Chase any nicer, and Nate wasn't in any more of a mood to deal with it. "If you want me gone, I'll go."

"Chase!" Elijah protested. "You could try to be a decent human. Just once." Elijah went into huff mode and started to push past Chase.

Chase's eyes immediately dropped to his ass, which he slapped. Elijah bared his teeth. "Stop groping me and listen. Holden wants him here, so quit being such a dick."

"Oh, I bet Holden does. And that's real sweet of him." Chase's smirk was ice-cold. "But if I was you two, I'd stop running your fucking mouths before you get yourselves in trouble."

Nate got to his feet. "Is that a threat?"

"If that's what it will take for both of you to stay out of Theo's mess, feel free to look at it that way."

They stared at each other silently for a long moment before Chase walked away.

CHAPTER ELEVEN

Fort Tryon Park was surprisingly beautiful. A huge green space full of centuries-old trees, stone archways and walls, and an amazing view of the river. It was the last thing Nate had expected to find in a city made of concrete and blacktop.

The park wasn't by any means empty, considering the joggers and bicyclists speeding by alongside the groups of teens and strolling couples, but the open air brought him peace after his first overwhelming experience riding the subway. Scores of hostile people had closed in on him, and he'd been defenseless against the Molotov cocktail of impressions his mind had sucked in. By the time he'd burst out of the train car, it'd felt too close to suffocating, and he'd left the subway despite having gotten off at the wrong stop.

Good thing he'd headed uptown to meet Trent early. Elijah and Chase had shockingly left him alone in their apartment after they'd gone to work. His snooping had turned up nothing of interest, so if they *were* hiding something, it was in a place so secure they'd known he wouldn't find it.

Nate stopped walking near the stretch of green space dubbed Billings Lawn, and scanned the vicinity for a spot to wait for Trent. He was drawn to a stone terrace overlooking the Hudson, and stretched out on a bench near the edge. The wind coming off the water reminded him of his vision of Theo. For the hundredth time, Nate replayed the vision. He could smell the river, feel the cool breeze whipping back his hair, and sense the imminent danger of another presence nearby. But the voice remained garbled and genderless. Impossible to discern and attach to one of the many people Nate had met the night before.

He dozed off with these thoughts in mind and was quickly overtaken by a dream. A rush of sound and color, all red and black and full of sharp edges that left him feeling inside out and exposed. He heard Theo's voice, fierce and accusing, and a lower one snarling to "leave it alone." Nate didn't know what the *it* was, but when the dream became lucid, he was once again trapped in his brother's aggressively thin body as the dance floor of Evolution spun around him. Chase's face, taut and intense, glared down.

The dream shattered when, in the real world, a hand touched Nate's arm. Pieces of it fell just out of reach and the sound drifted away.

"You can't be sleeping in parks, Nate," a voice chastised. "I told you about that shit."

Waking up to the sight of Trent's dark, shaggy hair escaping a backward baseball cap, warm eyes, and the concerned shape of Trent's mouth, was a relief. When Trent knelt beside the bench and brushed his fingers against Nate's cheek, he loosed butterfly wings and a delicious crest of good vibes. It activated Nate's touch addiction for the man beside him.

Still caught in the limbo of sleep and awareness, Nate covered Trent's hand with his own. He reached out with his gift and took as much as he could get, all while gazing at Trent from beneath his lashes, watching the distance between them close. They were kissing before Nate's eyes fully opened.

There was nothing questioning about the crush of their mouths or the glide of their tongues. Nothing hesitant in Trent's motions as he cupped the delicate base of Nate's skull to dig his fingers into tangled hair. And there was no stopping the tidal wave of impressions crashing over Nate—lust and hunger and bits and pieces of imagery flying across his mind like he was seeing into Trent's head. Seeing what Trent wanted to do to him. Shimmery flashes of Trent on his knees with Nate's dick in his mouth, and clearer images of him taking Nate right there in the park—rucking their jeans down and fucking into him with deep thrusts.

The ache of Nate's own arousal doubled when joined with Trent's. His hands shook and his body burned. He had to yank away with a ragged gasp and a pounding heart when it hit him that the dual sensations would make him come in his pants.

Trent responded by latching on to the side of Nate's throat. He sucked hard and cupped the bulge in Nate's jeans.

The trembling in Nate's limbs intensified. "Oh God." Teeth scraped his burning flesh. His balls drew up tight enough to rip a moan from his mouth. "Stop."

Trent sat back on his haunches. His eyes were wild and his deep-golden skin was flushed. "What's wrong?"

"We're—" Nate cast a harried look around. "We're outside."

"It doesn't matter."

"Someone will see."

"I don't give a fuck. I passed three couples dry humping on my way up here." Trent leaned in again to brush a more delicate kiss to Nate's swollen lips. "I love kissing you. And I missed you."

Nate shuddered. He reminded himself this was a bad idea. He wasn't even supposed to be meeting Trent at all, let alone allowing Trent to grab his hand and lead him away from the terrace, but the attempted reality check couldn't penetrate the hazy bubble surrounding them. His feet moved of their own accord, stumbling after Trent's purposeful strides, and the adrenaline coursing through his body wouldn't allow him to pull it together enough to stop.

Excitement pumped into him and a nonstop chant of *He wants me, he likes me, I can feel how much he wants me. Nothing's changed since yesterday.* The chant didn't stop until they hopped over the side of one of the crumbling walls into a more neglected-looking section of the park. Trent backed him up against the faded stone.

They kissed again, but Nate couldn't focus enough to respond skillfully. His technique consisted of heavy breathing, nipping, and barely muffled groans when Trent began sucking on his tongue. Things were moving fast, and the feel of Trent's erection outlined by denim as it ground against Nate's thigh was exhilarating. Even after everything that had happened while they were on the road, he wasn't prepared for the onslaught of impressions while a tongue invaded his mouth and a hand tugged down his zipper. The physical and mental feel of Trent was everything.

His mouth was a brand against Nate's as their hands worked. They jerked each other off with fast, furious upstrokes—gripping hard and swallowing each other's hoarse gasps. Nate opened himself to Trent and selfishly sucked in every drop of his pleasure. When Trent came with a strangled moan and Nate's name on his lips, everything intensified.

Nate slumped against the wall with shaking knees. They nearly gave out when Trent sank to the ground. He sucked Nate's dick with absolutely zero self-consciousness given his lack of experience, and lapped up Nate's pre-come and the remnants of his own release before taking Nate down deep enough to gag. He tried twice before bobbing his head in earnest.

Eyes rolling back, Nate tilted his head against the wall. His coming ejaculation built so steadily that he had to bite his fist to keep from shouting when it finally hit him. The reality of Trent swallowing it all down was absolute perfection.

"No—" His voice came out craggy. "No one's done that before."

Still licking his lips, Trent stood up. "Swallowed?"

"Sucked me off until I came. Uh, the guys I hooked up with were never really . . . interested in me finishing. So."

"They're jerks." Trent wiped his mouth with his forearm. He was still giving Nate that wild-eyed stare. "I'm not sure why I was struck with this need to give my first blowjob in a park, but . . ."

Nate's heart stilled in his chest. "But what?"

"Something comes over me when I'm with you. I don't understand it, but it's there."

Trent was smiling shyly even as Nate's body was going cold. His mind went back to Elijah's words about empaths influencing people. Was it possible? And had he done it?

Why would Trent choose him as the first guy to fool around with? Trent was gorgeous. In the age of social media and hookup apps, he could have had any man he wanted when he'd wanted them. But only Nate had driven him to make a move, and it always happened when Nate was already wired up and turned on. Almost as if Trent was keying into his feelings.

Nate fumbled with his jeans.

"Hey, what's wrong?"

"Nothing."

Maybe Elijah was right. Maybe none of this was real.

"Nate." Trent's voice cut through the clambering thoughts. "What's wrong? You're whiter than usual."

"I'm just . . ." Nate combed a hand through his hair and looked everywhere but at Trent. "I, uh, just— It hit me that I'm here fooling around instead of trying to figure out what's going on. I'm a terrible brother."

"You hitchhiked across the country to figure out what happened. You're anything but terrible."

"That's true." Nate fixed his clothing and kept his gaze on the ground. He could feel Trent's eyes on him, but avoided them. There was so much to process, and it was impossible to think with Trent so close. It was too easy to be sucked in by his smell and touch. Nate skirted around him to create a safe distance. "I'm a little overloaded. There's a lot going on."

"I figured that."

Trent zipped his pants. He paused as if waiting for a cue from Nate, and then boosted himself up to sit on the edge of the wall. He patted the space beside him, and Nate jerkily made his way over.

"How did the city treat you last night?"

"I'm still trying to figure that out. It's so different here."

"In a good way or a bad way?"

"Right now it's good." The fact that they'd hooked up without him expecting to get smashed in the head with a bat by some redneck with a confederate flag trucker cap was a good start. The suburbs of Houston weren't as hillbilly as some places in west Texas, but he'd almost always possessed a sense that he was in danger when around certain people or in certain places. And he doubted New York City was entirely safe, but . . . the specter of violence hadn't overshadowed the feeling of being touched. "Last night not so much."

"What happened?"

"For starters, you may have been onto something about the entire X-Men cast existing."

Trent arched an eyebrow. "Come again?"

Nate launched into the full tale about the club, the Community, and the apparent existence of countless psychics. Through it all, Trent just watched him intently and asked questions mostly relating to the logistics of the Community—what the function of Community Watch was, and what on Earth "the Farm" was. Nate couldn't answer that question, but he was relieved to not have Trent giving him one of those skeptical stares.

"This shit is wild," Trent said.

"I know, right?" Nate hit the heels of his shoes against the wall. "It sounds weirder unloading it all at once to you. Do you even believe they're as good as they say?"

"I mean . . . there's definitely a cultlike feel about it," Trent said slowly. "Like this whole Scientology vibe or whatever, *but* I can see why they'd want to band together? Back during the Cold War, the CIA used to experiment on psychics, didn't they? The Community people have a point about needing to protect each other and keep it on the low."

"That's true." Nate turned sideways on the ledge so he could watch Trent's profile. "I felt like an idiot standing there while Holden explained everything to me. It doesn't help that all of them are so trendy and sophisticated. I'm sure they think I'm a hick with subpar psychic abilities."

There was another pause. Trent's plush mouth was flattened into a line, brows lowered in an expression of annoyance. Even without articulating his thoughts, it was clear Trent was on Nate's side. But as good as it felt to have someone at his back, Nate forced himself not to show the fondness growing in his chest. He couldn't afford to get used to feeling this way if it was possible Trent's feelings were nothing more than a reflection of his own. Trent further involving, and endangering, himself was bad enough without him doing it based on an attraction that potentially didn't even exist.

"Don't get mad for me."

"I'll do what I want."

"It's just me. It's my problem. I don't trust any of these people, which is gonna make it pretty damn hard to keep pretending I like them enough to talk to them about Theo. I need to stop being on edge when I meet new people."

Trent brushed hair out of Nate's face. "You didn't do that to me."

"Because you're different. From the start you—"

"Fucking fags."

Nate's spine snapped straight. Hands tightening into fists, he glared at the asshole's retreating back. His Knicks jersey glimmered in the sun like a flag.

"Wow. I guess some things don't change no matter where I am."

Trent responded by kissing him. The warm press of his mouth was there and gone before Nate could decide if he should respond. He exhaled shakily and licked his lips. Trent's eyes followed the movement, intent and hungry.

"Do you want to go to my place? I asked the girl I'm subletting from, and she said it's okay."

Yes. No. Yes.

"I don't know." Nate looked in the direction of the jackass Knicks fan. "We should probably slow down."

"Slow down with what?"

"Us fooling around. There's a lot going on, Trent. I don't know if me getting involved with you makes sense right now." He winced. "I mean, I have no idea who killed Theo. This could be dangerous. So . . . maybe we should keep some distance? I obviously can't help myself once you touch me, but what if someone decides to silence me the way they silenced him, and sees you as a way to get to me?"

He was rambling. He knew he was. And a silence followed his words. Nate couldn't bring himself to watch his rejection crossing Trent's face.

"Fine. Then tell me what happened with your brother, and we can just stick to that."

And of course now that Trent was agreeing, Nate regretted suggesting it. He missed the feel of Trent's hands on him already. God, he was a mess.

Even so, he filled Trent in on everything he'd learned the previous night, leaving nothing out, explaining everything from the clawing anxiety that had accompanied him in the line at Evolution to the tangled nightmare that he'd woken up from only minutes ago. Trent listened to it all without interrupting. From time to time, Nate glanced over, expecting to see a skeptical pull to Trent's lips or a perplexed scowl, but Trent only nodded.

Nate exhaled slowly once it was all out. Trent frowned and looked around the park as if he, too, was now wondering whether someone would be after Nate.

"Do you think one of the people you met last night is involved with Theo's death?"

"I don't know," Nate admitted. "The only person who seemed okay was Beck. Elijah is nice, but his blind loyalty to the Community makes him an untrustworthy source of information."

"Yeah, his perspective is skewed. Also, he might repeat whatever questions you've been asking to other people."

"Exactly. Probably to Chase. That dude just seems to want to get rid of me. He outright told me to stay out of Theo's mess, which is suspicious as hell. And then there's Holden—I didn't trust him at all, but it seems like maybe *Theo* did. I don't know what it is about him that puts me off. Elijah was coming down on Theo just as much if not more than Holden, but Holden . . ." Nate frowned. "Maybe his suave, smooth shit automatically put me on my guard? Or the fact that he wasn't forthcoming about Carrie disappearing?"

"And he's connected to higher-ups in the Community," Trent said. "Generally, I don't trust any corporate motherfucker. Even if it's a psychic corporation."

Nate laughed. "Yes, that too."

Trent winked. "Also, he owns Evolution. It's weird for that club to have had a disappearance and then a murder attached to it. Can't be a coincidence."

"Right. It *has* to be connected. Sure, Theo had it in him to piss everyone off, but if he knew something about that Carrie girl's disappearance, it makes sense that someone from the club or the Community shut him up because of it. The simplest explanation is usually the—"

"Right one," Trent finished. "Occam's razor. I agree."

"You don't think I'm being paranoid?" Nate drew his legs up and wrapped his arms around them. He realized he was mimicking a pose he'd defaulted to as an insecure teen, and dropped his legs again. "I told you my entire family is made up of people with mental illness. My aunt is incredibly paranoid. I sometimes worry that I'm—"

"Well, don't. Stop doubting yourself." Trent grabbed his hand, squeezed, and quickly pulled it away. It was a far cry from the lingering caresses he'd bestowed upon Nate only a few minutes ago. "I come from totally boring stock, and I can tell you that your conclusions are my own as well. The clues all point to this shit being connected. It's the most logical answer." He frowned. "I mean, not that my word means anything or that it should automatically make you feel better."

"It does, though. I second-guess myself constantly. Talking to you makes me feel a lot better." Nate exhaled slowly. "Thanks."

"Glad to be of service."

Was Trent being passive-aggressive? Nate couldn't tell. His peopling skills were not good enough to handle this level of intimacy.

"So," Trent said. "What's next?"

"I'm going to call one of Theo's other bandmates and hope they're not as gung ho about the Community as Elijah."

"Do you want some company when you do?" Nate's lips started to form a *no*, but Trent flashed an impatient glare. "It's not like we're going to the club. I can go with you to talk to some musicians if you want me to." Nate hesitated again, and Trent sighed. "It's what I want, Nate. You're not forcing me into anything."

Nate hoped that was true. He really did, and so he felt himself nodding. "I could use the backup."

"I was thinking I could be more of a sounding board later. You can handle yourself, kid. You're a lot tougher than me."

"I guess we'll see about that."

It turned out that of the Dreadnoughts, only Elijah hadn't known of Nate's existence. He counted that, along with Elijah's loyalty to the Community and his relationship with Chase, as three strikes against him, even if two of them were knee-jerk responses.

Trent accompanied Nate to the band's practice space in Williamsburg, and tried to talk him down the entire way. But repeated comments that Nate could do this, and he had his story straight this time, and these were people Theo had actually trusted, didn't stick in Nate's head. He was sweating and worried about fucking up.

Or trusting the wrong person. Making the wrong move or placing his bets on the wrong side. Were there even sides to this, or was this entire conspiracy in his head?

There was no telling.

When they got to the Dreadnoughts' place, Trent knocked on the door while Nate took deep breaths. He wiped his sweaty palms against his jeans and tried to act like a normal adult and not a fucking basket case.

The door was opened by a woman with long black hair and light-brown skin covered liberally with ink. Her eyes went round at the sight of Nate. "Holy shit, you really are identical."

"Um. Yeah."

She kept staring and only quit it when Trent cleared his throat.

"I'm Trent. A friend of Nate's."

"Right on." She nodded and backed up so the two of them could enter. "I'm Taína. Lia and Jericho are setting up in the backyard. Trying to take advantage of the weather before we get hit with thunderstorms later on," she said with an awkward chuckle.

"As long as we don't get any freak hurricanes, it's all good," Trent said.

"I know, right? I've been living in terror since Hurricane Sandy."

They went off about wacky New York weather, and Nate checked out the surroundings. The ground-floor apartment was small, dark, and cramped, but even when he reached out with his gift he didn't pick up on anything insidious. The only thing that *did* hit him was a strange sense of déjà vu. The same sense he'd gotten while walking to the pier along the Hudson River.

There was a longish corridor leading from the main part of the apartment to the backyard. Sunlight streamed through the gridded screen door and slanted across the walls in random patterns—the same patterns in the dream from earlier. The dream that obviously had not been a dream.

"I'm taking all the abuse out there, J. Y'all sit up here and stay hidden while I'm asking the questions about what happened to her."

"Nate."

Blinking, Nate jerked to awareness and found himself in the backyard with everyone staring at him. Trent was giving him encouraging looks, as if that would take away from the fact that Nate was, as usual, coming off as a total fucking weirdo.

"Oh, sorry. I was thinking about something."

"Understandable. I'm sure you have a lot to think about." The woman who stood up was short and slight, and her bright-red crewcut contrasted starkly with her dark-brown skin. Like Taína, she had tattoos liberally covering her body, but these were more of the watercolor style than the stark black lines sloping across Taína's skin. "I'm Lia."

"Nate. And this—"

"I already introduced myself."

Great. He was being a weirdo to the max.

"And this guy here is Jericho," Lia said. "He's not too friendly, but don't take it personally."

Jericho was over six feet of solid, tattoo-covered muscle. Just as imposing in person as he'd been in photographs. His dark hair was shaved close to his head, a silver hoop circling one nostril, and a cigarette sticking out of the corner of his mouth, as he stared down at Nate without emotion.

"Nice garden." Trent grinned at Jericho, unfazed by the brooding glare and the muscles busting out of a skintight black T-shirt. He indicated the small, well-tended garden tucked to the side of the backyard. It looked out of place next to the slab of concrete currently littered with thick extension cords and instruments. "I wouldn't take you for one of those organic freaks, but then again, this is Williamsburg."

Jericho's gaze slid to Trent as if he'd just noticed him. "Who are you?"

"I'm Trent. Like I said."

"His boyfriend?"

"No." Nate ignored the sideways stare Trent aimed at him. "He's my friend."

"I'd have brought a friend too if I was dealing with something like this," Taína mumbled. Her kohl-rimmed cat eyes were still wide as she perched on a wooden patio table, clad in fishnets and a crinoline skirt, a gothic lawn sculpture in a hipster's backyard. "I can't believe how much you look like him. He barely talked about his family."

"Did he with you?" Nate asked Jericho.

"Yes. And I figured you'd come around."

Nate's eyebrows flew up. Trent looked at him sideways.

"Why didn't you say anything?" Lia demanded. She was about a foot shorter than the bass player, but her voice was commanding. "It would have been nice to know that Theo's brother would want to meet with us. I thought they were totally estranged."

"What difference does it make? I figured he'd show up after Theo died, but that doesn't mean he gave a shit about Theo before. And Theo didn't give a shit about him or the rest of their fucked-up family." A defensive edge crept into Jericho's voice. "Even when he should have been contacting them for help, Theo choked every time he started to pick up the phone."

"Contacting us about what?"

"Forget it."

A thousand thoughts coalesced into the memory of that morning's dream. J had to be Jericho. The speech patterns were the same. And that meant Jericho knew things. Things Nate needed to know. Without thinking, he reached out to touch the larger man's hand. Jericho nearly growled in response.

"Don't try your shit on me, kid."

Nate recoiled. Trent tensed up next to him, and for a moment, everyone froze.

It was Lia who broke the ice. "Taína, why don't you show Trent where some of Theo's things are? Their uncle didn't get everything, and I'm sure Nate will want to take them when he leaves."

"But—"

"Go," Lia said, her tone leaving little room for argument. There was no mistaking who was in charge here.

Trent seemed ready to argue right along with Taína, but after exchanging a long look with Nate, he followed her back into the apartment.

"This conversation is easier without the voids present," Lia explained.

"You're psychic too."

"I inherited a touch of precognition from my mom so I'm more perceptive than most."

Jericho said nothing, clearly unwilling to divulge his own talent.

"Look, Nate," Lia began, moving closer. "I don't know how much you know about things up here, but we have reason not to trust anyone from the Community. If you count yourself as one of them, fine, but it's going to make this conversation a lot tougher."

"If you're not friends with people from the Community, why do you regularly play at the club that is basically their home base?"

She smiled. "You're quick. So was Theo."

Jericho scoffed. "I'm going inside. I can't deal with this right now."

When he stalked back into the house, shitkicker boots pounding against the concrete, Lia didn't look surprised. She didn't apologize for him either.

"Jericho's having a hard time, and he was already an asshole before all of this happened, so this is the result."

"I get it, but why is he so pissed at me? I just got here."

"He's not pissed at you. He's just pissed." Lia walked over to the table, taking Taína's spot on the edge of it. She slipped a hand into her pocket and pulled out a vaporizer. "Want some? It's apple flavored."

"No, thanks. Look—folks keep trying to distract me every time I ask a question, and I'd appreciate it if you didn't do the same. I came here hoping I'd get some solid answers."

"Which folks would that be?" she asked, putting the vaporizer to her lips.

"Listen, Lia, I didn't come here for games. I came here to find out why my brother was pulled out of the Hudson River."

Lia exhaled a cloud of smoke, and the apple scent drifted between them. "I'm not in the Community. Neither is Jericho. I'm not playing their games."

"Then how did you meet so many Community people?"

Lia thought for a moment before speaking. "Not just psys hang out at Evo. Taína is a void, but she's a woman of color so I gravitated to her when I first started going to the club. Holden bills it as being so inclusive, but it's really not. There's queers from all shades of the rainbow, but only about thirty percent on a given night are nonwhite. So, me and Taína became friends, talked about forming a band, and then met Jericho. It just so happened that we'd all attempted to spend time at the club before realizing it's not for us."

"Now you just play there," Nate said.

"Yes. And since not every psy drinks their Kool-Aid, neither me nor Jericho ever joined the Comm. Elijah was already knee-deep in it when we met him."

"Fine. Then tell me this—what did Jericho mean about telling Theo to call the family?"

"I don't know. He doesn't tell me all of his deep darks."

"He had no problem referencing his deep darks right here in front of you, though."

"That doesn't mean he'll explain himself to me," she said, sharper this time. She set the vaporizer down with a *clink*. "I told you I'm no fan of the Community, but Jericho takes it to a whole other level. A radical one. I don't know what he told Theo or what the two of them were up to—I wasn't privy to that info. What I do know is that not all Comm members are the noble allies they claim to be. Yeah, they help people out sometimes, but it comes with a price."

"And what price is that? Elijah made it sound like they're all a bunch of Boy Scouts working hard to get their merit badges by taking in poor isolated psychics like me and my brother."

Lia looked away. "Yeah, he would say that. It worked with him. He came here from Wisconsin after running away, and they saved him from survival sex and sleeping on the street. Told him if he followed their rules, did what they said, and basically signed his life over to them, they'd help him find his place in life. Show him how to reach his full potential as a psychic and build the family he never had at home. And honestly? They did. He's happy, and he has the infamous Chase Payne fawning all over him. Well, his version of fawning."

"That's great that he thinks he found a family," Nate said slowly, unable to keep the skepticism from his voice. "But from here it sounds like their philanthropy with the CW could be a front to bring in disenfranchised kids and use this talk of family and potential to lure them in."

Lia nodded, eyes slitting at Nate. "And who's more disenfranchised than queer psy kids of color like Elijah? What you just said has always been my thought about the CW. Maybe even Evo. You're more likely to find a lone psy desperately seeking a home if that lone psy was shunned by their family for their identity. It's a trap for kids like Elijah."

It was all conjecture of the most cynical kind, but in Nate's bones . . . it felt true. Even if the Community didn't know about the disappearances, it still seemed like a fucking cult.

"What do you mean Elijah signed his life away?"

"Once you're in the Community, you're their property." She spread her hands, sunlight flashing over her colorful tattoos. "You tell them everything they want to know, talk to who they want you to talk to, and cut out anyone they don't approve of."

"People like Theo," Nate said.

"Yes. People like Theo. It wasn't there yet, he wasn't officially blackballed, but it was getting there."

"Just because he asked some questions about his friend disappearing?"

"Asking questions is the worst thing you can do." Lia hunched forward. "Listen," she said, voice going softer. "I don't want to drag you into this. Some people do think the Community is a great place, but I'm not one of them. And I'm not objective about it. What I can say with certainty is that there's been strange things going on in the Community and more recently at Evolution. In the past couple of years, more than one baby psy has disappeared from Evo. I don't know how or why, but they come, they make friends with the upper crust of the Comm, and they go poof." Lia waved her hand, fingers flicking at the air. "I was dating one of them. A new kid on the block who'd run away from home after his talent developed. His parents thought he was schizophrenic and kept putting him in residential treatment centers."

"Did the Community induct him before he disappeared?"

She nodded. "Yeah. *Inducted* is a good word. They snatched him up from one of the treatment centers, told him they'd give him a new life, and he never looked back. I met him at the club, actually. Anthony wasn't queer, but he'd gone there looking for Holden. Everyone thinks you're golden if you get in with the Paynes." Her expression softened and a slight smile appeared. "And he liked being in the cool kids club even if the cool kids were all queer guys with a jones for his big ole green eyes, and the fact that he was multitalented and had some serious power coursing through his veins."

"And he just vanished one day?"

"Yep." Lia's smile faded. "Like I said, he went poof. Just like Carrie. I tried to look into it, but I didn't get very far. And just like with Carrie's girlfriend—they stonewalled me at every point. And when the case went cold, I hired a PI. Hoo boy, did that piss them off." Lia rolled her eyes. "Man, it was serious drama. They *hated* that I had a stranger sniffing around the club."

"When you say 'they' . . ."

"The people on Comm's board of directors. Not Holden," she said. "He was surprisingly reasonable about it, even though he wished I'd consulted with him before hiring someone. But when the PI's trail also went cold, Holden went against the recommendation of his father, and let me continue playing at the club."

Nate wondered whether Theo would have wound up as another missing psychic if his body hadn't floated to the surface so soon. Had he been another targeted multitalented psychic? Or was his death different because it had been personal?

"So two suspicious disappearances associated with Evolution. No wonder Holden wasn't thrilled with Theo for harping on it," he said. "He probably wished all talk of it would go away."

"Oh, he did. Especially after his father put Beck there to babysit him. When I asked him about it after Carrie's disappearance, all he had to say was 'This is the last time I look out for another baby psy.'"

"But does he really look out for them?" Nate pressed, leaning forward. "It seems like they're not doing too well under his watch."

Lia looked down at her pipe, seeming to weigh her words. "You know, Nate, I try to be fair. But I've had too many run-ins with Community assholes who keep a tight grip on their people to be fair when it comes to them. If you want to know about the Community, about the good they do for people like us, I would talk to Elijah again. Or Beck."

The back door squeaked open, and Trent stepped out, a guitar case strapped to his back. "You ready?"

Nate glanced at Lia. "I don't know. Am I?"

"I've got nothing else for you right now," she replied. "Anything else you'll want to know is locked up in J's thick skull."

Taína's voice drifted over Trent's shoulder. "You guys should come to our show next week. We're not having luck finding a new guitarist, but we'll be at Evolution regardless."

"We thought about taking time off," Lia added. "But gigs pay my rent. We can't find anyone as good as your brother, and frankly the idea of playing with fresh meat so soon feels wrong, so Taína will probably be on guitar and singing."

Trent looked between them and Nate. "Cool. I don't know if it's really my type of place, but I'll go if Nate wants me there."

Nate immediately said, "I do," and regretted it just as fast. Why was it so hard to keep Trent at arm's length?

They left the house and made the three-block walk to Trent's car where they finally broke the silence to exchange information. Trent was carrying Theo's guitar and another bag of his belongings, and informed Nate that his twin hadn't had a permanent residence. He'd couch surfed with various friends for the entire time he'd lived in New York.

"What's with that Jericho dude, anyway?" Trent asked. "Seems like a fucking asshole."

"He could just be upset. I think he's definitely hiding something, though. Maybe I can get it out of him when they play at Evolution next week." Nate strapped on his seat belt before Trent could lecture him. "Either way, they're definitely not on the same side as Elijah and Holden when it comes to the Community."

Trent pulled away from the curb, guiding the Nova out onto the cramped street. "Why do you think Jericho knows anything more than Lia? She seems more trustworthy and forthcoming."

"It's not just a feeling." Despite everything, Nate hesitated to admit the next part. "I know he knows something. Earlier I had this dream . . ."

"About what? Him?"

"Yeah, but I don't think it was just a dream. It was the same sort of vision I had of Theo's death. I was in someone else's body, but this time I had no idea who. And I was in that hallway leading to the backyard of that apartment, eavesdropping on Jericho and Theo having an argument. I think they were talking about that girl Carrie."

"And you have no idea whose body you were riding along in?"

"No. Not at all."

Trent tapped his fingers against the steering wheel. "I hate to say it, Nate, but I think you're going to have to make friends with someone who actually understands all this psychic shit. Once you figure out those visions, you'll be a lot closer to learning the truth."

CHAPTER TWELVE

Nate went so far as to call Dade's phone before hanging up. Mystery or not, he couldn't bring himself to ask his uncle for advice. The idea of talking to him was so repellent that Nate willingly decided to enter the part of adulthood where he had no one to depend on but himself. No family. No parents. No people he could look up to as the grown-up, not that he'd had that in years. He was on his own.

Except that wasn't entirely true, because he had Trent.

After picking up Nate's belongings from Elijah's place, Trent had admitted to being late for dinner plans with family, and Nate asked to be dropped off at the subway. Going back to Trent's place to wait for him was the more desirable option, but there was more to do and Nate wouldn't get any of it done by hiding.

Trent double-parked and stood with Nate outside the train station at Union Square.

"I know you don't like Holden," Trent said. "But you can use him. You claimed he offered to be big daddy psychic, right?"

"Yeah, but I'm pretty sure that's just because of my last name." Someone brushed against Nate while hurrying into the station, and he flinched. "I just don't trust him."

"I know you don't, but using him to figure out the visions and your power is a good excuse to hang out at the club and get more information from him and others. Two birds with one stone."

"True." Nate thought about Holden's eye fucks and constant touching, and wondered if he'd have to endure more flirting. "I can head over there before I go get my stuff from the apartment. I'll need Chase or Elijah to let me in, anyway."

"Good plan." Trent looked around the crowded subway. "How about I come with you? I'll tell my aunt I'll come another time, and I can drive you. The train situation isn't gonna work."

"No. I can do it."

"I know you can do it, Nate. I don't doubt that. But just because you're strong enough to endure it doesn't mean you should force yourself to suffer. You tense up every time someone gets too close to you."

People rushed around them, hundreds going in different directions while heading for streets that seemed to confusingly zig and zag. The combination of fast-walking commuters, looming police, and random musicians was turning the idea of him riding the subway alone into a real horror show.

"I want to try," Nate insisted. "I can't rely on you for everything."

"Even if I want you to? I'm not trying to baby you. I *want* to help you. I care about you."

"Why? You barely know me."

"Maybe so. But that doesn't change the fact that I care."

"Goddamn it." Nate brought a hand to his face, pressing the heel of it against his eyes. "I'm sorry. I'm a mess. I'm fucking nervous. I just don't want to talk to Holden."

"I know you don't, but you can use your need for psychic training as a way to pump him for info."

Or maybe he could find a way to talk to Beck. She hadn't been as defensive as Holden, and if she was monitoring him, it was more likely that she was onto anything shady he'd been up to.

"I'm just worried that I'll screw this up. Last time I wasn't going in with this whole plan of action. Now that I am, I think I'll get nervous and start stammering and fuck up."

"It'll be fine. Seriously. You said he's a real slick motherfucker, right?" At Nate's nod, Trent nudged him with a smile. "So play on that. Let him feel like he's working you over, amp up the flustered baby psy bullshit, and slide in some questions to trip him up. Easy."

"I probably won't have to pretend to amp it up," Nate said bitterly. "I hate that I get so flustered."

Trent sighed, clearly recognizing that his attempts to motivate Nate were in vain. "Are you sure you don't want me to go with you?"

"No. You're right. I need to get information, and it won't work if you're there."

"Okay. Good luck, then. You'll be awesome." Trent brushed a kiss to Nate's forehead right there in the middle of everyone. "Let me know when you're headed home."

They parted ways and, as he tried to find the right train, he wondered about the word *home*.

The ride was only ten minutes, but by the time he lurched out of the train at Forty-ninth Street, Nate was sweating and nauseated. He made it to Evolution in a blur of uneven steps. Not getting run over by a taxi while trembling and being shoulder checked all over the crosswalk had to earn him some NYC survival points. It *had* to. Navigating the city while in his right frame of mine was already a feat. Making his way through the maze of subway tunnels and enormous avenues while spots danced before his eyes was a miracle.

But he did it.

Chase was at the door when Nate arrived. After a single once-over, he sneered and jerked his chin at the door. "Don't throw up on the floor or I'll make you lick it up."

"Eat a dick."

One of Chase's brows quirked at the retort, but he went back to his hostile contemplation of every human passing the club.

Too irritated to be mortified, Nate hurried to the bathroom as bile surged up his throat. He crashed through the battered door and squeezed his eyes shut. It was dim and the AC felt stronger in here. It felt good. After several deep breaths, he found a calm center. The need to vomit receded, and he peeled himself off the wall.

When he opened his eyes, he saw that the bathroom was covered in graffiti. The walls were grimy and had been tagged over preexisting tags for years, resulting in a jumble of colors and illegible scrawls. There was a single toilet, a claw-foot sink with no mirror above it and a cluster of postcards and flyers for raves and parties dating back thirty years. Nate splashed water over his face and stared at a red flyer stapled to the wall where the mirror should have been. The paper was thin and dry, curling at the edges, the color faded from time, but the words were just barely legible.

"You okay in there?"

Nate started at the sound of Holden's voice. "Yeah," he called. "I'll be right out."

In the daylight, the club looked less glamorous. Without the red lights, the din of a hundred drunk-slurred voices and pounding bass, it barely resembled the sophisticated establishment he'd been too intimidated to approach. The same could not be said for Holden. In the light of day, he was just as gorgeous—hair perfect, muscular build showcased by a tight, gray button-down and dark-blue jeans.

"Interesting bathroom," Nate said, because in his world that was a good conversation topic. "I've never heard of a rave called Digital Domain."

"Probably because it went out in the mid-nineties. Before your time."

"You're right. I was born in 1990." Make small talk. Pretend to be affable. Be normal. "But not your time?"

"Don't be fooled by this lovely face." Holden smirked. "I'm a child of the eighties. Apparently that makes me an antique in the gay world."

"I'm barely part of the, uh, gay world. So I have no idea what to say about that." Nate hurried on to avoid explaining his lack of functional relationships with other men. "How old is your brother?"

"He's two years older than you. I told you—I'm an antique. The oldest person in this establishment besides Beck. She and my father are the same age. They met in the early stages of the Community forming, which is why they're so . . . close."

Nate tucked away the continuous undercurrent of bitterness in Holden's tone for later. He couldn't tell if it had anything to do with the matter at hand, and was way too aware of how much these Evolution folks tried to redirect and distract him with useless bits of information.

Holden flashed a tight smile and headed to the staircase leading to his office. "So, what happened to you?"

"The subway freaks me out."

Holden led him to the office and shut the door behind them. It had been cleaned up slightly and a sitting area with two small couches were now visible. Previously, boxes had been stacked there. "Does that happen a lot with crowds?"

"Well, I don't make it a habit. It's not like I have anxiety attacks for the fun of it." Nate ran his hands over the thighs of his jeans. "This city is an enormous, sweaty clusterfuck."

Holden smirked and sat down. "Are you claustrophobic?"

"No." Nate plopped onto the couch across from Holden. The toes of his beat-up sneakers bumped against the table. "But all of those people surrounding me and pressing up against me? I can't handle it. It makes me feel like my head is going to explode."

"Well, can't you shield yourself against it?"

The judgmental tone set Nate's teeth on edge. How did someone grow to be such a condescending dick?

"Not when people are transmitting their pissed-off hatred and aggravation as strong as they do when commuting in this city. It's sensory overload. The same thing happened the first time I came into this club."

Holden rested his ankle against the opposite knee, one arm thrown over the back of the sofa, and stared. Nate fidgeted under the scrutiny.

"I don't understand your family. Why wouldn't they teach you how to use your talent?"

"I'm not close to them. My mother kept us away from the rest of the family. She didn't like to talk about what we could do."

"What was her talent?"

"Like I said, she didn't like to talk about it, but I suspect she was an empath too."

"A good one?"

Nate shrugged. "Like I would know? I'm not even sure what I can do besides receive unwanted impressions. For example . . . is it possible to get an impression in the form of a vision?"

"Of course, if whoever you're touching is giving off strong enough impressions."

"What if you're not touching something or someone?"

Holden cocked his head, flashing a bemused half smile. "I've never heard of such a thing, although it would be amusing for empaths, say like you, to receive visions of everyone who had a sexual fantasy about them. Say, like me."

"That's really special, Holden." And useless. If receiving visions wasn't an empath ability, then either Nate had latent talents he didn't know about or someone had been sending them to him on purpose. "If I was able to protect myself with a mental shield like you and Chase do, I wouldn't have to worry about your perverted aspirations."

"Heh. You like the attention. Even if you pretend not to."

"That's bullshit," Nate said.

"Right." Holden winked. "Anyway, you shouldn't compare yourself to Chase. He's an exceptional psychic. He has so many different talents that he can't even be classified." Holden held out his fingers to tick them off. "Empath, precog, telepath . . ."

Telepath. The idea sent a chill down Nate's spine. How much of what had been going on in his brain had Chase heard when he'd first approached the club?

"He's lucky. I wish I had talents as useful."

Holden uncrossed his legs and leaned forward. "The disdain in your voice when you talk about your talent is so fucking unfortunate, Nate. Some people would love to be able to do what we can do. You just don't know how to use it to your advantage. You weren't taught properly. Or at all."

"What's the good of knowing how much everyone in Brookside despised me?"

"Knowing the truth is always valuable if you have a goal. But that's not the only good thing about being an empath."

Holden pressed his fingers to Nate's cheek. Nate ignored the instinct to jerk away and avoid skin-to-skin contact. In the recent past, that had only been safe with Trent.

He tensed, unsure of what to expect, and a jolt surged between them. The blankness he'd come to expect from Holden was replaced with such a strong surge of energy that Nate was struck speechless. Holden's vibes were all calm rays of self-assurance, and Nate reached out with his gift, wanting more. If only he could blanket himself in that feeling, everything would be better. His ability to speak to other people, to trust his own judgment, and to trust the people around him . . .

"Imagine how good that would feel if I fucked you."

Nate realized that he'd listed forward. He yanked away. "What the hell was that?"

"People walk around exuding energy all day, and because you can't control your gift, you take it all in whether you want to or not. You let it affect your mood, your body, your health, because you don't have a defense mechanism against it. And because of that . . ." Holden shrugged. "Well, what do you think the flip side of that would be?"

Nate's thin shirt felt too warm all of a sudden. Sweat had gathered in a fine sheen on his skin. "If someone is exuding good vibes, it makes me feel good. But I've never felt it like *that* before."

"I turned it up for you. You can control how much you give and how much you take." Holden smiled slyly. "And you were taking a lot, gorgeous."

"Could you feel how much I was absorbing from you?"

"Yes." Holden brushed hair out of Nate's face. "And I could feel how much it was turning you on."

Nate turned his face. "Stop."

"It was, wasn't it?"

"Yeah, but don't get too excited. It's just because it felt good in general."

"Ah. The hypersensitive type. Elijah will enjoy that."

Nate said nothing. Holden could tease and flirt all he wanted, but his words were nothing compared to the panic in Nate's head.

He'd hoped Elijah had been bullshitting—a vain attempt at justifying why Theo and Holden had been close. But this was proof. Proof he couldn't deny or shake off. One shot of Holden's mojo, and he'd been leaning forward while his blood had warmed, wanting more of *something*, even if he hadn't known what. If that was all it had taken, how much had *he* unknowingly influenced Trent during the past few days? How much of what had happened between them was real?

His stomach clenched, and he felt sick again.

He tried to focus on the sounds coming from outside, horns honking from the steady flow of traffic, people laughing, music floating up quietly from the lower floor—anything but the man sitting across from him. He looked around the office, taking in the wall of monitors, an old calendar, and a thumbtack board that was filled with notes and pictures. Frowning, he stood, glad to have a reason to move away.

He'd assumed the pictures on the board were primarily of Evolution employees. There was an image of Elijah in his "work outfit"—denim booty shorts and unlaced Doc Martins—wearing a sweater that looked like chain mail and a Santa hat. From what he saw, many of the photos were of Elijah individually, hugging someone at the club, or photobombing someone else. The three pictures of Holden were candid, one in which he appeared to be in a serious conversation with Beck near the front of the club. Each photo told the story of the club, of its employees, and the relationships between them. They seemed close, even Chase who was so detached and withdrawn. Nate had assumed he just was using Elijah for easy sex, but photos of them cuddled together on the maroon lounge chairs implied more.

The idea of the Community had immediately made him suspicious, but looking at these pictures, these talented men who'd formed alliances and found friends in each other, Nate wondered what it would feel like to have connections like this. People he could trust and talk to about his gift, and people who would understand how it felt to grow up thinking he was a freak before learning there were others out there just like him.

But he wasn't part of their Community, and he didn't have these sorts of allies. And until he found out who'd killed his brother, he couldn't trust any of them.

A twinge constricted Nate's chest. He shoved it aside and started to turn away from the board. Before he could, a small Polaroid caught his eye. It was of a wisp of a boy, maybe twelve years old, with platinum hair. For a moment, Nate was sure it was a picture of him or Theo as a child.

"That was taken when Chase first came home from the Farm."

Nate looked at the Polaroid again. The child in the picture was at an amusement park, standing in front of a sign that said, *Cyclone.* "What's the Farm?"

"Another Community property upstate. He was troubled, and he received extensive counseling there."

"He was always this powerful?"

"Yes. Chase is special. He must come from good psychic stock."

Nate frowned at the phrasing. It was a weird way to describe someone's parents, but maybe Holden didn't see biological family as important since he had the Community.

"Who was his mother?"

"No idea. All I know about her was that she was one of my father's mistresses." Holden smiled again, but it seemed more default than genuine. Like he tried to show a pleasant face so no one would see his anger or bitterness. "My father doesn't talk about her, but apparently she was a drifter or a whore or something. She dumped Chase on my father after trying to blackmail him for money, and moved back to wherever she'd come from. I don't even know if Chase is *really* my father's son, but abandoning him would have been horrible. Everyone says it was obvious he was special since birth. He learned everything ten times faster than other babies. His talents were so sensitive that they put him on psy suppressants."

"Am I supposed to know what that is?"

"It's a chemical that temporarily slows psychic activity in the brain. For powerful psys who can't control their talent, it's invaluable. And Chase was like that at first." Holden pressed his thumb against the corner of the picture. "Do you know what he could have become without the Community to guide him?"

"Voldemort?"

"Cute."

"I'm not trying to be cute. You're just trying to sell me on how amazing your Community is."

"Not really," Holden said. "If anything, you tried to change the subject away from the fact that your dick got hard when I let you feel my vibes."

Nate moved away to sit on the sofa. He felt Holden staring at him, eyes raking over his body with filthy intent. "Look, I'm not going to have sex with you."

Holden laughed. "Everyone says that about me and Elijah. And then they see him in those tiny shorts one too many times and find themselves trying to get into his bed. Even my brother wasn't immune to his charms."

It was said with such nonchalance that Nate was at a complete loss for words. This conversation was going sideways.

Another low chuckle tumbled from Holden's mouth. "You'll see."

"No. I really won't. How old is he, anyway? Is he legally allowed to hang out here?"

"He turns twenty-one in the fall." Holden flicked his fingers dismissively. "If he's legally allowed to vote on who runs the country and can join the military, why can't he have a drink? It's not very logical."

"But won't you get in trouble?"

A flash of impatience streaked across Holden's expression. "You're a lovely young man, Nate. But not too bright."

Here they went again. "Fuck you, Holden. I knew it was a mistake to think I could talk to you."

"Fine. I take it back. You're bright, but you're not imaginative in the slightest. This club alone houses empaths, telepaths, people with precognitive abilities. Do you seriously think some void cop would stand a chance? A psy can do whatever they want if they master their talent."

Holden was right. Nate wasn't very imaginative, because he'd never considered the possibilities of using his gift that way. His thoughts returned to things his mother had said about Eveline and her desire to control the family. At the time, it hadn't made sense, but now it clicked together. If Eveline controlled the family, she controlled their gifts. And in the same vein, that would also be true for the Community.

"Get that look off your face, Nate. Your brother was thrilled once he started taking advantage of what he had."

"I'm not my brother. And I'm not judging you. I don't have to. You're smart enough to know that shit is shady."

"Maybe it is, but I'm not going to feel bad about it. How many people use money to get what they want? How many people use status? We just use something we were born with."

"What difference does that make?" Nate pressed his hands flat against the cushion, poised to push himself up. "You're still manipulating people to get what you want. And I know what you're saying makes sense, but I still wouldn't do it. It wouldn't feel right."

"Oh, give me a fucking break," Holden said, an edge making its way into his tone. "Why are you so hung up on what's right? Have you been treated right by your family? The people in your hometown? Your own brother? No, I don't think so. He told me all about it. You of all people should want to take advantage of what God, or whatever higher power, gave you. There's nothing evil about knowing what people want and being able to give it to them."

"So then what do I want?" Nate asked. "Because you must know it's not to fuck you."

Holden flashed one of his smiles again, this one chillier than the others. "You want to know why your brother killed himself. And whether the Community helped him off that pier."

Nate's heart skipped a beat. "Did it?"

"No."

"Are you sure?"

"I am positive," Holden said, enunciating each word, "that I did all I could to help your brother."

"Did you do anything to stop him from being blackballed once he asked about the missing girl?"

Holden's steady gaze flickered, but he squared his shoulders. "Elijah talks too much."

"I think he talks just enough. But don't start arranging his exile just yet—he only mentioned it while ranting about what a traitor Theo had been for daring to question the Community's involvement."

"Because it was bullshit!" Holden's voice boomed in the small room. Not a yell, but sharp enough to cut through the air in a slice. "He wasn't just questioning the Community. He was questioning Evolution—*me*. After all I tried to do for him. My father had already been doubting my ability to control this club, which is why he sent Beck here to babysit me." Holden scoffed. "Lot of good it did. Carrie disappeared *after* she showed up."

"You're saying the Community is also concerned about the disappearances? Then why is no one out here asking questions about why Theo was—why he killed himself? Why is it just me, while everyone else rushes to bury what happened or put the full blame on him?"

Holden finally jerked away to glare at the monitors. "What would you have me do?"

Nate balled his hands into fists and returned his gaze to the bulletin board of pictures again. "I'd have you, any of you, admit that isolating someone after you make them believe they have something resembling a family, just because they asked questions, is a good way to fuck with their heads. Especially when they come from a family like mine. Maybe if you'd shown more concern in helping him rather than icing him out, he wouldn't have wound up floating in the Hudson."

The temperature in the room dropped several degrees. Nate almost regretted saying it. Except, he didn't. It was true. Even if Holden hadn't been the one to shove Theo into the brackish water, he hadn't been there to have Theo's back either. It seemed like any one Community person who could have supported Theo in his quest to learn the truth about the disappearances had merely turned their backs and closed their eyes and ears to the possibility that his suspicions had been true. That was apparently better than admitting that someone in their clique was complicit in a crime.

"Your brother was *starved* for attention," Holden said, his voice sharp and vicious. "He would do literally anything to have someone give him the time of day so he could pretend he belonged at the top of the Community's hierarchy instead of back in the white trash town you both grew up in. So, excuse me if I didn't immediately take him at face value when he was accusing the Community I'd grown up in of hurting one of our own."

Nate wanted to argue, but it made sense.

Even after all his family—and Theo—had done to him, he still defended them. He couldn't imagine how he would react if he'd grown up in a family that had actually supported him the way the Community had done for Holden or any of the others.

"You're right."

Holden's eyes narrowed. "Am I?"

"Yeah. But you can still go fuck yourself."

Nate strode toward the door and evaded when Holden tried to grab his arm.

"Wait. I'm sorry."

"Don't backtrack now."

"Damn it, just stop." Holden dug his fingers into Nate's arm. To his credit, he didn't try any of the influencing crap. "I'm sorry. I swear. I liked Theo. I cared for him. I'm just sick of being blamed for what happened to him."

Nate looked over his shoulder. "Who else is blaming you?"

Holden's lips parted, and he looked uncertain. Before he could respond the door opened and nearly slammed into them. Nate stepped away.

"Nate." Beck stopped just inside the doorway holding a clipboard. "Am I interrupting anything?"

"No," Nate snapped. "I mean, no, ma'am. You're not."

Her lips twitched. "'Ma'am.' That's a new one. Are you sure you're not calling me old?"

"Not at all. It just means . . . I'm showing you respect."

"I see." Beck's gaze glided over to Holden. "It's nice to meet someone who has respect."

Holden scoffed and turned away. He showed Beck his back, which only seemed to please her. These two seemed to love getting a rise out of each other. She looked at Nate again.

"How long will you be in the city? I'd like to show you around if you have the time."

"I don't know yet. I . . ." Think, fucker. *Think.* "I met someone here, so it's a little complicated. I'm going to be staying with him."

Holden frowned, and Beck didn't bother pretending not to smirk.

"Well. If you have interest in learning more about the Community, let me know. I'd love for you to become a member, but it only works if you understand how we operate."

"Actually . . ." He turned away from Holden. "I do have some questions."

"Excellent. I'm headed to Community Watch, and you're welcome to accompany me."

Nate nodded and started for the door, but not before catching a glimpse of the worried look creasing Holden's face.

CHAPTER THIRTEEN

They left the club to go out onto the sunshine-drenched streets of New York City. Honking horns and a steady hum of voices greeted them. It was like the pulse of the city never slowed, and Nate didn't know how he'd be able to handle the steady beat. He felt too slow, too lost, and too unsure of his next move to ever keep pace.

Seeing Nate's slow headshake, Beck smiled. "How much of the city have you seen?"

"Just a few places," he said. "Here, Elijah's apartment, and my friend's place uptown. I haven't had much time to explore."

"Do you want to?"

They began walking toward Eighth Avenue, and the crowds increased. Nate wondered if the crowds would be similarly thick without the tourists.

"I'd like to," he said. "I'd never been anywhere except the town I'm from in Texas, but at the same time I don't think my anxiety could handle all this on a regular basis."

"Social anxiety?"

"No. Well . . ." Explaining this for the second time in an hour didn't really put him at ease, but there was no way to avoid the question without being rude. And he wanted Beck as an ally. "You could say it's social anxiety stemming from my inability to block my own talent. Constantly picking up on people's vibes has a way of messing with your head after a while. Sometimes I think it's going to turn me into a complete recluse."

Without missing a beat, Beck switched their path from the subway to the corner. She held out a hand for a cab, and Nate could have hugged her if physical contact with strangers didn't make him want to hurl.

"I can't imagine being unable to block at all," she admitted. "It must make it hard to function in a relationship. No one should be able to know what everyone around them is feeling all the time. It's not healthy."

"Definitely not." But at least it wasn't like that with Trent. Unless he was safe only because Nate had been influencing him . . . He shook the thought away. Later. He'd deal with that later. "I wish I could learn."

"That's part of what we do in the Community, you know." Beck scowled at the cabs rushing by without pausing. "We find unconnected psys and give them the tools they need to survive in this world."

"How do you do all of this outreach and help?"

"Good question." A cab finally pulled to a stop at the curb beside them. Beck slid in and gave the driver an address on Thirty-fourth Street. She spoke again after Nate had pulled the door shut. "There is an organization run by Richard Payne—Holden's father. That's actually where we're going now. It's called Community Watch." Beck lowered her voice and leaned closer to Nate. "To voids, it's a mental health rehabilitation center, but in reality it's a rehab and intake center for psys who have developed issues as a result of going their whole lives without understanding that they're psychic."

"And Holden's father founded it."

"Technically the idea began with his grandfather, but it was Richard Payne and some close friends of his who brought the idea to life."

"I see." It was more organized than Nate had expected. He wasn't sure how he felt about cover organizations and office buildings run by the Community. It sounded like a psychic IMF from Mission Impossible. "One thing I don't understand is how you find the people you end up helping. For example, how did my brother stumble on Evolution? It can't have been a coincidence."

"It wasn't." Beck glanced out the window. They were already near Thirty-fourth Street according to the street signs. "There are all kinds of websites online where psys connect and word spreads about the Community—especially on Reddit and Tumblr. Many people come to us. Like Elijah. And your brother."

"And those who don't?"

The cab slowed to a stop. "There are people within the Community who can sense and track other psys. Richard is one of them. I'm another."

The cab driver glanced at them in the rearview mirror. He lost interest once Beck swiped her card. She'd been talking low, but it would have been easy for the cabbie to overhear their conversation. Maybe she didn't care. Or maybe she had faith that the average person would immediately dismiss any discussion of psychic powers.

"Let me get this straight," Nate said after getting out of the cab. Another pedestrian shoved by him and dove inside. No one looked twice at him or Beck even though dozens of people moved around them in a steady flow. "You and Richard, and probably others, track psychics in need and bring them to the Community, where you help to train them, or rehabilitate them as needed, and then . . . nudge them into the workforce?"

"If possible we try to help them advance their education so they can find a suitable career, not just get any random job. And if they need more help than we can handle here—" she indicated the building behind them "—they go to the Farm for a while."

"The Farm," Nate repeated. "Sounds like a horror movie waiting to happen."

She tried to hide a smile and failed. "The Payne family owns two hundred and seventy acres of farmland in Dutchess County, New York. On it is a large farmhouse." She snorted. "Well, they call it a farmhouse. Compared to where I grew up, it's a compound. Psys in need of extended rehabilitation go there until they're stable enough to rejoin the rest of us. The program is run by a man named Jasper. He's one of the most devoted members of the Community, and a dear friend of mine. He's essentially dedicated his life to studying and rehabilitating multitalented psychics who've experienced trauma. Chase spent a lot of time with him as a child, but most people learn to acclimate faster than he did."

"Okay . . ." Nate glanced up at the building. A shining high-rise in the center of what appeared to be one of the busiest parts of the city. All around them were subways and buses, and too many stores to count. It was a far cry from a farm in upstate New York where mentally unstable psychics were shipped off for extensive therapy.

"And the Payne family started this organization out of complete altruism?"

Beck led him to the building, her shoes clicking on the concrete as she navigated a crowd that seemed to part around her like the sea.

"It's not just run on warm fuzzies and helpful desires," she said. "It would be impossible since we don't receive funds from the government to operate. We have donors and most people involved in the organization pay an annual fee."

"A fee," Nate repeated. "Even Elijah?"

"Yes. It's agreed when you sign the contract."

"A *contract*?" Holy shit, maybe Lia hadn't been kidding when she'd mentioned people signing their lives away.

"Don't look so surprised, Nate. There has to be a price for as many resources as we pour into members. So, to answer your question, the heart of the Community is altruistic, but there is still money exchanging hands."

"I see." Nate slowly nodded. "What about my brother?"

"Your brother wasn't officially part of the Community. He didn't have the money, and I don't know that he would have done it even if he had. It's part of the reasons his behavior became a problem. People considered him an outsider."

"I see." They paused by the glass revolving door. "Did you consider him one?"

"No. Chase and the others would say I didn't know him, or that I'm just here to bust Holden's balls, but it's not true. I believe in the Community, and the purpose of it is to help psys like Theo. We helped him even though we didn't have to."

A crowd of people pushed between them, putting the conversation on hold as Nate gathered his thoughts to figure out what he wanted to say.

"And why is that? Before now it sounded like you didn't even have a relationship with him."

"We didn't have a long one, but we spoke to each other." Beck glanced out at the city unfolding behind them, grid patterns of streets and a flood of buses and taxi cabs. "We had things in common. I came from a place not too different from Brookside, and I had a family not that different from yours, except they weren't psychics. The difference between me and you guys is that my talent allowed me to find allies, and that's how I got out. Your family should have been your allies, and they weren't."

Nate looked down. "It's weird that any of you even know who my family is. We're just a bunch of rednecks."

"Maybe. But once upon a time someone thought a redneck family full of psychics had potential."

She started to the door, but he put an arm out before she could go in.

"What do you mean? Who?"

Beck considered him for a moment before saying, "I remember when your mother showed up here, Nate. That's partially why I'd tried to pay attention to your brother."

"So, it *was* her," he breathed. "Can you tell me what happened?"

"I don't know the whole story," she admitted with regret in her voice. "But I do know that she turned up right here back when the Community was finally gaining steam on the East Coast, and everyone was absolutely taken with her because she was such a talented psychic." Beck smiled, but there was a trace of bitterness. "I'm sure it helped that she was gorgeous."

"What did she do while she was here? No one has ever—" Nate tried to collect his thoughts as a million questions sprang at him. "She never told anyone what happened."

"And again, I'm not sure of the exact chain of events. All I know is that she threw herself into becoming a Community member, even requesting to go to the Farm to work alongside Jasper and the others. But somewhere along the line, she decided this wasn't the right place for her."

"And she left?"

"Yes. Abruptly."

"But—" This couldn't be all of it. After all this time, Nate refused to believe this was the only story he'd be getting. "She didn't say anything before she went? There were no signs?"

Beck shook her head. "No. But, again, I wasn't close with her. I saw her from afar. The founders kept her for themselves once they realized the extent of her powers and the story of her family."

Nate digested this information, struggling with the disappointment building inside him. He knew his mother was capable of running off without notice, but there had to have been a reason why. Something she was running *from*. And unless Nate got in with the founders, he'd never find out.

"Thank you for telling me," he said. "I always wondered about that time in her life."

"You're welcome. I wish I could be more help."

They entered the lobby, and Beck did a retina scan before striding to the front desk. Nate had to do fingerprints and have a picture taken in order to sign in. He tried to redirect his brain to the matter at hand instead of focusing on the past.

"I gotta say, I didn't expect contracts and buildings with high security whenever Elijah and Holden started going on about the Community."

"I don't blame you." Beck put her hand on his as they walked to the elevator. She radiated such soothing vibes that Nate sucked them in like a vacuum. "It's a lot to take in, but the only way we can function is if we're organized. And over the past twenty years, since Richard took over, the changes in the Comm have been amazing. The only thing we haven't been able to change is the social aspect."

"Social aspect," Nate repeated. They stepped into the elevator, sleek and cold and completely empty. For such a large building, it was deserted. "You mean the fact that people like Holden think your worth is defined by how powerful you are?"

Beck faced him with her back to the wall, arms crossed over her chest. "Yes. Even Jasper, who has worked for years on the Farm, is treated as a lesser and his talent is . . . phenomenal. He can delve into someone's mind and learn exactly who people are and what makes them different." Beck flicked lint from her shirt, for the first time avoiding Nate's eyes. Her voice was neutral, but there was no hiding the bitterness. "The great flaw in the Community is that even if you provide significant value, it's not fully appreciated unless your gift can be utilized in many other ways. At the end of the day, we're here to provide support, but we also need to use our abilities as tools to achieve our goals. And some tools are more useful than others."

"Is that the case for you?"

She flashed a small smile. "I'll just say that at the moment, the only way to have influence in this organization is if you have money like the Payne family, or talent like Chase. Those of us like Jasper and me had to find solace in bonding with each other."

Jasper seemed like someone close to her, and yet she was apparently romantically involved with Richard Payne. Maybe that was how she moved up in the Community. Nate didn't know what was more depressing: that the Community was so focused on power and money despite their other claims, or that anyone wanted to climb a social ladder enough to sleep with someone to get a leg up.

But none of that was any of his business, so he nodded and let the conversation end.

Beck gave him a tour of the facility while Nate snuck texts to Trent. He documented everything he saw and heard so he wouldn't forget later, and Trent responded by suggesting other things to ask and compliments about how high level Nate's secret agent skills were becoming. Silly comments between boring monologues about the value of the Community to psychics, but they kept Nate from worrying that he was being lured into an evil lair. Strange how Trent could keep him at ease even when they were miles part.

Community Watch really was like a large psychic corporation. There were departments, a board of directors who made decisions, and Richard Payne at the top of it all. On the surface, it really did seem like a supportive place. There was counseling, educational resources, and career outreach. Pamphlets bragged about success stories—psychics who'd given testimonials about how the Community had helped them and where they'd be without it. Elijah was in one of them.

It seemed legit, despite their rules and fees that likely made the actual staff wealthy, but Nate couldn't figure out what was in it for Richard Payne.

"I can tell you're skeptical," Beck said once they finished the tour. "And that's healthy."

"I'm just confused."

"It's okay, Nate. If I was you, I'd feel the same."

"Why's that?"

Beck nudged him toward a corridor. "Because I've been in this for twenty-five years, and sometimes I'm still skeptical about whether I'm a cog in a bigger machine or whether anything I do or say will make a difference to the Community's goals."

"What are their goals?"

She smiled. "To make this world safe for us. That being said, there are still risks. Not everyone we take in is a good fit. Some people turn on us."

"Like my brother?" Nate asked sharply.

"No, not just him. Some people pretend to want help but then take advantage of us. Once, about two decades ago, we had a boy who was taken off the streets and turned out to be a thief. It was in the early days when everyone was idealistic and hopeful, and it changed everything. That's when security got so tight. We can't have people learning our secrets and then running off. It's a threat to all of us."

Nate stopped before they walked further down the hall. "What happened to him?"

"He was dealt with. Internally. We didn't throw him into the street," she said, as if that had been a serious option. "But he did spend a long time at the Farm. Now, he's a contributing member of our Community. It just took some time for him to acclimate."

Acclimate. There was that word again. First Chase and now this mysterious thief. Nate was beginning to wonder exactly what methods the Comm used to ensure psychics at the Farm adapted to the indoctrination and fell in line. Part of him wondered if that was what had happened with his mother.

"If all of this is about helping people . . . acclimate and become contributing members of society who won't fuck up the big psy secret, why is there so much obsession with who has what talent?"

"Like I said, our main goal is to make the world safe for people like us, and you can't do that unless you have power."

The city's age was continuously emphasized as Nate traveled around the city. The remnants of history saturated everything he touched, and Trent's building was no exception.

The tile mosaic of the lobby's floor and the brass gate attached to the elevator reminded Nate of a 1920s movie set. He ran his fingers over the panel where the elevator buttons were, watching absently as light hit the scissored gate through the tiny window in the inner door. The elevator reached the third floor with a jolt. It rocked alarmingly, and Nate pushed the gate open to step out into the hallway.

He was at Trent's door before he was fully prepared. Setting his backpack down, Nate squinted at his reflection in the broad brass strip encircling the peephole and tucked hair behind his ear. It stuck to his sweaty face despite his efforts. That was the other thing he'd noticed as he commuted everywhere—the heat in New York was somehow more unbearable than the heat in Texas. The humidity and high temperatures seemed to triple since he was always surrounded by hundreds of other people. Not to mention the fact that some places didn't have central AC.

The door opened before he could knock. Trent appeared before him with a smile. Even in a pair of baggy sweatpants and a ribbed undershirt, he was gorgeous. With the outline of his carved muscles and bulge? He was a god. Nate was definitely not worthy.

"Are you going to say hi or stare at my dick print?"

Nate could feel himself reddening. "Hi."

Trent didn't try to hide his smug smile as he stepped back and held the door open wider. He also grabbed the straps to Nate's book bag after Nate forgot about its existence and hurried inside.

"Everything all right?"

"Uh, yeah."

Trent kicked the door shut and flipped at least four locks. "Why? Did something happen?"

"No."

"Then . . .?"

Nate shrugged, looking around the living room he'd stepped into. It had hardwood floors and was decorated in shades of cream and beige. A wide archway led to a kitchen that appeared largely untouched. There was a door off to the left of the living room and a dark hallway on the opposite side of the kitchen. With the exception of a lone bowl sitting on the coffee table, it was spotless.

"Are you sure it's okay if I stay here?"

"Yes."

"Really? It's pretty nice."

"So?" Trent snorted. "What, are you going to sully the place with your presence? Calm down. I spoke to my friend about it, and she said it was cool."

"Why is it cool? She doesn't know me."

"Because she knows me and trusts my judgment." Trent stepped closer, his mouth drawing down into a frown. "What's wrong with you? I thought you were happy to be out of those Evolution punks' apartment?"

"I am happy. I'm grateful for you letting me stay here."

"You don't have to be grateful, dude. I want you here."

And Nate wanted to be here. Relief had hit him square in the chest as soon as he'd stepped into the spacious, mostly empty apartment. There was no glut of knickknacks and fabrics like at Elijah's apartment. No impressions springing off every surface. Most of all, Nate wasn't on his guard. As soon as he saw Trent's warm smile and glittering eyes, he felt safe. He just hoped this invitation hadn't come from him infusing his own desires into Trent.

Nate exhaled slowly. "Sorry I'm being weird. I'm just tense and exhausted."

"I can see that." Trent grabbed Nate's shoulder and guided him past the kitchen and down the short hall. "You look even more tired than you did earlier."

"I slept like shit last night."

"Me too. I waited up hoping some asshole would call me."

They entered the room Trent was staying in, and the sense of safety doubled. It was small and mostly empty, but sunlight streamed onto a full-sized bed and the sight of Trent's clothing and video game controllers were a welcome indication of normalcy. No psychic bullshit or big bad organizations. Just a regular human with a great smile and an apparent love for *Call of Duty*. Everything was white, from the walls to the tangled sheets on the bed. A whiteboard and bulletin board dominated an entire wall, while a flat-screen TV inhabited the other.

"That asshole dropped the ball," Nate said. "You sure you want to give him another shot?"

"After finding out how good he kisses? Fuck yeah."

The flush had likely deepened to a highly unattractive strawberry color by this point. Wonderful. He plopped onto a narrow armchair that had IKEA written all over it.

"I like your room."

"Yeah, right." Trent sat on the bed and kicked the Xbox controller out of the way. "I fully intend to live out of my suitcase for the next month and a half, so it isn't going to get much livelier than this."

"It doesn't need to. The room I crashed in was so cluttered, it triggered my empath shit all night."

Trent half turned on the bed, bracing his bare foot on the metal rail. "But you made out okay?"

"I guess. They're pretty uncomfortable to be around."

"Uppity New Yorkers?"

"That's definitely a factor, but they're also very . . . touchy-feely. In a way I'm not comfortable with." Nate cringed. "Casual touching in general is something I'm not okay with."

"Even with me?"

"Well, no. You're different." The upturn of Trent's mouth proved that Nate had no idea how to create space between them. Especially not when he wanted to cause Trent to smile like that again—bashful and adorable. "Anyway, I'm not used to people casually talking about fucking me and each other at random in a conversation. Even Holden was doing it, and he's some high-society big shot in the Community."

The bashful smile flattened into a slash. "That dude put the moves on you?"

"I think he was just trying to distract me."

"Uh-huh." Trent still sounded skeptical. "Tell me what else happened."

"I didn't get much information out of Holden about the visions except for the fact that empaths don't get them from impressions."

"Well, at least we know we can cross empaths off the list of people who may have sent you the vision."

"True, unless it's an empath who's also a telepath or something. Not Elijah or Beck—neither of them have the capacity. And Chase is multi-talented but he can't stand me."

"Sounds like he can't stand anyone. Maybe because he had to grow up on some weird psychic farm. What are they, growing assholes?"

Nate snorted out a laugh. "No. It's like . . . intense therapy or training or, shit, I don't know. Intense brainwashing maybe? This whole Community thing is wacky. Beck kept saying they're trying to change the world or keep us safe from the world."

Trent raised his eyebrows and leaned over to grab a beer from the night stand. "Uh, yeah. *Wacky* would be the correct word."

"Right?" Nate sighed. "I don't even know how much of this has to do with my brother, except the Community is really keen on people thinking they're amazing and not wanting anyone to say otherwise. And I get it now. They do seem amazing for the people that benefit from it. It's just shitty that they ice people out. And there's weird fucking social hierarchies."

"Where would you be in their hierarchy?"

"I have no money and a half-assed talent, so low." Nate shrugged. "Holden would be somewhere at the top. That asshole. He gets under my skin. I think he knows what he's talking about, and I think there's a chance that Theo trusted him enough to tell him about me and the family, but that doesn't change the fact that he is a complete dick. He thinks he's hot shit because he's handsome and rich."

Trent nodded slowly, but his lips were still pursed. "So him being rich keeps him at the top?"

"I'm not sure," Nate admitted. "He's also really talented. He's an empath like me and he's . . ." Nate trailed off, thinking about the explosion of heat and pleasure that had infiltrated him. How it'd left him hard and wanting. "Really good at it."

Trent didn't respond at first, and Nate looked out the window. There was a school and playground across the street. A group of children were chasing each other with water guns as the warm breeze carried their laughter. It was a foreign sound, and reminded Nate of times years and years ago when he and Theo had been that happy.

"Is this dude actually useful, or is he just getting all up on you?"

"Both. He shut down and got defensive when I implied he hadn't done all he could to help Theo. He also seems to have a thing about my family. Thinks we're all backwoods freaks, which . . . isn't far from the truth, I guess. It's hard to defend myself when all of this is so new to me. I had no idea there were potentially millions of other psychics out in the world, and I sure as hell didn't expect that they'd joined together in a community complete with a fucking high-rise and a farm."

Trent shook his head at the mention of the farm. "Do you think your family knew?"

"I know my mom did. Turns out she *did* meet these people when she was in New York, even though Beck wasn't able to tell me what happened while she was there." Nate thought a moment, frowning into space. "I also think maybe my aunt did. She was way too paranoid about unknown forces coming after us. I'm starting to wonder if she meant the Community since they're this huge organized group of rich and powerful psychics, but that doesn't really make any sense unless she was scared of losing control over the family if they started joining the Comm." Nate scowled and pounded his fist down against the arm of the chair. "Fuck, I feel like I'm getting nowhere. I got a tour of a fancy building, but the only thing to come out of this day was finding out that Beck is the only marginally normal psychic I've met so far who had at some point crossed paths with my mother."

"Just because we don't have the whole picture doesn't mean it was pointless," Trent countered. "At least you're using clues to come up with workable theories. And I doubt you're too far off. Just because some of these fools are acting all hunky-dory doesn't mean there might not be little factions who want to fuck shit up."

"It's true." Nate inhaled and exhaled again. "I just wish I wasn't so in the dark. I look like an idiot every time I speak to these people. I just grasp at straws and none of them are ever the right ones."

"And your point being?" Trent scooted forward on the bed and put his hands on Nate's knees. "Look—you came here to figure out what happened to Theo, not to do an exposé on Community Watch or whatever the hell it's called."

Nate grinned. "We've known each other like a week. How are you this good at keeping me focused?"

"You worry so much about everything that I had to figure out ways to do it." Trent squeezed Nate's knees. "Now tell me if you found out anything new about Theo. Let's CSI this shit."

They wound up rehashing everything while writing the details on the whiteboard.

They started with a list of Theo's potential enemies. Jericho, the allegedly scorned boyfriend, went on the list. They also added individuals connected with Evolution and the Community who would have been angry about Theo's preoccupation with the disappearances that had occurred there. They added Chase's name with a question mark because of his thinly veiled threat, and his obvious loathing of Nate.

"What about your boy Holden?"

"What about him?"

"You said he had the most to lose if Theo was going around blaming his club for the disappearances?" Trent pointed at the board with the marker. "Also, he'd look like shit to his father."

Nate chewed on the inside of his cheek. Trent smacked him on the head with the dry-erase marker.

"Nate, be realistic. His father even put Beck there because he didn't trust Holden with the club, and you said it drives him insane. I'm not saying the guy planned it, but if he was already on edge about having a babysitter, and now he had this tweaked-out punk running around stirring up more gossip while Beck is hearing all of it, he might have gone off the deep end and shoved him into the damn water."

"I see what you're saying. And I do think the murder was personal. But . . ."

Now that all the pieces were on the table, Holden being the killer didn't add up. The moments before Theo's drowning, a voice had whispered for him to run. Someone had known the meeting on the pier was dangerous, and they'd tried to warn Theo about it. And somehow . . . someone had prevented him from turning away. They'd also prevented him from swimming to the surface of the water. They'd *psychically* held him down. An empath couldn't do that. Even if empaths could influence people, they had to use their own emotions to do it.

Nate shook his head, frustrated. "I just don't know."

"Seriously, Nate?"

"I think there's more to it. Whoever killed Nate was far more powerful than Holden is. Probably someone strong like Chase. And besides that . . ." Nate sneaked a glance at Trent's increasingly unimpressed face. "I didn't get that feeling from him. He opened himself up to me, and the connection was stronger than any I'd ever had before. I got no hint of danger. If anything, he's probably guilty of stonewalling people who investigate because he *knows* the outcome will make him and his club look bad if something was going on under his nose. Not to mention him wanting to protect the Community."

"Fine." Trent rubbed the name off the board with a sharp swipe of the palm of his hand. "Don't look into him, then. It's your show." He dropped the marker onto the table with a clatter.

"Why are you getting pissed? All I said was that I don't get bad vibes from him."

Trent gave Nate a scathing look. "What, you think murderers go around carrying signs that announce it?"

"I'm not stupid—"

"I didn't fucking say you were."

"Well, you're sure acting like you think I am." Nate got to his feet. "I got this attitude from people all day long. I don't need it from you too."

"I'm not acting like a goddamn thing." Trent planted his hands on his hips and loomed over Nate. "It just gets on my nerves when people put on blinders about someone just because they have some stupid crush. I mean, that's what this is, right? Dude did his empathy thing and gave you his warm, glowy, horny feelings, and now you're ignoring basic investigation shit because Mr. Awesome Empath knows how to withhold bad feels."

A shred of embarrassment shot through the comfort Nate had basked in for the past hour. He backed away from Trent, hands curling into fists. There was nothing he could say that wouldn't sound defensive or hurt. It was the first time Nate felt uncomfortable around Trent, and he hated it.

Trent sighed. "Forget it. Sorry."

"You know, I'm not a social person. I'm bad at talking to people, and I tend to shut down rather than make a real effort to get to know someone. But I'm trying really hard with you, and now you're the one shutting me out just because we had one disagreement. I'm not naive. I'm making a judgment call based on . . . my gut. And I'm trying to learn to trust my gut, which is why I fucking trusted *you* to begin with."

Trent looked down, his shoulders sagging. "You should trust your gut. Don't listen to me. I'm just a void, anyway."

"You're not *just* anything." Nate grabbed Trent's arm and pulled him forward. He flinched at the self-doubt coming off Trent, but didn't let him go. "I want to listen to you. I just don't want you to be an asshole when we don't agree."

"Well—" Trent shrugged in frustration. "Well, I'm being an asshole because I'm fucking jealous."

"So don't be," Nate said. "You and I are friends. I trust you, not them."

"I'm not talking about trusting me versus them," Trent said irritably. "I'm talking about your boy, Holden. The club owner who made you go all red-faced and glassy-eyed when you talked about his awesome connection. Stronger than you ever felt before, apparently."

"I never—" Fuck, yes, he had. Shit. "That's not what I meant! I barely know him. I know *you*. We were in a car together for like forty hours or something. That's basically the equivalent of ten dates." Bad choice of words. "Or ten days of people hanging out, or something. I don't know."

"Right." Trent set his jaw. "Is there a reason why you're not into me?"

"What? How can you say that?"

"Because that's how it seems. Like we get off together, and that's cool and all, but . . . I don't know. I'm just not feeling real clear on what we're doing. You get close and then back off."

"That's not true."

"Yeah, it is. It's totally fucking true. You just think I can't tell you're all hesitant and weird because I'm not a psychic."

"Dude, you can't really think I'm being like . . . like . . ."

"I'm sure there's a sentence in there just dying to get out."

Nate frowned. "Don't be a dick. I'm just afraid. I love the way our relationship is, even as fast as it happened, and I don't want to mess it up."

"I love our relationship too. Believe me, I do. I just don't see what you're so afraid of."

Nate looked at the whiteboard. The words glared at him accusingly as they were ignored.

Trent growled in frustration. "All I mean is, fuck, dude—I feel like we really get each other. Don't we?"

"We do. You get me better than anyone ever has before. And it's been that way since I first sat in your car."

"Then what's the problem?"

"The problem is that I'm afraid this whole thing is an extended fever dream and none of it is real," Nate blurted. "I'm afraid I'm going to wake up one day and realize this was all in my head, and lose the one good thing that has come out of this entire fucked-up situation."

They looked at each other for a long moment before Trent moved closer, putting his hands on Nate's shoulders. "It's not in your head. I like you. I *want* you. If you think I'm trying to experiment or something just because I don't have a lot of experience, I'm not."

It hadn't even crossed Nate's mind. After getting to know Trent, Nate had no doubts that Trent made his decisions based on careful thought. He didn't give in to random whims. If he wanted to fuck Nate, or date him, or wherever this was going, it was because he really wanted to go down that road.

Unless it wasn't his own thoughts and feelings guiding him.

"I . . ." God, he couldn't say it. "The thing is . . ."

"What? What's the thing?"

The frustration and insecurity rolling of Trent was awful. Nate tried to think of ways to phrase what he was thinking without . . . saying the awful truth, but he couldn't. Yet again, he wished for Theo's articulate side. "I just don't think this is the right time to figure out our relationship."

"When would be a better time?" Trent asked. "After you figure out what happened to Theo and hitch another ride back to Texas?"

Nate hadn't thought that far in advance. The possibility of going home and never seeing Trent again caused his chest to go hollow and his stomach to bottom out. "Trent, I just don't want to fuck things up. I know this sounds really selfish, and I know I'm probably putting a lot of pressure on you by admitting it, but . . . you're kind of my safety blanket right now. My—my rock. Or something. Shit. I don't know how to use words, okay? You're the only person I can count on to have my back and to take me at my word, and I don't want to lose that! I need you."

Trent searched his face with parted lips and quickening breath. The flush rising up his neck made Nate want to run his fingers along it, feel the warmth he always exuded like an inferno, and bask in the overwhelming sense of desire Trent would almost certainly be feeling.

Nate could almost feel it now, and his body reacted. He was already hard when Trent grabbed the front of his shirt and drew him closer. And there was no way Nate could stop once he heard the raspy groan Trent released when their lips touched again. It wasn't their first kiss, but it was still different because this was the start of something new.

Nate parted his lips, and their tongues slicked together. Trent tasted like peppermints, which prompted Nate to attack his mouth harder. He sucked that sweet-tasting tongue into his mouth and relished in the hoarse moan that followed.

Everything about the moment, from the tight grip of Trent's hands on his upper arms to the thick rod of his dick pressing up against Nate's thigh, was perfection. No one had ever worshiped his mouth this way. Had ever drawn him close and drank him in with such hunger. And he'd never experienced the wondrous sense of such a massive onslaught of impressions—affection, lust, love.

Nate clung to Trent, desperate for this to be real, or to pretend it was for this one moment.

Breathing heavily, Trent guided Nate over to the bed and guided them down until their bodies were smashed together. His fear crumbled more with each swipe of Trent's tongue. The thoughts that churned in his head and pulsed with each waking moment winked out one by one as Trent's hands moved over him. One clenched the back of his shirt and the other slid down to grip his ass, forcing their bodies to fit together in a press of hard lines and angles.

The channel between them opened wider without Nate trying. The dual sensations of both his and Trent's desire made him cry out. He canted his hips up, abandoning everything in a desperate attempt to feel more of Trent's body. The answering hardness in Trent's sweatpants only encouraged him, and Nate bucked up again, demanding more. The kissing turned into openmouthed panting as Trent undid Nate's jeans. The zipper slid down with a whisper.

"Touch my dick," Nate demanded hoarsely.

"Shit."

The word was nearly lost in Nate's mouth. Trent pulled away, eyes dilated when he sat up on his knees. A growl of frustration escaped Nate. The need to be touched, to come, was excruciating, but the ache was satisfied when Trent ripped his jeans off and wrapped a hand around Nate's throbbing cock.

"Oh god."

The connection between them sparked hot and bright, blotting out everything except the energy that seared between their bodies. It linked them so strongly that Nate wasn't sure he'd be able to untangle his emotions from Trent's again.

He could feel how badly Trent wanted to fill and fuck him, and how deep he wanted to drive in. Nate shuddered, incoherent and dizzy from the force of their lust. He wanted nothing more than for Trent to flip him over, ass in the air, and bury himself to the root.

"I want—" The sentence broke off when the speed and tightness of Trent's grip increased. "Oh fuck, not yet. Please don't make me come yet."

Trent pulled away, and Nate shuddered at the loss. He shuddered again when Trent licked the fingers that had just been clutching Nate's pre-come–slicked cock. Their eyes locked, each long digit disappearing into Trent's mouth, and Nate had no fucking idea how he'd resisted Trent for the scant few days that they'd known each other. How had he resisted for a moment?

Still reeling, he groped around on the bed until he could push himself up. A flurry of motion followed—him ripping Trent's undershirt off, and then him leaning forward to bury his face in the fabric of Trent's pants. He rubbed his face against the outline of Trent's cock and enjoyed the feel of fingers fisting in his hair. Nate mouthed at Trent through the fabric, inhaling, before lifting his face just slightly to glide his tongue over clenching ab muscles and soft skin.

"Why don't you do that to my dick?" Trent asked, voice strained.

"Take your pants off, then."

Trent removed them with shaking hands, and sat back so Nate could swallow him down. He wrapped his palm around the base of

Trent's dick and pumped, simultaneously bobbing his head. Hands gripped his hair, forcing his head down faster, fucking his throat and using him hard while a cacophony of swears and increasingly loud moans filled the room.

Nate pulled away with a wet sucking sound.

"Why'd you stop?"

"Because I want you to fuck me." Nate licked his lips. "Do you have a condom?"

"Yeah. In the—the thing." Trent nodded at the suitcase. His fingers caught in the sheet. "But just . . . you can suck me for longer. That was the best fucking blowjob I've ever had."

Nate couldn't help a smug grin. "Good. But if we keep going I'm gonna make you come before I can feel you in my ass."

Trent made a tormented sound as Nate slid off the bed to attack the suitcase. Trent leaned over, grasping at him and trying to pull him back, but Nate evaded. He all but dumped the bag inside out before finding his prize—a gold-wrapped foil square. Nate turned to find Trent jerking himself off, gaze so smoldering that Nate's balls clenched and fluid pearled at the tip of his cock.

He ripped the condom open and knocked Trent's hand away, covering his pulsing dick with the ribbed latex. The texture was oily with lubricant so he reared up on his knees and straddled Trent, grabbed the base of Trent's cock once more, and guided it into the tight ring of his ass.

"Oh my fucking God."

Trent seemed to short-circuit. He shook and panted as Nate seated himself and braced both his hands on either side of Trent's head, eyes nearly shut. It burned, but it burned good. He hadn't been fucked in so long that it was almost too much—the mix of pleasure and pain as his hole was stretched open and the feeling of fullness as Trent's hips bucked up to sheath himself entirely.

"Shit." Trent pressed his head against the pillow, eyes squeezed shut. "Fuck, I'm gonna bust."

"Just don't move for a second."

"Nate, I can't. You feel so fucking good."

"I can feel everything you're feeling, Trent. When you come, I'll be right behind you."

"But—"

Nate brushed his lips against Trent's stubbled jaw, and began to ride the thick cock lodged inside of him. Trent restrained himself for a second more before the hot length of him began slamming into Nate with deep, jarring thrusts. His body overloaded with the combined force of fucking and being fucked. It was so intense that Nate went back on his word. He hit his peak while Trent was still nailing him. He was aware of coming, of the mind-blowing and all-consuming pleasure of his body's release, but it was eclipsed by the impressions he leeched from Trent—a tangled knot of pure bliss and affection that made Nate feel like he was losing his mind.

When Trent released, Nate felt like he was coming all over again. They both cried out until they were hoarse.

Lips turning to lead and mind spinning, he crushed Trent into the bed. Minutes ticked by until Trent forced him to shift to the side. Finally, Nate opened his eyes to find Trent gazing at him.

"I like looking at you."

"You're not so bad yourself." Nate smiled and closed his eyes, pressing his forehead against Trent's. He didn't pull away when a heavy arm swung over his side, tugging him closer.

"That was amazing. Are you sure you're not a hooker?"

"Way to ruin a moment."

Trent snickered and brushed his lips against the side of Nate's face.

They lay together silently, the sun warm on Nate's bare back and the sheets damp beneath their tangled limbs. It felt too good, but his eyes inevitably returned to the whiteboard.

"Hey."

"Hmm?" Nate said, bringing his attention back to Trent.

"I'm not going to distract you from your purpose here, Nate." Trent nodded at the whiteboard. "Tomorrow we got this shit. Just let me have one night to make believe you're mine."

When Trent touched his face and drew him in for a kiss, it occurred to Nate that he'd never been this happy in his life. He'd never had a friend like Trent, let alone a boyfriend or a lover or whatever it was they were on their way to becoming. But once again there was that nagging question in his head of whether any of it would be happening if he wasn't a psychic.

CHAPTER FOURTEEN

"**S**ocial networking sites make it too easy to stalk people."

Nate looked up from his phone. Trent's bare chest and sprawled legs were a more welcome sight than the newspaper articles he'd been scrolling through for the past couple of hours. "What did you find?"

"Carrie's girlfriend. Her name's Felicia Tate."

Trent spun his laptop so Nate could see the screen. There was a Facebook page called Find Carrie Williams. An image of Carrie, a striking young woman with pale skin and a shaved head, smiled from the page's banner. Most of the status updates had been posted by Felicia—a woman with long braids and high cheek bones stretching over mahogany skin—but there were other people as well. Friends, family members, and coworkers had posted their memories or condolences. The most useful thing was contact information for Felicia as well as her cobbled-together timeline of events.

"We can call her."

"Yeah. There's contact info on the website. Did you find any other missing people?" Trent asked.

"It's hard to say. There's Anthony, Lia's boyfriend, and I found another missing psychic—this guy Oz. I can't find a lot of information on him except for an old Instagram account with a few pictures. He looked like he was in his thirties. There were some from a pride parade, so I'm assuming he was queer, but that was all I found. There were no comments from loved ones or any information about people pushing the investigation forward." Nate slid off the couch and sat next to Trent. "This Facebook page has more information about Carrie than any of the newspapers. Why do you think everything on Oz and Anthony is so vague?"

"Maybe they're not supposed to be giving so many details since it's an ongoing investigation."

It was possible, but Nate wondered if it was a combination of lack of family and the Community blocking investigations like they'd done about both Carrie and Anthony. If the stats on young psys running away or being institutionalized held true, there wouldn't be an army of people to fight the power and keep pushing the way Theo had.

"Do you think it's possible the Community is covering it up?"

Trent rubbed his chin, looking down at the laptop again. "Like, the entire organization?"

"Well, no, but . . . Holden made a comment about how psychics could use their talents to do anything they wanted if they were strong enough, and he's right. For some reason I'd never considered exploiting my abilities, but even Theo did." Nate hunched forward, frowning as he tried to work out his own theory. "How likely is it that everyone in the Community is good? Don't you think there are potentially tiny factions who want to use their gifts to get more out of it?"

"You mean like breaking the law."

"Yes. Exactly. They could infiltrate the police department if they wanted. Change the course of investigations. Hell, even geopolitics. If there were people powerful enough, they could take over the—"

Trent held up a hand. "Okay, dial it back."

"Sorry." Nate took a deep breath. "I read a lot of dystopian novels. But what I'm saying is, if there really is a psychic killer lurking around, what's to stop that person, or people, from covering it up? Especially if they can count on the Community to automatically want to bury anything that will make it look bad."

"I agree." Trent reached out to run his hand through Nate's hair, pushing errant strands out of his eyes. "I just wish we could come up with a motive. What would anyone have to gain from taking out other psys? What do they even have in common? Oz and Carrie are both queer, but they're different ages. Then there's Anthony, who was straight as far as we know." He kept playing with Nate's hair, frowning thoughtfully. "Were they all connected to the Dreadnoughts? I know Carrie and Anthony were."

Nate perked up at that. "Oz was apparently a musician, but I couldn't find more than that. It could be, though."

What if they'd been off the mark all along? Maybe someone in the band was the culprit and they'd thrown this Community idea at Theo as a red herring. The problem with that theory was that, with the exception of Jericho who was still a mystery, the Dreadnoughts had limited talents. Whoever had pushed Theo and held him down had to have been extremely powerful.

"I want to meet with Felicia. Maybe she'll be able to tell us something that would make this all make sense."

"You got it." Trent stood in one long stretch. His basketball shorts slipped on his hip bones, exposing the V of his torso. Nate stared. "Call her, and maybe pick a time when I can come with you? If you get nervous, I can take over." When Nate didn't respond, Trent laughed. "Stop checking me out and make the phone call. We have plenty of time to play with each other later."

Nate's eyes moved along the smooth flesh of Trent's body. He couldn't see exposed flesh without thinking of Trent's mouth, his strong hands, and the electric shock of the connection once they were wrapped up in each other. He didn't think he'd ever get used to it.

"What if we don't?"

Trent grabbed his arm and pulled him up. Their fingers slid together. "Don't what?"

"Don't have time. Anything could happen."

"Don't get morbid, Nate."

"I'm not." Nate glanced down at their joined hands. He flexed his fingers. "Whoever is behind all of this doesn't want anyone snooping around. I really believe that's why Theo wound up dead. He asked the wrong questions and pushed the wrong buttons until someone he knew, someone who felt betrayed by what he was asking, lashed out. Yet here we are . . . doing exactly what he did."

"That's true, but . . ." Trent lifted their hands and pressed his lips to Nate's palm. "Your brother didn't have me watching his back."

Nate smiled despite himself. "I can't ask you to put yourself in danger, Trent."

"And you can't keep me away." Another kiss brushed Nate's wrist. "I may be a void, but I'm a pretty smart one. We make a good team."

They did, but without knowing what was coming at them, there was no way to guarantee they could keep each other safe.

Being in the Nova with Trent was as close to home as Nate would likely ever get.

The feel of the worn leather at his back while watching the sun set to the tune of AC/DC was a good memory to have. With nowhere to go back to and nothing to look forward to, another moment of being on the road with Trent was as much as Nate could ask for. A scrap of normalcy amid the confusing tornado of his life.

They left the bustle of the city behind and headed out to a suburban area full of names like Massapequa, Ronkonkoma, and Patchogue. Trent said they were going out to Long Island, and Nate was left wondering how much of New York was attached to the mainland. Everything appeared to be surrounded by water, which was a nice change. Brookside was near the Gulf, but he'd always felt landlocked.

The drive to Felicia's home took over an hour. Trent bypassed signs to parks and beaches, and rolled up to a mansion protected by a large gate. After they were buzzed in, Nate realized the pebbled driveway was twice the size of Eveline's.

Trent shut off the engine after stopping at the end of the driveway. The house was even larger up close. Like something out of *The Great Gatsby*, except Nate had always thought the descriptions were exaggerated. He'd never imagined that real people, outside of movie stars and British royalty, lived in houses this large. He thought back on the little trailer he and Theo had lived in with their mother. It had been narrow, barely six hundred square feet, but it had been theirs.

"Holy shit."

Trent released a low whistle. "This is where the rich folks be at."

"Jesus."

"Mm-hmm." Trent yawned and slumped back against the driver's seat. His eyes watered, and he reached up to rub at them wearily. "You ready?"

"No." Nate pulled down the mirror in the passenger's seat and stared at his reflection. Hot mess. As usual. Hair everywhere, dark circles lining his eyes, and his deep-cut sleeveless T-shirt looked too grungy for this area. "Maybe it's a bad idea."

"Why?" There was an edge of incredulity in Trent's tone. "You serious? I just drove for an hour."

"I know but . . ." Nate flipped the mirror back up. His nostalgic mood had faded, leaving him drained and anxious. Pouring his guts out to a stranger was bad enough. Doing it to a filthy-rich stranger was unthinkable. "I don't know, I'm not good with talking to people. Especially not people like this."

"People like what? Rich people?"

"Yeah."

"Oh. Well, who gives a flying fuck?"

"I do," Nate snapped. "And they will. You don't get it."

"What is there to get?"

"I'm white trash. People can sense it as soon as they set eyes on me."

"That's just what you think and you project it at others," Trent countered. "Don't be so intimidated. They're just people."

Nate looked around at the sprawling green lawn and shrubbery sculpted into bizarre shapes. The mansion itself was made up of white columns and ivy-covered red bricks. It could easily devour three of the old Black home. If the family thought that was a mansion, they'd think this was a palace. It practically was.

"I look like some street urchin who turned three tricks to get a ride up here."

"Yeah, it's true."

Nate slammed his hand into Trent's shoulder. "You're a dick."

"I'm just saying—you do." Trent laughed when Nate hit him again. "You owe me like three blowjobs."

"Shut up, Trent."

"Fine." Trent unsnapped his seat belt and turned in the driver's seat. A hint of amusement was still brightening his face as he snagged the front of Nate's shirt. "Stop being so self-conscious. She wasn't expecting bankers. She's probably expecting the type of people her girlfriend hung out with." Nate didn't stop frowning at the house.

Trent dragged him across the center console. "Okay, you look hot. Perfectly fuckable. In fact your mouth is so goddamn gorgeous when you frown that I'm stuck on that blowjob thing. How's that make you feel?"

"It feels like you're a tease since we won't be able to do anything until we make that long drive home."

"That's what you think."

Trent drew him in, and his kisses were so magical that Nate told himself, just for these moments, that there was no way he could have this much power over Trent. There was no way he could be influencing him this much, for this long, and for these kisses to feel so real if they weren't. Nate had been telling himself that for days, a constant battle until Trent touched him again. As if he knew to reassure Nate even though he couldn't have known about all these doubts. Even now, Trent's kisses felt like promises that things would be okay.

Trent's hands were snarled in Nate's hair as he dropped his own in Trent's lap. He was on a wonderful path of being tongued out of his mind when someone knocked on the window. They pulled apart, both flushed and swollen-lipped.

"Shit." Trent rolled down the window and peered out at the woman. Felicia. "Uh, hi there."

"Hi." Felicia looked between them, but her attention fixed on Nate. "Are you the one who called me?"

"Yes," Nate said quickly. "Yeah. Yes. I'm really sorry. There was— We were— We got distracted."

"I can see that." Unfazed, Felicia gestured for them to get out. "Come on. We're going around back."

"Fuck," Nate hissed once she was away from the vehicle. "Great first impression."

Trent rolled his eyes and opened the door.

Together, they made the walk around the side of the house. There were statues dotting the property, cracked angel faces that were likely designed to seem aged, and a massive fountain in the middle of the lawn. Felicia led them to the back of the house where she'd laid out lemonade and snacks.

"Thank you for coming all this way. I promised my parents I wouldn't go into the city."

"What do your parents do?" Nate said. Trent shot Nate a look, and he realized that was too blunt a question. "Sorry."

"No, it's fine." Felicia watched Trent tuck into the mini sandwiches. "My father works on Wall Street. My mother is a corporate lawyer."

"Wow," Nate said.

Felicia didn't react to his awed tone. Trent consumed a sandwich in two bites and asked, "Why'd your parents make you promise not to go to Manhattan?"

A glimmer of displeasure crossed her face. "I figure they caught on to what I was doing and put a stop to it before I could cause them trouble. Or myself when they're not around to save me."

"You mean putting up the flyers?" Nate asked.

"Yes. They think I'm shit stirring." The vein of her displeasure widened into an inferno of anger. "In their eyes, it's more plausible to believe powerful psychics are wandering off on their own rather than being abducted by someone inside the Community. But they're not ones for rocking the boat. They told me to stay out of crazy white people's business."

"Good advice," Trent noted. "But what are they afraid of? You being abducted as well, or you making a scene and messing up their reputation within the Community?"

Felicia studied Trent. Nate couldn't decide if she liked his forthright attitude or if she found it off-putting. Whatever the case, she answered.

"Both. They have high standing within the Community, and they don't want me to press the wrong buttons. If I don't stop, there's a good chance the board will tell them to blackball me."

"Wait," Nate said. "They'd be told to blackball their own daughter? That's ridiculous."

"It is," she said. "But it's happened before. Once you get on their bad side, it's over. They don't want you talking to their people. They don't really want you talking to anybody, to be honest. Too big a chance of an ex-Community member telling their secrets to get revenge."

"Well, how can they control that?" Trent asked. "Do they spy on people if they leave or something?"

"I've heard they do. There are a lot of rumors about it, but I don't know for sure. Anyone who leaves doesn't really come back to chat about it later."

Trent's brow was creased in thought, the look he got whenever he was puzzling over a situation that didn't make sense no matter how he tried to put it together. After a while, he said, "If the Community really exists to help disadvantaged psychics and keep powerful psychics all safe and on the same page, why the hell are they exiling their own people?" He dusted the crumbs from his hands and sat back in his chair. "Because that sounds more like they just want to have *control* over both disadvantaged and powerful psychics. And they go off the deep end when that doesn't go down the way they want."

"I don't know where the deep end is for you," Felicia said. "But I'd be inclined to concur. The Paynes like things their way, and so does everyone else who has drunk the Kool-Aid."

"So, what, they're just using everyone?" Nate asked. "People in the Community are just a means to an end and get kicked out when they're not useful anymore?"

"That's how I've always seen it. Even my parents know the Community isn't above cannibalizing their own, whether it's someone being completely cut off from their friends and families for speaking to the wrong person or being too open about their abilities, or whether it's people challenging the rules and getting into power struggles." Felicia shook her head. "Believe me when I say I know there is good in the Community. They've helped my parents a lot. I'm not sure how much my parents' success is because they're ambitious and how much is from Community connections, but it's a big group with a lot of people and not all those people are good."

They were nearly the same words Nate had used earlier to Trent.

"How likely is it that . . ." Nate chewed on his own question, trying to figure out how to ask without coming off like a conspiracy theorist. "Carrie, Oz, and Anthony did something to . . . to challenge the status quo like Theo did?"

"I don't know," she admitted. "Carrie loved the Community. She loved Evolution. I'm not sure how she would have rocked the boat. She was powerful and rare—a dreamwalker by night and she had kinetic powers by day."

"Dreamwalker with kinetic powers," Trent repeated. "Baby Jesus on a bicycle, this shit is blowing my mind. I don't even know what the last part means. Like telekinesis?"

Felicia laughed and covered her mouth as if the sound surprised her. "Yes. She could control things and people if she really wanted to, but she wasn't very skilled at it."

"Wasn't very skilled at it? Shit, she has a ton up on me." Trent elbowed Nate. "I can barely control myself."

She laughed again. "You're funny."

Trent winked. "The sidekick usually is. It's the only way I can keep up with my superhero."

"I'm pretty much the opposite of a superhero," Nate muttered.

Trent knocked their knees together. "You're trying to uncover corruption in this mega powerful organization and find out who's kidnapping or killing psychics. Sounds pretty heroic to me."

If they'd been alone, Nate would have pressed him to the ground and kissed him until they both lost their breath. But they were on the job, so he just bit back a smile and looked at Felicia again.

"Do you think someone may have thought Carrie was rocking the boat just by hanging out with my brother?"

"Maybe," she said. "I hadn't thought of that, but they were fast friends. Both fringe kids with more than one talent. They traded stories a lot, and I think she was fascinated to hear the fucked-up stories he told."

And boy, would Theo have had a lot of those.

"Sometimes it's a relief to know someone's life is more fucked up than your own," he offered.

Felicia nodded. "Exactly. They started partying together. Doing drugs. Staying out late. And he introduced her to people at the club I'd have preferred she stay away from."

"Holden and Chase, and that whole crew?" Trent asked.

"Yes. I know Holden well enough to be able to reasonably say he's a spoiled brat who started that club with his daddy's money, but he's probably harmless. But his brother?" She shook her head emphatically. "Uh-uh. He sets off all of my red flags. So does their father, and the girlfriend."

"You mean Beck," Trent said.

"Yes. She was the one who threatened to have me arrested if I continued to put up missing-person flyers."

Nate leaned forward so abruptly, he nearly knocked over the plate of snacks. "Was this the other night?" When she nodded again, he pushed on. "Do you think she was personally invested or just speaking on behalf of the Payne family?"

"I don't know," Felicia said. "But between her and Chase, I got the sense there would be major problems if I didn't leave and not come back. There was a point when I almost felt . . . compelled to walk away even when I wanted to argue. Like my body was on autopilot."

Or like someone had been controlling her actions the way they'd controlled Theo's when he'd drowned. He and Trent exchanged glances.

"Do you think someone compelled Carrie to go somewhere with them?" Trent asked. "We know she disappeared from the club, but not how."

"I don't know how either." Felicia's lips flattened. "That's what first tipped me off that someone at the club was hiding something. She texted me the night she disappeared and told me she was heading home, and that was the last I heard of her. When I went to Evolution to ask the staff, they iced me out. Seemed pissed off that I was questioning them, even though, at the time, I'd just been hoping for help. Their attitudes are why I got so suspicious."

"And they didn't tell you anything?" Trent pressed. "They must have surveillance tapes. When the police got involved, they had to have taken them as evidence."

She laughed bitterly. "You'd think so, but they didn't. They didn't do anything. They were completely useless."

"Yeah," Nate said. "I guess they would be."

"Especially if there's a Community connection there. Or . . ." Trent looked between them. "If the Community isn't above doing a little mind control on some cops."

Nate sighed disgustedly and hunched over the table. "What about that other guy? Oz? Do you know anything about him?"

"Not much," she said. "But he was another flavor of the month for a while."

"Flavor of the month? What does that mean?"

Felicia's chair scraped as she scooted it back. "Every now and then, everyone at Evolution hyperfocuses on fresh blood. Someone totally new to the club and the Community. He was a medium. An extremely rare gift. Everyone wanted to get to know him, before he up and vanished. When he did, Theo popped up, and it was his turn to be Evolution's new flavor."

But unlike Oz, Theo had turned up dead.

CHAPTER FIFTEEN

O n the day of the Dreadnoughts' show, Jericho was as grim as he'd been on the day Nate had visited them in Brooklyn. He stalked around the stage, setting up equipment and plugging in amps while the rest of his band stood down below. They'd given no indication to Elijah that they'd already met him, and so the slight drummer rocked on the balls of his heels, indignant and annoyed in his skintight shorts and a shredded Evolution tank top as Jericho ignored Nate.

"Aren't you going to say anything?" he demanded.

"What's there to say?" Jericho looped a wire around one hand and stared at Nate, nothing in his face other than the same distant look of dislike he'd worn the first time they'd met. Nate was unsure whether his presence truly inspired that reaction, or if it was part of the act of them not knowing each other. "If he's got something to talk about, he can do it some other time. I have shit to do."

"Oh, nice. How sensitive." Elijah crossed his arms over his chest. "You know, it was his brother—"

Jericho turned away and crossed the stage, not looking back. The tread of his boots was heavy, each footstep a resounding boom against the stage floor. He didn't flinch under the weight of their stares, and knelt down, faced away, his black T-shirt straining across his shoulders. It was easy to see why Theo had wanted him—big, mean, and unattainable had always been his weakness, and Jericho's quiet anger made him mysterious.

"Wow, what a dick." Elijah was wringing his hands. "I'm sorry."

"It's okay," Nate said. It was probably for the best. He wasn't good at pretending, and since the rest of the band apparently didn't trust Elijah enough to have told him about their secret meeting, lying in a room full of psychics wouldn't have ended well. "I'll try to catch him later."

"Well, what the fuck did you expect him to be like?" Chase asked. He was sprawled on one of the purple sofas, a cigarette dangling from one hand. "Jumping up and down because his dead fuck's Doublemint is here?"

"Theo was more than just his dead fuck," Lia said from her position by the stage. "They cared about each other."

"Oh right, I forgot. They were in a serious relationship. Two steps away from getting gay married." Chase arched one pale eyebrow, and blew hoops of smoke in their direction. "Too bad Theo was still blowing half the psys in the city."

"Wow, Chase. Can't you shut up?" Elijah shot Nate an apologetic frown. "Sorry. Chase thinks he's going to one day play the villainous queer on some horrible reality show about dramatic white gays, and likes to practice daily." Chase flipped him off, but Elijah didn't look. "Anyway, Nate, this is Lia and Taína. My more awesome bandmates."

"Hi," Nate said awkwardly. "Any chance Jericho will chat with me later?"

"If you catch him in a good mood," Taína said. "Maybe after the set when he's full of adrenaline? He's on edge about performing without Theo for the first time."

Nate hadn't even thought of that, and now he felt insensitive. Except . . . he was positive Jericho knew whatever Theo had known, and that was the priority here.

"I suggest you leave the man alone," Chase said. "Unless you're in a real mood for shit stirring."

"What shit would I be stirring just by asking him about my brother?"

Chase got to his feet and crossed the space between them. He was wiry but half a head taller than Nate. "Don't be stupid, kid."

"I don't know what you mean."

Chase's hand clamped down on Nate's upper arm, and he was hit with a sense of foreboding so strong that he stumbled back. They stared at each other, Chase with narrowed silver eyes, and Nate suddenly out of breath and panicked. The imminent danger that had slammed into him had nearly stopped his heart.

"I told you before—watch yourself."

Nate said nothing as Chase walked away, his long wallet chain jingling with each step.

"Jesus," Elijah said softly. "I'll go talk to him."

Again, Nate stayed shut. He continued to track Chase's movements until the man was out of sight. Taína mumbled something about going to talk to Jericho, and then Nate and Lia were alone. Or as alone as they could be in a building full of surveillance and people packed with extrasensory abilities.

"Does Chase know about the other day?"

"He shouldn't," Nate said. "I don't trust any of these people. Especially him."

Lia moved closer. She wasn't as visibly nervous as Elijah, but her face was tight with worry. "He has a point though, Nate. You need to watch your step. This whole thing is getting weird. Beck grilled me and Jericho as soon as we walked in."

"Grilled you about what?"

"She wanted to know if anyone had been asking us questions. Or if anyone has been hanging around our practice space." Lia's voice grew lower with each word. "And then she warned us about Chase."

"Warned in what way?"

"She told us to stay away from him."

It kept coming back to Chase. People commenting on how dangerous he was, him threatening Nate, and then that negative energy coursing between them. It'd been a nonverbal threat of *shut the fuck up and get out of here or you will get hurt.*

"Does anyone know you came to see us in Brooklyn that day?"

Nate stopped scanning the mostly empty club. "No. Only Trent."

"And he's just a void, right? Not connected in any way."

"He's not *just* anything, but he also isn't connected to the Community. He only knows what we've discussed."

She slowly nodded. "Maybe you should keep him out of it. The tension around this place is amping up. Something's going to happen soon, Nate. And it's connected to Theo and everything else. I can feel it."

"Something happened," Nate said. "It's not just a feeling, is it?"

Lia stepped well within his personal space. Her voice was barely a whisper. "Last night J woke up in a panic. He said he'd had this nightmare that he was in the club, but he wasn't himself, and he was listening in on this . . . this conversation."

It sounded exactly like some of the visions Nate had had in the past. Especially the one when he'd been spying on Theo and Jericho.

"What was the conversation about?"

Lia look around again. The music in the club turned up abruptly. Lia had to press her lips to his ear to be heard. "Someone was talking about J being in Ex-Comm. About J being quiet now but that not changing the fact that he knew too much. That's all he told me, but he was freaked out when he woke up. Kept saying it had felt so real . . ."

Nate thought back to the second vision he'd received from their mysterious benefactor—Theo had mentioned Ex-Comm in it.

"What's Ex-Comm?"

"A group of people who left the Community. Some people just want to get off the radar so they're not subjected to surveillance after breaking their contract, and a lot of people don't trust the Community because of whatever corruption they think is in it."

"Are they investigating the disappearances too? Maybe I can talk to someone—"

"No," she said, stepping away. "I can't set that up even if I tried. I wanted to warn you that if J is getting this spooked, that means things are getting weird. Please be careful."

Lia backed away and rejoined her bandmates. The quiet sounds of their conversation was masked by the music filtering through the club. Even with the darkness of the Community pressing in around them, they seemed safe with each other, and Nate wondered how Theo had fit in.

The cagey feeling of pent-up frustration made Nate jittery, and he wondered if it wouldn't be a bad idea to have a drink. It was tempting, but Chase was lingering around the bar with Elijah. Everywhere he turned, there was another red flag, another point that condemned the club and the people who ran it.

Wanting to leave but also wanting a chance to talk to Jericho, Nate headed upstairs to the VIP area. He sat in a chaise lounge and checked his phone for messages from Trent. There weren't any yet, but maybe that was a good thing. The way they were playing house in the apartment and running around like detectives . . . he was losing himself in how Trent made him feel while actively ignoring all the things that could go wrong. With the Community and with them.

Hunching forward, Nate covered his face with his hand. His head felt like it was being torn in two different directions, and he wondered when all of this would resolve. When would the sinking feeling cease? Maybe it wouldn't. Maybe this was how his life would be from now on—total awareness of a conspiracy and murders, but absolutely no power to stop it.

Fuck. He really needed to talk to Trent.

Nate made the call and ignored the little voice in his head that told him it was a bad idea.

"Hey."

Nate took a deep breath. "You're still sleeping?"

"I can sleep for fifteen hours if you let me. Where are you?"

"Evolution."

"Without me." Trent didn't have to voice his displeasure. "Okay."

"I didn't want to wake you, but I was hoping you wouldn't mind coming down here before the Dreadnoughts' show."

"You sure?"

"Why wouldn't I be?"

"Dunno," Trent said. "There's a lot of suave psy bros there. I'm just some void. The amusing sidekick."

"Don't be an idiot. This isn't a coolness contest. I want you here."

"For what?"

Nate stood and paced the lounge. His hands trembled as he formed the words in his head. It felt like giddiness warring with fear. Pouring his heart out was only as good as the response, and he still wasn't sure how much of this was real, and how much was wishful thinking and psychic bullshit and him clinging to the hope that there was one person on this goddamn planet he could count on.

"I'm afraid. And you're the only person I can trust. And even though it's selfish of me to drag you into this, even though we could both end up in more trouble than we can probably handle, I know I can count on you to have my back."

At first, Nate worried Trent wouldn't respond. He was asking this man to put himself in danger for a stranger who'd labeled him as a friend not even a full day after they'd been intimate. Anyone else would have probably asked for time to think. Or said no outright. But Trent wasn't anyone else.

"I'll be there in an hour."

Each time Nate saw Holden, the man seemed more stressed. He was still polished and untouchably handsome in his tailored indigo suit, but he was restless. Pacing the tiny office after having summoned Nate there, and looking at each surveillance monitor without really seeming to see what was on them.

He never once took stock of the square that showed Chase and Elijah outside the back door of the club. Chase was towering over the slender drummer, and speaking harshly enough to make it clear he was delivering orders. Orders that Elijah wasn't taking if Nate went by the furrowed brow and frequent head shakes.

"This is going to be a bad night."

Nate agreed, but he was too busy watching Chase and Elijah to respond. Elijah had shouldered past and said slowly and clearly enough for Nate to read: *I'm not leaving. You're being paranoid.* Chase grabbed for his shirt, but Elijah avoided him and dashed back inside. The frustration and anger sliding over Chase's features were made plainer when he punched the wall.

"I can feel it. Everyone is off."

"What are you talking about, Holden? And why are you talking about it with me?"

Holden stopped running his hands through his sandy-brown hair. "A little bird told me they saw you leave the CW building with Beck. Why were you with her?"

"She was showing me around. Trying to sell me on the Community."

"That's it?"

"More or less."

"Your vagueness pisses me off." Holden stopped pacing to stand in front of Nate. He stared down, maybe weighing his words. "Things have been off since you got here."

"Things have been weird since my brother turned up dead. You're going to have to excuse my lack of compassion for your anxiety."

Holden frowned. "Why are you here? I assumed you were finished with us and the Community after you left Chase and Elijah's place."

"I'm not allowed to come here?" Nate stood so he was eye level with Holden. "I didn't realize not taking your Community offerings made me unwelcome. Do I have to sign my life away in a contract to be allowed entrance?"

"I didn't say you were unwelcome. I asked why you're here. I get the sense that you, like your brother, are here to kick up dirt." Holden jerked his thumb toward the monitors. "Just like Beck is here to kick up dirt. Prove I'm incompetent and have my father bounce me from this club since he owns a larger share."

"You think Beck wants to dethrone you as club owner? Like . . . that's her goal in life?"

"Yes!" Holden rocked back on his heels and scowled. "And I am fully aware of how ridiculously childish that sounds."

"It's good to be self-aware."

"You think this is a game?" Holden stepped closer. "It's not. This is a safe space in the Community for queer psys, and she just wants to use it as a way to scout rare psys for my father, which will never happen."

Rare psychics like mediums and dreamwalkers, and people with multiple talents. "And what would that get her?"

"A good reputation for scouting and vetting powerful psys?" Holden said it as if it should have been obvious. "She thinks it will get her on the board if she can prove how valuable she is, but it won't happen. Board members aren't chosen based on their talents. They're the original founders—the ones who created the Community for the sole purpose of supporting each other. She can't force her way in by having a good scouting résumé."

"Right. I was under the impression that the Community cared more about charity and good will," Nate said. "Why does she think they'd want so much rare talent?"

"I have no idea. It's her obsession. She goes on and on about how high you can climb if your talent is rare and strong, which hers isn't." He released a sarcastic laugh. "In a way, I can't blame her for fixating.

You and I are fucking mediocre compared to Chase, so imagine what someone like *her* must feel. She's basically a void, and it was like he was born with a touch of everything. His mother's lineage must have been incredible."

"Why his mother? What about your father?"

Holden shook his head. "If it weren't for my grandfather, I doubt my father would even know he's a psychic, because his empath abilities are so weak. But my grandfather was in the Stargate Project—the military's attempt to use psychics during the Cold War. It mostly failed, but while in it, he met other psychics. They got the idea to form a support group after the project was over. When my father learned of it, it turned into CW." Holden slipped his hands into his pockets. "So, yes, they started the Community, but at the end of the day, neither of them are very powerful. My father is a spotter like Beck, and all they can do is find powerful psys and wish all that power was theirs. It's a sad excuse for a talent. I'm just an empath, and I'm worth more of a damn than either of them."

"Your criteria for what a person needs to be worth a damn is shitty." Nate planted his hands against Holden's chest and pushed him back a step. "And as far as I'm concerned? This Community you people have going sounds like a shitty place to be. Maybe you do some good here and there, but part of me wonders whether that's just a cover for having a fuck-ton of psychics all under your thumbs. Everyone seems to be in it for what they can get from the people who are stupid enough to sign the dotted line. Unless they're lucky enough to not have the kind of power to get them noticed."

"You're lecturing me on methods of obtaining power?" Holden's eyebrows flew up. "Your family inbreeds to get higher birthrates for psychic babies. Everyone who's heard of your family knows that."

"Fuck you," Nate said.

"No, fuck you." Holden shoved Nate against the desk. He went full body on him and pinned him there. "You don't even know how to properly use your abilities. You don't know how easily I could manipulate you right now."

Nate's breath caught. "To do what?"

"Anything I wanted. Think about how much I want to give you a fucking blowjob until it becomes *your* urge to get blown. Turn up those vibes until you can't do anything but lay still while I suck you down to the root." Holden pressed a hand to the small of Nate's back. Their chests rubbed together, and Nate could feel Holden's racing heart. Once the shields crashed down, he could also feel Holden's energy as well as his body. "I know Elijah's been running his mouth about how he thought Theo influenced me, but he didn't. I can protect myself unless I let my guard down."

"If you're so worried about why I'm here and what I'm doing, why do you keep coming on to me?" Nate asked roughly.

"Because I have nothing to hide from you. I didn't hurt your fucking brother."

Nate searched every corner of the connection that had opened between them, and found nothing but anger, frustration, and lust fueled by loneliness. Lonely? How could this rich, successful psychic be *lonely*? Whatever the reason, it had nothing to do with him being a depraved killer.

"You can feel me," Holden said. "And I can feel how hungry you are."

"Not for you."

"It doesn't matter. I'm the one that's here. And now you know I'm not hiding anything."

Holden leaned in for a kiss, but Nate turned his face. That well-formed mouth crested along the side of his face and latched on to his jaw. Nate shuddered.

"Fuck off, Holden. You may have me beat when it comes to psychic shit, but I can fuck you up in a fist fight."

"Maybe. But I just want to fuck you."

Nate grabbed the back of Holden's jacket. "Get off me or you'll regret it."

"Please, Nate." The words pitched low and desperate. "I could make you feel so good. I did it before." Holden canted his hips forward. "I could show you again."

"No, thanks."

"Are you sure?" He dropped his hand to Nate's crotch. "You're tense. Anxious. Full of self-doubt. I could wipe it all away and make you feel nothing but pleasure."

"You're out of your mind." The words weren't as forceful as Nate wanted. He was overtaken by wave after wave of lust knocking into him. He could practically see Holden kneeling at his feet. His light-brown hair messy from Nate's clawing hands. His head bobbing. The wet sound of sucking. The image grooved in his mind, hooked in, and Nate suddenly wanted it. He wanted to spread his thighs and lean back and get his cock sucked. He could practically feel it.

"You want it," Holden whispered. "You can feel how good it would be, can't you?"

"Shit."

"You want it."

"I— Fuck, I—"

No.

Trent.

Holden had Nate's jeans undone by the time he snapped out of the daze. Even then, his arms refused to cooperate. He couldn't move. A frantic desire to get away swelled up. It wasn't until Holden caught the likely dismayed expression on his face did the connection slam shut again.

Holden stepped away. "I'm sorry. I just thought—"

"You thought you had the right to control me."

"I never said—"

"You didn't have to. Even if you didn't hurt my brother, you're just like the rest of them."

"That's not true," Holden said, his voice insistent. "Don't be like this, Nate. I don't want you as an enemy."

"Then keep out of my head and stay the hell away from me."

Nate fled the room and slammed the door shut behind him.

CHAPTER SIXTEEN

The evening crowd had grown by the time Nate went downstairs. The urge to get out and go home to Trent tripled. He didn't want to be here. He didn't want to be around these people. He didn't want to put himself and Trent in danger.

He wanted to go somewhere far away and never ping on the Community's radar again. Be safe. With Trent. Just the two of them. Forever.

Wheeling away from the thickening crowd, Nate found his way to the back door. He was desperate for a safe haven until Trent arrived, and had expected Chase to be gone from the small courtyard behind the club, but no luck. Not only was Chase there, but he was with Jericho.

They both looked at Nate when he appeared. Chase continued sitting in a beat-up lawn chair, but Jericho flicked his cigarette to the ground. He muttered something about sound check and went back inside. The door slammed shut behind him, and Nate was left alone with Chase and the flickering white Christmas lights that were wound around the gate.

Nate could barely see Chase's expression, but his posture was relaxed. Judging from the sweet smell permeating the air, he seemed to be making a conscious effort to stay that way.

"Want a hit?"

"No."

"You straight edge?"

The question was packed with such disgust that Nate almost wanted to say yes. "I just don't want to smoke."

"Suit yourself."

Nate watched the smoke pour from Chase's mouth, and tried to read him. As always, it was a dismal failure beyond the obvious fact that Chase was more at ease than usual. His slim body was elegantly slouched as he tilted his buzzed head back against the gate. The metal of his piercings, as well as the various buckles and his wallet chain, glinted in the shadows. He crossed one knee over the other and swung one long leg. For all intents and purposes, he was exactly the kind of person who should have gotten along with Theo. They were both awful smart-asses. Mercenary in their view of other people. And they'd both mastered the art of cool unimpressed stares. It reminded Nate of Eveline.

"Why did you hate my brother?"

Chase flicked his lighter and sucked on the tip of his pipe again. When he finally spoke, his voice was higher as he held the smoke in. "I didn't."

"Then why do you talk so much shit?"

"Because."

"You just enjoy being a dick?"

"Nah." Chase exhaled, and a cloud of smoke exploded from his lips. "I like keeping all these fake assholes real. There's nothing wrong with brutal honesty."

"'Brutal honesty'? That's what you call it?" Nate stood over Chase the way Holden had towered over him moments ago. "I'm talking about the way you try to shut me down every time I ask anyone a question. What the fuck does it matter to you if I ask about my brother?"

"It doesn't matter to me personally. But it's my job to keep this place in check." Chase unfolded his legs and stood, his sharp features exposed more fully by the light. "I don't like you. Don't take it personal, though. I don't like anyone until they give me a reason to, and all you've done so far is stir the pot, even though I keep trying to tell your punk ass to quit." He slipped the pipe into the pocket of his skinny, black pants. "You want answers? Learn how to get them on your own. Whether people want to give them or not. You got the goods, so use them."

Nate didn't back away as Chase's razor-blade smile held in place and his hooded, red-rimmed eyes unflinchingly bored into Nate.

"Is that how you keep everyone quiet about the truth? You use your goods?"

"You'd be fucking surprised what I use my goods for. That's the reason why Big Daddy Payne keeps me around."

"I thought this place was Holden's."

"You thought wrong, fuck-rag. Holden just thinks it is. He's stupider than you and Theo. Totally oblivious to everything that happens right under his pointy gay nose."

"I see."

"No, you don't." Chase flicked Nate's hair and broke their standoff. "If I was you, I'd stop running my mouth and take my inbred country ass back to Texas. You're gonna find yourself in a world of trouble, and when it happens, I'm going to be the dude pointing at you and saying I fucking told you so."

For the second time in only a few minutes, Nate couldn't restrain himself from lashing out. He wasn't tongue-tied or worried. He didn't shrink back in shame when faced with the truth of his family. He was fucking done.

"You don't know me. You don't know my family. And if you think mine are fucked up, how about you consider your own. A father who uses you to keep an eye on a club so his spoiled-rotten yuppie son and girlfriend can pick and choose which psys are worthy and who should be cast off. Or maybe you get off on that part too."

"Nah," Chase drawled. "If that was the case, I would have let them bounce Elijah out of this club long ago. And believe me, they tried."

"And you actually cared what happened to him?"

"You trying to dig deep and find a heart somewhere in my chest? Sorry, motherfucker. You're shit out of luck."

"I'm not that naive," Nate said. "I can tell you don't feel anything. I can tell how twisted you are. Maybe you were born this way, or maybe it's all of the synapses in your head switching on and off with your ten million gifts, or maybe you get it from the mother who left your ass here with this fucked-up Community."

Chase's eyes lit up. "You got it, Nate. You hit the nail on the head. I got it from my mama. We both got shortchanged in that department, didn't we?"

The urge to punch Chase was almost impossible to ignore. Nate balled his hands up, seething, and waited for Chase to keep punching buttons until he hit the right one. It'd been a long time since Nate had gotten into a fight, but his tendency to go for weak points and low blows would come back in a snap. He was already considering where he could strike out to down Chase the fastest. It played out in his mind like a movie as Chase kept smiling. Wider and more terrible like he knew what Nate was thinking.

But if he did, Chase didn't rise to the promise of a fight. He brushed past Nate, shoulder-checking him, and returned to the club.

When the door shut, Nate sat down in the chair that Chase had vacated. He gripped the chair's handles so tight that the sides bit into his fingers, whitening the skin. Just when he thought he was over letting people get to him, something happened to undo the scant amount of progress he'd made. But there was something about Chase that irked him. A knowing quality mixed with his smarmy mocking that slid under Nate's skin like a million splinters.

The din of talking and laughter had grown steadily louder inside the club and from the front of the building. Nate cringed, not ready to be around crowds of people just yet. He needed to find his calm center.

He closed his eyes and pictured Trent's bed. Their damp, flushed skin sticking together as their bodies lay tangled and the fan blew warm air. The glimmers of red and golden light coming through the slatted blinds as the sun set. Then he pictured the car ride from Houston. The hot breeze blowing in open windows as he dozed off, only to open his eyes and periodically find Trent gazing at him. It replayed like a loop in his mind until the straps of discord that had tightened around his chest weakened, and he could breathe evenly.

Sliding down in the chair, Nate let the negative energy flow out of his body as he thought of Trent. His smile and voice. His hands and lips. He'd never meditated before, but thinking of the one lucky star in a sky full of darkness was a good way to find peace. After a while, the hum of noise and soft beats of music mixed together like a lullaby, and he felt himself dozing off.

"Nate?"

Nate started, surprised to see Trent standing on the patio. Like Nate's semiobsessive thoughts had summoned him from Washington Heights.

"You got here fast."

"It's been over an hour."

It hadn't felt like that long, but he did notice the volume of music and voices had steadily increased. The club was probably packed.

Nate pushed himself out of the chair, gaze moving over Trent. He hadn't bothered to dress up for the club, and wore jeans and a faded T-shirt emblazoned with barely decipherable words. But he didn't need anything else. He was perfect. It was quickly becoming clear to Nate that he would never be able to look at anyone else, or consider anyone else, as long as Trent was in his life. Which made him panic.

"I need to ask you something." The words were out before he could pull on the reins of his fear. "About what's going on with us."

Trent frowned. "What about it?"

"There's some things we need to figure out."

"If you tell me it was a mistake, there's a very big chance that I might get pissed off and walk away."

Nate paused in his struggle to verbalize the questions that had been dogging him for days. "Why would I say that?"

"I have no idea. Maybe you found someone better."

This time, it was Nate scowling. "Your lack of faith is starting to be insulting."

"Who are you, Darth Vader?" Trent stepped farther onto the patio. "Look—I'm a very blunt person. You've known since New Orleans that I wanted you, and you've been dancing around it ever since then."

"That's not true. We've been fucking every day."

"Yeah, but you get sketchy whenever I start talking about what happens after you find out what went on with your brother." Trent released a rough sigh. "And maybe that's on me. Maybe I should stop trying to force shit."

He was giving Nate a way out. Which meant he thought this was just a fling for Nate. Or worse—a stress release. The idea couldn't have been farther from reality. At the end of it all, after the mysteries were solved and Nate found out who'd killed his brother, Theo was still gone and Nate was still alone. No family. No friends. No one to trust. Except Trent. He wanted Trent to still be there after the dust settled.

"There's a reason I've been avoiding talking about . . . what we are. Or what we're doing."

"And?"

"And, again, it's going to sound ridiculous."

Trent snorted. "We've crossed that bridge, dude. Just tell me."

Nate gave him a searching stare, but was prevented from going further by Holden stepping out to join them. The patio was a popular spot tonight. Or maybe Holden had just been spying on them via the surveillance cameras.

"Gentlemen," Holden said. "There are VIP areas if you want privacy. This spot is for employees only."

Judging from the way Trent was sizing up Holden, Nate had little doubt that he'd already put a face to the name they'd been arguing about the other day. "That Elijah kid told me I could find Nate out here."

"It's not a problem. There's no need to apologize."

"I know. That's why I didn't."

Nate put a hand on Trent's arm. "Let's go upstairs."

"I'm curious as to how the two of you know each other," Holden said. "I was under the impression that Nate just arrived in the city."

"We're friends," Trent said. "What does it matter to you?"

"I was under the impression that Nate didn't have any friends."

Trent shot Nate an incredulous look. "Well, it's good to know that boundaries and social cues aren't needed to own night clubs. I'll keep that in mind the next time someone says engineers are awkward."

Holden's gaze moved over to Nate. "Am I being offensive?"

"Yeah. But I'm used to you being an asshole by now."

"Oh. I'm sorry. You teasing me to the point of having blue balls didn't leave me feeling very charitable."

For a moment the only noises in the patio were the bass of a dubstep song, the high pitch of someone's laughter down the street, and the clank of multiple shot glasses hitting the bar at once. But then Holden grinned, and all of the made-up meditation techniques fell by the wayside as the full force of Trent's pissed-off aggression slammed into Nate. He dropped his hand from Trent's arm.

"You people are a bunch of freaks." Trent shoved past Holden and stormed into the club, leaving a trail of rage in his wake.

"Sensitive, isn't he?"

As he hurried after Trent, Nate was sure that Holden was laughing at him, but he didn't care. His eyes refocused to the darkness, and he saw Trent was already halfway down the corridor. He sprinted after him and grabbed his arm, forcing him to stop.

"Where are you going?"

"Seriously? You really can't figure it out?"

"Just wait," Nate yelled over the music. Frustrated, he dragged Trent toward the bathroom. Trent pulled away once, but Nate shoved him inside, kicking the door shut behind them. The sound of the latch sliding into place echoed in the tiny room. The music was a faint, muffling throb in his ears.

Nate looked at Trent in the dim, flickering light. He was standing with his back pressed against the sink, framed by the graffiti and concert flyers that covered the walls. The tension in Trent's body caused the muscles in his shoulders and arms to stand out in stark relief under his T-shirt. That, combined with his messy, dark hair and the angry curl of his mouth was enough to make Nate want to say to hell with explanations and drop to his knees.

"Just relax. He's full of shit."

"Yeah? Then tell me what happened."

"Nothing fucking happened!"

The words had little effect. Trent's anger was a blinding starburst of energy that made sweat dampen Nate's brow. A thousand impressions of hurt chipped away at Nate like little daggers, forcing him to feel the betrayal that Trent was feeling. He tried to block it out, but his mental shield increased only in tiny increments as the seconds ticked by.

"He's twisting what happened," Nate said. "He used— He does this thing where . . ." The impatience on Trent's face prompted Nate to launch into a frantic incoherent explanation. "I told you he's an empath too. A strong one. He can . . . redirect his emotions to the people around him, and he did it to me. Tried to influence me to want him. And all this time, when you thought I wasn't being serious about us, it's just that I've been worried I was influencing your decisions."

"Give me a break." Trent released the sink, and moved forward to crowd Nate against the door. "You don't have to lie, Nate. I'll fucking forget about the fact that I thought we had something."

"We *do* have something! All I think about, when I'm not trying to figure out what happened to my brother, is you. When I get freaked out or scared, I picture us together. About that car ride and sleeping next to you, and you touching me. It's the only thing that makes me feel normal anymore."

"Then why were you letting him get all up on you again? You knew he was scheming to get your ass, and you still went off to be alone with him."

"That's not what happened!" Nate's voice rose in frustration. "Why the hell would I do that?"

"Gee, I don't fucking know, Nate. Maybe because you're thirsty for them to accept you since my void ass isn't good enough."

Nate had trouble breathing for a moment, but then he asked softly, "That's really what you think of me?"

"What the fuck else can I think?" Trent's voice echoed off the tiled walls of the bathroom. "You're good with me when we're alone, but as soon as you're out of my sight, you have this rich asshole all up on you."

"I already told you it wasn't the way he made it sound! Goddamn it, Trent." Nate slammed his fist into the door. It shuddered behind him. "Why can't you just listen to me?"

"Because I'm tired of this hot-and-cold bullshit. I'm tired of feeling like an idiot for falling for you so fast and hard when we just met, only to have you push me away. Jesus Christ, Nate. You have no idea how badly I want to walk out right now."

Trent pressed his palms against the door, penning Nate in. It wasn't just jealousy pouring off him. It was anguish. Loneliness. A crushing sense of defeat. Was it possible that Nate meant this much to Trent? If Nate trusted his talent, and his ability to read Trent, it wasn't just a possibility—it was a fact.

Desperation tore through Nate and shredded his fears of accidentally influencing Trent. There was nothing accidental when he put his hands on Trent, yanked him forward until they were slamming back against the door, and opened the channel between them. Driven by the naked fear of Trent leaving him, Nate crushed their lips together and poured every ounce of his affection and desire into that connection. He had no idea what he was doing, no clear knowledge of how to force those emotions into Trent, but he tried.

A constant mantra of *feel me want me love me* went through his mind until Trent stopped trying to detangle their bodies and get away, and sagged against him. What should have been a simple kiss and a last-ditch effort to calm Trent enough to listen, escalated into scorching lust. It ping-ponged between him and Trent, reflecting like sunlight off two mirrors, until their tongues were tangling and the knee-buckling sound of Trent moaning filled the bathroom.

The sound seemed to startle Trent. He jerked back, eyes wild and dilated, and panted openmouthed as he stared down at Nate. His brows drew together, a clear indicator that Nate's efforts had worked, but Nate wasn't ready to give up on this moment just yet. He wasn't ready for Trent to walk away.

Tangling his fingers in Trent's shaggy hair, he dragged him in for another deep kiss. Their bodies were completely aligned, but he wanted to get closer. The feeling tightening his chest demanded it, and his own breathing shuddered as insuppressible tenderness clawed its way out of him and manifested in a desperate press of tongues.

He needed more. He wanted that channel open while their bodies were connected in every possible way.

The thought stuck in his brain, ricocheting, until he was ripping open their jeans and doing his best to force that mental image into Trent's head—a silent plea to be breached and fucked while curtained in the delicious sensation of Trent's pleasure as well as his own. The connection they shared was addictive. It was dangerous. And Nate stood no chance of ending it once their bodies were bared and sliding together. He could no longer tell the difference between whose raw need was building and whose heart was racing in anticipation for the moment they were joined.

Nate found himself naked and sitting on the edge of the sink. His thighs were spread wide enough to twinge with pain as the faucet dug into his lower back. Trent shoved down his jeans and boxers, and pulled out his cock.

It was the wrong time and the wrong place, but Nate didn't care. It was impossible to tell where his frantic desire started and where it became Trent's, or vice versa, but neither of them hesitated to get into position.

Even with a messy mixture of spit and pre-come, it hurt when Trent entered him. The pain was nothing but a prickle compared to the reality of feeling both his own fullness as well as Trent's side of their joining. Nate dropped his head back, doing nothing to swallow his increasingly loud groans. Trent's hands tightened on his hips as he moved faster, and Nate responded by working his hole around the thick intruder in his ass. And god—he felt that too. As if it was his cock being milked while his ass was fucked, and it was too much to handle.

Nate's eyes watered, and the sharp tang of blood filled his mouth. His gut tightened, body stiffening with an impending ejaculation, and he released a guttural shout. He came without laying one finger on his own dick. Semen striped his stomach, his torso, and even his face, stream after stream covering him. It was barely a moment later when Trent came deep in his ass.

The echo of Trent's harsh guttered breaths, and his own heartbeat, filled Nate's ears. There was a raw feeling moving through him, something wrecked and exposed and vulnerable, but the affection was overtaken by the reality of what he'd just done.

Trent stepped back, still shaking from the force of his orgasm. He watched as Nate cleaned himself up with trembling hands, and turned away to do the same as the bathroom filled with oppressive silence. It wasn't until Nate had wiped himself down and dressed again did Trent speak.

"You did something to me."

"Yeah. I did."

Nate turned to face Trent, and was afraid of what he would see. Judgment? Hate? Disgust? He expected any or all of those things, because he deserved to have them hurled at him. He'd done exactly what he'd been afraid of doing, and now Trent knew. But he couldn't read Trent's face. It was expressionless. That was almost worse.

"Trent, ple—"

His desperate plea was cut off by the sound of shouting filling the corridor behind them.

CHAPTER SEVENTEEN

The shouting grew louder, and the door shook under the weight of a sudden onslaught of knocks and kicks.

Trent swung it open and leaped back as several people poured into the small space. One man's face was bleeding, and another's shirt was practically torn off.

"What the hell is going on?" Trent demanded.

"I wouldn't go out there if I was you," the guy with the ripped shirt yelled over the noise. "People are rioting over that fucking band. They had the bass player on the floor. It makes no sense. It's like everyone's possessed."

"What does that mean?" Nate pressed. "How?"

"I dunno, man. Things were fine, and then all of a sudden, they were angry."

Nate sprinted from the bathroom without waiting for further explanation.

The shouting got louder the closer he got to the dance floor. With his mental defenses completely down to the connection he'd made with Trent, Nate nearly buckled against the attack of negative impressions that rocked him upon approaching the main part of the club. He stopped abruptly, insides roiling, and flattened a hand against his stomach.

In the space of fifteen minutes, Evolution had transformed. The music had stopped and security pushed through the crowds. Small clusters of fights had broken out all over the place. People were pushing and shouting as they tried to get away from the stage, but it was so crowded that it resulted in more frustration and anger boiling over into aggression.

Nate scanned the crowds for a familiar face. He saw nothing but a sea of rage and flailing limbs. He waded into the confusion despite the way his instincts were attempting to rebel and force him to go in the opposite direction.

The focus of the activity seemed to be around the stage. The Dreadnoughts' instruments were abandoned and, through the din of a hundred angry voices, Nate heard Taína screaming.

Nate shoved to the front of the crowd. When he got there, a bubble of fear and horror exploded inside of him.

Elijah was on his knees, hunched over Jericho and pressing his hands against a bloody wound in the bass player's stomach. Elijah's russet skin was ashen, face slick with tears, and he barely managed to keep his hands still as Lia forced Taína to stay back.

"What— What—" Nate stammered, unable to rip his eyes away from the carnage.

"Jericho!" Taína crumpled to her knees, wailing. "He's dead! They killed him!"

At the words, Elijah ripped his hands away from Jericho as if realizing the body he touched was void of a soul. He grabbed the side of the stage with blood-slick hands and staggered to his feet. It snapped Nate out of his daze, and he rushed forward, turning the smaller man so he wouldn't have to see. It put Jericho's body directly in Nate's line of sight. He stared, unable to look away from the savage way someone had butchered Jericho's torso. Only an hour ago he had been whole, humming with energy and smoldering anger. Now he was gone.

Elijah had wound his arms around Nate and was weeping bitterly against his chest as the club raged around them. His sobs were so loud and violent that they tore through the shouts. Nate had only just managed to respond, to press a hand against Elijah's back and open his mouth to call for Trent, when vertigo hit him.

A column of energy slammed into him and the darkness rushed forward, dimming his surroundings and muffling Elijah's hysterical cries. When the curtain of blackness parted, it was as though Nate had been yanked through space and time.

Once again, Nate found himself in someone else's skin. Someone who had been standing on the fringe of the crowd as the Dreadnoughts performed, just before chaos rocked the club and sent it spiraling into horror. The vision was fragmented and the sounds warbled unevenly as Nate remained locked within his mysterious host.

He saw glimpses of Taína singing, and then another glimpse of her flying to the side with a pained cry. There were remains of a broken bottle beside her. Jericho jumped into the crowd, which converged around him. There were flashes of the crowd swarming. As if a switch had been flipped in the minds of the club goers, their faces abruptly contorted with anger. They trampled each other in their sudden need to get at Jericho, which was when the blood-curdling screams began.

The vision shifted, the crowd parted enough for a single figure to exit the maelstrom. It exited the club, and Nate's host followed. He pushed people out of the way as sirens faintly wailed in the distance. There was another shift in the vision, a flash of concrete stairs and the blue-circled letters of a subway station, and then Nate was in the present again.

He pulled away from Elijah and spun toward the exit. Without explanation, he threw himself back into the now-thinning crowd. There were voices that stood out above the others, familiar voices, but he didn't stop for them. The mist of the vision swam around him like a film over his eyes. He couldn't focus on anything else but what he'd seen.

Nate shoved through a knot of people at the exit and burst outside. Sirens screamed in the distance, coming steadily closer. The figure and Nate's host had either just entered the subway or were doing so now.

The police cars careened around a corner just as he crossed the street. Nobody stopped him from running away from Evolution.

Someone shouted his name, but Nate didn't turn back. The urgency wouldn't let him. The panic that the person in his vision would get onto a train and disappear into the depths of the city.

He turned onto Eighth Avenue and nearly collided with a group of teenagers huddling on the corner. They pushed him away, but his eyes fell on the subway station on Fiftieth Street instead of their angry faces. The kids shouted at his retreating back. He ignored them and squeezed between a taxi and the bumper of a truck in order to cross the street. The station loomed before him, just a few feet away, and the sight of the sign juxtaposed with the brief flash from the vision.

Sound seemed muffled as his feet pounded down the concrete steps of the subway. His surroundings went by in a blur until he entered the empty station and hopped the turnstile. Nate froze, breathing hard, and looked between two separate staircases that led to opposite tracks. He hesitated before heading to the side that said *Downtown* and *Brooklyn*.

The entire station appeared deserted after he descended. He didn't know if it was always this empty or if a train had just come, but he prayed for the former. The only sounds were the echo of a distant drip and Nate's erratic breathing.

He paused just beyond the foot of the steps and stared down the long platform. It looked empty, but the eerie sensation of distorted energy made it clear he was not alone. Whoever he'd followed, whoever he'd seen, was still there.

The adrenaline that had coursed through his veins slowed. Self-awareness hit.

What was he doing?

He had no idea who he'd followed or who his host had been— whether it was someone who was going to hurt or help. This could be a trap.

Nate sucked in breaths to steady his quickly expanding lungs. He steeled himself, and walked farther down the platform, eyes scanning the perimeter for the person who had killed Jericho and potentially his brother. It wasn't very wide, but it was lined with columns thick enough for a person to hide behind. Graffiti adorned a few places on the white-tiled wall, but other than that, the long stretch of concrete and tile was empty. A glance across the two sets of tracks told him that the Uptown side was the same.

The sound of his own heart was a steady drum in Nate's ears. The eerie feeling persisted, but an attempt to reach out with his gift resulted in no insight. He didn't get any impressions from anyone in the area or even from the surroundings. It was wrong. These walls should have been vibrating with decades-old energy like the rest of the city, but the station was blanketed in nothing. The vibes had been muted.

Nate stopped walking and stared down the platform. His instincts screamed at him to run, but he didn't. He just stood and waited.

"Nate!"

The voice floated from the upper part of the subway station. Nate's head jerked to the side.

"Nate, where the hell did you go?"

The distant rumble of a train broke the silence. It grew steadily louder. Light streamed onto the tracks and reflected onto the tile walls.

"I'm down here," Nate shouted. "In the downtown—"

A hand closed around his shoulder, cutting off his words.

Nate only managed a hoarse gasp. Terror exploded inside of him. The hand tugged him back, but before Nate could react, a force jolted inside of him and guided him to the edge of the platform, away from the person standing behind him. In a mindless wash of uncontrollable motion, he threw himself over the edge. The world tilted as he fell to the track bed, and he saw only a flash of torn denim, a wallet chain, and booted feet before he realized he was inches from the third rail.

Nate's head slammed into the filthy concrete, and for a moment, he was stunned. He stared up at the ceiling, so high and dark above him, and didn't move. Couldn't move. A faint impression of thoughts and feelings, seductive and coaxing, told him that he should stay there. That it was okay if he stayed there sprawled across the tracks. It was okay to die.

Then another voice burst into his head. One that screamed, *Get up!*

That voice was so familiar—the same hiss that had entered Theo's head before he'd made it to the pier. The same one that Theo had ignored as he was shoved into the river, as he sunk below the surface because an invisible force had kept his limbs weighted at his sides.

Get up, Nate!

Nate tried, but he couldn't. His legs wouldn't follow the directions from the lizard part of his brain.

"Nate!"

Trent's voice ripped through the tunnel. It was then that Nate realized that he was going to die.

Light flooded the tunnel and the ground trembled beneath him. Wheels screeched against the rails.

"Nate, get up!"

Nate's eyes snapped back to the platform, which seemed so far away. He saw Trent's horrified face on the platform, but no one else. Whoever had touched his shoulder was gone, and their footsteps had been masked by the deafening roar of the train. And whoever had mind controlled him into the tracks wasn't there either.

"Get up, goddamn it!"

The train was coming fast, the headlights visible, and then the conductor sitting in the front. Nate stared at the train, at the man guiding it, and saw the sparks of the wheels against the rails. It was coming closer, faster, the wind from the speed causing a whooshing sound to fill the station.

This was it. He was going to die in a filthy New York subway station while rooted to the spot by unknown forces. It was going to happen.

But then strong hands grabbed him, and he was being dragged to the side and partially lifted. An indistinguishable shout that couldn't rival the shrieking of the rails filled his ears. Nate recognized the way Trent smelled, the feel of his hands, and he instantly complied. His legs moved, following Trent's lead. He stepped over the third rail, and then the train was hurtling by instead of crushing him to the tracks. The wind whipped his hair around wildly, slapping into his eyes and blinding him.

"Fuck!"

Nate opened his mouth to speak, but his eyes widened when light flooded the tunnel on the Uptown side of the station. Another train was coming on the other set of tracks.

"Stay still!" Trent shouted.

He crowded Nate into a space less than three feet wide between the two sets of track beds. It was lined with metal bars that shot up to the ceiling. The trains were only inches away from them on either side.

Nate shuddered, fear consuming him. Trent pulled him close, and kept Nate's arms down at his side. Their torsos crushed together while they remained trapped in the narrow shelter.

"Oh God. Oh fuck."

Nate squeezed his eyes shut. He didn't want to look at the train that had nearly crushed him. He didn't want to see just how tightly they were pressed in the miniscule space. One false move and they were dead. Trent was dead. Crushed beneath the wheels or electrocuted by the third rail, all because of him. All because, for the second time in weeks, he'd blindly followed a vision. This time, to his own death. Because he'd thought he was strong enough to confront people and forces that he couldn't hope to challenge with his own pathetic talent.

He couldn't do this. He wasn't strong.

He couldn't stop anyone, let alone avenge his brother.

Hot tears welled in Nate's eyes and slicked down the sides of his face. Shame filled him.

The trains began to pull out of the station with more squeals of wheels against rails.

It should have been a relief, but Nate was trembling uncontrollably. He didn't move from the near-painful grip that Trent had him in, and he didn't look up at the platform. All he could think was that Trent had nearly died because of him, and the person who'd forced him into the tracks could very possibly still be there waiting.

CHAPTER EIGHTEEN

The park on Forty-sixth Street and Tenth Avenue was eerily quiet despite the shadow playing in every corner.

After climbing out of the tracks, they'd staggered out of the subway and had scaled the park's locked gates. With nowhere to go in the vicinity, and with no desire to go back to Trent's house and potentially be followed, they'd holed up in the corner of the handball court. The long stretch of concrete felt like protection, and the angle gave them a view of each exit. If someone came up on them, they'd know.

Neither of them had verbalized these facts, but Nate had instinctively known they were on the same page.

"We have to tell the cops."

They were on the same page about everything except for that.

Nate rubbed his hand along a filthy tear in the thigh of his jeans and hissed in pain. Other than the laceration that lay beneath, skinned palms, and a headache, he'd escaped the fall into the tracks nearly unscathed.

"Nate, this isn't fucking TV, okay? Someone tried to kill you. The same person probably killed your brother. We can't handle this on our own. We need to—"

Nate's gaze drew away from the ruins of his jeans. Trent was pacing the length of the wall, his rangy form throwing a long shadow over the orange-gold glow of the street lights. It was the first time he'd spoken since they'd entered the park. The walk to the park from Fiftieth Street had been silent as Nate peered at everyone they passed, wondering if the seemingly carefree pedestrians knew danger was lurking just beyond their line of sight.

"What would we tell them?" Nate asked. "About the visions? There's no way I can explain how I knew to go to the station, let alone why I'm here investigating Theo's death to begin with. A cop is more likely to give me a ticket for making up an insane story and wasting their time than actually show interest in my version of events."

"What if we told them what we know about all those disappearances?"

"We don't actually know anything that doesn't stem from more psychic shit. We have no hard facts. Besides, remember what Felicia said? They didn't even help with Carrie."

"Shit. You're right." Trent stopped pacing. He rubbed his hands together and stared at Nate with a hunted look in his eyes. "What about the Community?"

"What about it?"

"There has to be someone there who would want to crack down on all this shit. Like Beck—you said she's there to keep an eye on the club because of everything that's been going down. Maybe she could tell us about some psychic contact in the NYPD."

Nate slumped down lower, his back skidding against the wall. "I don't know."

"Why not? You don't think she's trustworthy?"

"Maybe."

"You said they want rare psychics and all of that shit, right? I bet they want people like that to put them in key positions in different government agencies where they can affect policy. Including the police."

"Yeah, but—"

"Then you need to let someone know. Someone tried to kill you. We can't just sit here and—"

"Trent, just stop for a damn second!" Nate bolted to his feet. He moved away from Trent and the nervous impressions pouring off him. Every time Trent fidgeted or his leg hopped in agitation, a spike of anxiety shot through Nate that made him want to crawl in a dark corner and attempt to block everything, including Trent, out. "You know as well as I do that we can't trust anyone right now. And believe me—I am fucking terrified. I have no doubts that we're in way over our heads. But . . ." Nate dug his fingers in his hair, knotting them together. "But I don't know who's safe and who isn't."

Trent looked ready to argue, but he swore softly instead of pushing the issue. "You think they're all in on it?"

Nate shook his head. "There's . . . I know this sounds unlikely given I've only met assholes, but I know there's at least one person who's on our side. The person sending me the visions is the same person who yelled at Theo to run. They did the same thing to me tonight."

"What does that mean?"

Nate surveyed the park for the fifth time, and for the fifth time he saw nothing but a stray cat sleeping on one of the benches.

"Nate, don't hold out on me." Trent crossed the distance between them. His broad frame blocked out Nate's view of the rest of the park. "Despite . . . the weird shit that happened between us before this all went down, I know I can trust you and you know you can trust me. That was never in question, was it?"

"No. It never was for me." And after Trent had literally jumped in front of a train to save Nate, how would he ever doubt it in the future? Trent's loyalty wasn't just a gut feeling anymore. It was a fact. "There was someone on the platform with me, but they didn't push me. I jumped down myself. Some force . . . guided me there. And when I was lying on the tracks, I couldn't move. It was like . . . the part of my brain that wanted to panic and send me scrambling for the edge was blocked. All I could do was lie there like there were ten tons of concrete holding me down."

"Like Theo in the water."

"Yes," Nate said. "Someone was controlling me. And it wasn't the same person who sent the vision—*that* person tried to yank me away from the edge of the platform. That was the person who was mentally screaming for me to get up and run, just like they'd done to Theo the night he died."

"There were two people down in the subway?" Trent started pacing again. He shook his head in disbelief. "I didn't see anyone, but by the time I was on the platform, you were already in the tracks. Whoever it was must have taken off like a bat out of hell. And we still have no idea what the reason behind any of this is."

"Sort of?" Nate sighed and sank down to the concrete again. He dropped his head into his hands and kept talking, his voice muffled but still too loud in the deserted park. It was the only sound besides the breeze blowing an empty can down the stairs. "I know that for some reason, a really strong psychic in the Community is targeting multitalented or rare psys. And I know they're using Evolution to find victims. I also think that Jericho and Theo had found out what was happening and were trying to do something about it. Or maybe Jericho had already known about it and drew Theo into the conspiracy once Carrie disappeared. They may also have been involved in something called . . . Ex-Comm."

"What the fuck is an Ex-Comm?"

"A group of people who grew disillusioned by the Community and . . . escaped?"

"Nate, I'm telling you, man, this sounds like some cult-level Scientology shit."

"Maybe it is," Nate said. "Based on what Felicia and even Chase have said when he went on a rant, it seems like it *is* sort of like a cult. Or . . . maybe it has cultlike aspects? They draw psys in with the promise of great lives, and yeah, that does happen for some people, but they mostly ignore people like me, Elijah, and Holden, and root out anyone with powerful enough gifts to be useful for . . . for whatever. I have no idea. Maybe it's like you said and they want to plant psychics in key places so they can have control."

"Then maybe your idea that they want to take over the government or the world wasn't so off the mark after all," Trent said.

"Maybe. Or maybe it's not that big and it's just them wanting to use powerful psychics as protection, the way Holden does with Chase at the club. Either way, whatever they're doing has concerned enough people to have joined together and created Ex-Comm."

Instead of looking at him like he had three heads, Trent was nodding. Nate could practically see the wheels in his brain turning as he sorted through the information.

"This could either be a larger conspiracy within the Community regarding what those powerful psychics end up doing, or it could come down to people leaving the Community because they don't like the hierarchy that formed. Dude, it could even be that someone at the club is targeting the powerful psychics who get this star treatment, and taking them out."

All valid points, but Nate had no way of knowing which was the truth. The only people he could think of to ask, who might have some insight into the Community, was his own family. And that was only if he was right that at some point they'd crossed paths enough for the Blacks to get paranoid and start lying low.

"You think it could have been Holden or Chase?" Trent asked.

"I don't know. It's definitely someone with the ability to influence others, but not the way empaths can—" Nate broke off before the entire sentence was out of his mouth. Mentioning the shit he'd done before Evolution had descended into chaos was a very bad idea at the moment. "It has to be someone powerful enough to convince a man to let himself drown. Or to convince me to jump in front of a train."

"Or for dozens of people to drag a guy off a stage and beat him to death."

"Yeah. That too." Nate didn't mention that Jericho had been stabbed. He didn't want to continuing picturing the torn flesh and darkening pool of blood. An involuntary shudder racked his frame. "The problem is, I don't know anyone with the kind of kinetic or telepathic abilities to do that level of mind control. I don't even know what sort of psychic can do it."

"Jesus Christ." Trent joined him on the ground. "We're down to two options. Get the fuck out of Dodge and forget about all of this while hoping *it* forgets about *us*, or go back to Evolution—"

"—and confront Holden and Chase."

"Yeah. And hope whoever is sending you those visions will show up to have our fucking backs."

Nate rested his head against Trent's shoulder. He closed his eyes when one strong arm slid around his shoulders and pulled him close. The comforting gesture, so reflexively performed, dredged up all of his guilt again.

"I'm sorry, Trent. I didn't know everything would turn out this way. I thought it was just about my brother, that all of this was just tied to him and someone he'd made an enemy of. I didn't think someone would go so far as try to kill me. To fucking kill Jericho. Maybe he'd even still be alive if I hadn't made it clear I was zeroing in on him." Nate brought his knees up to his chin. "I fucked all of this up. I never should have gone to the club tonight. I never should have called you there. If you get hurt, it's all my fault."

"Shut up with that." Trent gently pulled Nate's hair, forcing him to look up. "If you hadn't called me, your narrow ass would be crushed against the tracks right now."

"I know."

"If you know, then stop. We'll figure it out, but I think confronting them is the right move. If either of them wanted you dead, they would have killed you the night you spent in Chase and Elijah's apartment."

A thousand scattered thoughts tried to coalesce in Nate's mind. The fragments of information he'd learned over the past week were floating around without coming together in a way that he could comprehend. For every possible answer, another question popped up. Why would Chase and Holden wait to kill him if they'd known what he was after all along? Why would they have given him access to the club at all? To Chase's home? Who was actually calling the shots, and what did this have to do with the string of powerful psychics who had gone missing for the past two years?

None of it made sense without a motive, and so far the only motive he could think of was that someone, or more than one person, in the Community was hungry for rare powers. And that person was willing to make people disappear in order to achieve their goal—whatever that was. They were also willing to kill to cover their tracks.

Again, Nate closed his eyes, but this time he opened himself up to Trent. The outpouring of concern and affection was almost too much to bear considering what Nate had done in the bathroom.

"Why are you still here with me?" he asked, voice rough. "After everything that happened tonight?"

"Because you need me to be here. Tonight proved it."

"I do," Nate said. "But . . . why do you care? I'm nothing. I'm no one. Just some guy you picked up by chance on the side of the road. Some fucking freak who's drawn you into a mess."

"Because since I first saw you in that goddamn liquor store, there was something about you that drew me in. I can't explain it. I don't even understand it. But I wanted to know more about you. And when

I saw you walking along the side of the road, I knew there was no way I could leave you there. I went against every instinct and came back for you, and I haven't regretted it since."

"And how do you know this unexplainable intrigue doesn't just exist because I forced it on you?"

"Nate . . ."

"No, I'm serious." Jaw clenching so hard his teeth ached, Nate sat up and faced Trent. He searched his face in the darkness, trying to see through the concern and find a glimmer of the suspicion that had flooded Trent's expression in the bathroom before everything had gone to shit. "You felt what I can do."

"I didn't feel anything."

"That's bullshit, and you know it. You . . . you wanted to leave that bathroom. You were *furious* at me. And then I put my hands on you, and suddenly you weren't. Suddenly you weren't thinking about leaving the bathroom anymore. And that's because I influenced you to stay. I influenced you to touch me and kiss me and fuck me." Nate nearly spat out the last few words. "I got so freaked out by the idea of you leaving me that I manipulated your emotions. So fucking easily, I did the thing I'd been terrified of doing all along."

Trent shook his head. "Nate, stop."

"Don't *Nate* me!" He jumped to his feet in an effort to end the connection between them, but the chasm was still open. He could still feel Trent. "Fuck, Trent. Why are you like this? Why aren't you angry?"

"Because regardless of what you did in the bathroom, it doesn't change the fact that I've wanted you all along." Trent stood as well, and promptly dragged Nate against him. He slid his fingers into the tangled hair at the nape of Nate's neck, and braced Nate's skull with his hands. "And you know what? Thank God I didn't leave that bathroom, or you would have died tonight."

"But that's not the poi—"

"So what's the point?" Trent asked. "You fucked with my head and you're an asshole? Yeah, okay. And if you do it again, you can rest assured that I will lay down the fucking law. Regardless of whatever fight we're having, you've got no right to influence my decisions and take away my autonomy."

Nate flinched at the words even though they weren't as harsh as what he'd expected.

"But," Trent went on, "your mistake is thinking I couldn't tell what you were doing."

Nate was poised to pull away and put space between them, but Trent's grip on him tightened. "What . . . does that mean?"

"It means what I said, dumbass. I could feel what you were doing. Maybe it's because I'm already aware of all of this psychic shit, so I didn't just cast it off as me changing my mind despite my better judgment, but I knew. Rageful Trenton was screaming at me to get the fuck out of the bathroom and away from you, but all of a sudden . . . the anger was gone. I was still conscious enough to know it was weird, but that didn't stop me from staying."

"But I still forced—"

"You didn't force anything." Now Trent sounded pissed off. "I knew you were trying to show me what you could do, and I knew you were doing it out of fear of me not believing you and walking away, so I gave in. I wanted to believe you, Nate. I never wanted to walk away. My pride was just down in the goddamn gutter."

Even with everything else going wrong, and with the menace of the Community pressing in on them, hope blossomed in Nate's chest. He was already losing the quest to find his brother's killer, and there was a strong chance he would never get out of this city alive, but at least he could have this. A tentative possibility that just maybe . . . maybe this thing that had built between him and Trent was real.

"And you never felt that way before?"

"Not once."

"But you wouldn't have been able to tell earlier on," Nate said, voice hushed. "And think about it—you'd never even been with a guy before, but you found yourself attracted to me at the liquor store. You made moves on me in New Orleans. You've been doing things out of character since you laid eyes on me. How do you know it's not just because—"

"Because that was all *me* making a goddamn move for the first time in my life because I knew I wanted you, and I didn't want to let you go without giving it a shot." Trent huffed out a quiet laugh. "Is it so hard to believe that I want you?"

"Yes."

"Then you're an idiot, and you don't see how special you are. How beautiful you are."

"Trent—"

"Don't *Trent* me," he said, mimicking Nate's words. "It's not just me who sees it. Holden does too. That's why he's trying his best to take you from me."

"But I didn't want him!"

"You sure?" Trent gazed deep into his eyes. "You weren't tempted even for a second?"

"No!"

"Do you swear?"

"I fucking swear. You're the only person I've ever felt this way about, Trent. You're the only person I want to be with. It's gotten to the point where I'm almost terrified of all this ending because—because then it means it's over. I go back to wherever I came from, or go wherever I'm going next, and you move on with your life. And I can't handle that."

Trent continued searching his face, maybe for a sign of dishonesty or even a hint of hesitation. Whatever he was looking for, he didn't find it, because he pressed their lips together. The world was raining down around them in fiery pieces, but at that moment, all Nate cared about was the taste and feel of Trent, and the unmistakable emotions coursing between them—love.

When they pulled apart, Trent brushed hair out of his face. "You never have to go back home if you don't want to, Nate. You never have to talk to those people again."

"Except I sort of do."

Trent cocked his head. "Why?"

"Because at this point I really think the Black family knows something about the Community. And at this point they're sadly the only people besides you who won't fuck me over."

"Nate?"

For days Nate had dreaded hearing the syrupy quality of Dade's voice, and it had the exact effect he'd expected. His stomach curdled.

Sweat broke out on his forehead. He immediately saw those horrible images. The ones in the photo album and the ones that had flashed through his mind as soon as they'd made contact.

"Nate, you there, son?"

"Don't call me 'son.'"

"Okay," Dade said quickly. He wasn't slurring. In any other circumstance, his low voice would have been reassuring. Now it brought only pangs of shame. "Anything you want, Nate."

Nate's stomach did another somersault. He had to swallow repeatedly to keep from gagging. Everything about this made him want to shut down the way he'd done in the past. The way he'd done after all of those beatings at school. There were only so many times he could get his face smashed in before he gave up on believing it would ever stop, and that was how he felt now. Like the hits would keep on coming.

"Nate?"

Hang up, he told himself. *Hang up and find another way.*

Nate sat up and started to do just that. His thumb brushed the end call button, but he didn't press down.

This was necessary to find out the truth. For this to go any further, he had to ask the right questions and he had to ask the right people. For the first time, he needed his fucked-up family.

"I want answers."

"Anything you want, so—Nate." Dade was so eager to please. So goddamn desperate for some kind of validation. "Where are you?"

"I'm in New York." Shit, he'd sworn not to cooperate before Dade did. Nervousness already had him by the balls, and it wasn't letting go. "What do you know about the Community?"

There was a sharp inhalation of breath on the other line. "Nate, stop this. Now. I am not kidding around."

"Stop what?"

"Whatever the hell you think you're doing up there. It's not safe."

"So you *do* know something." Hope exploded in Nate instead of trepidation. "Tell me everything."

"Get on a bus, a plane—"

"Tell me what you fucking know!"

Beside him, Trent tensed up and leaned closer.

"There's a reason our family stays under the radar," Dade said, voice dropping low. Like he didn't want someone else to hear. Eveline. "After what happened with Lore—"

"What *happened* to her?" Nate's heart stopped. "Did she not kill herself? Was she—"

"No, I—" Dade got quieter. "I think she did. But going to that place is what drove her to it."

"Oh, and not the fucking incest?" Nate's voice was sharp as a whip, and he hoped he was flaying Dade alive. Making him feel shame about what he'd done. "You think finding the Community was the worst part of her life?"

"Nate, please don't do this."

"Stop fucking begging me and tell me."

"But Eveline—"

Nate slammed his fist against the ground. "If you don't tell me, you will never hear from me again."

Silence followed for nearly a minute. The only signals that Dade hadn't hung up were the soft whirring of a fan on his side of the call and the clink of ice in a glass. Undoubtedly, he'd decided he needed the reassuring burn of whiskey to get through the call.

Nate took a breath. "Did someone in the Community do something to my mother while she was in New York?"

"Yes, but she wouldn't go into details." More clinking. The smacking of lips followed. "When she went up there, she said there was a growing group of people who were trying to get organized. Psychics had been coming together for a few years and had a plan to help each other out. And find people like them. Your mama—she was such a kind person. She—"

"Stick to the story."

There was another pause and more clinking. "She wrote me a letter about it and, at first, she half convinced me to follow her up there and get away from Eveline. I was fixin' to move until I got a weird phone call from her. Something about . . . how she'd gone to some farm, and the guy in charge had changed on her as soon as he found out about our family, and she felt like she'd put us all in danger. She'd been up there for over a year by then, and I guess she realized not everyone in the group cared about psychics singing kumbaya. Someone had shown their true colors."

"True colors," Nate repeated. "What does that mean? What did she see?"

"I don't know. She said not all of them were good, and that she'd trusted the wrong man. Said he didn't have a real gift of his own, but he'd figured out a way to take power—I don't know, Nate. It was all garbled. She was terrified. Even more so 'cause she thought she'd brought harm on her family by bringing us to their attention."

"But nothing ever happened to the family," Nate said.

"Right. 'Cause Lore said she'd made a deal. She'd give them everything if this mystery man left her and us alone."

"Everything like what?"

"At the time, I had no earthly idea. Far as I knew, she didn't have nothing."

More bits and pieces of information that didn't make sense. Nate would have to put it all on the board later and try to make the pieces go together. Right now, everything was a blur of information running through his brain.

Dade's sigh was slow and heavy, and punctuated by a heavy swallow. "Eventually, she escaped, but she wasn't all there when she came back."

"Escaped," Nate said. "How? Stop telling me half of a goddamn story."

"I don't know it all, damn it. I already told you she wasn't all there." Another ragged sigh exploded in the speaker. "She said . . . they took everything from her. And it was true. When she came back, she was changed."

Nate's eyes turned to slits. "Changed, how?"

"Not all there in the head, but also not as powerful. And she was paranoid. Thought everyone was after us. Never told me why, though. She and Eveline talked about it, but they kept it to themselves even after Eveline started saying the family needed to get strong again. That we needed strength to defend ourselves when evil came calling."

"By fucking each other and popping out powerful psy babies." The lack of a response was answer enough. The taste of revulsion was bitter in Nate's mouth. "You're all sick."

"You don't think I hate myself?"

"If you don't, you're sicker than I thought." Nate looked at Trent but saw no judgment, and no surprise, in his face. Nate had hinted at the incest in the past few days they'd spent together, but had never had the courage to say it aloud. Until now. "Last question and then we're done." He'd meant to ask if Dade was his father, but the words wouldn't come out. He knew without having to ask. Without having to hear the words. "What did she mean by them 'taking everything' from her? Was her gift not as strong? Was it the trauma of whatever had happened?"

A raspy scoff scraped out of Dade. Nate could clearly visualize the bloodshot gray eyes, stringy blond hair sticking to the sides of a damp, tear-stained face. It would have been no different from the other times when he'd found his uncle facedown in a puddle of drool, crying and incoherent. But now Nate knew what haunted him. Now he knew why Dade had lived for years on a scorching path of self-destruction.

"No, it wasn't no trauma that stripped her power away. She was too strong for that. That little gal didn't just have *one* gift before she left Texas, son. Sometimes I thought she had them all. But when she came home, they were gone."

CHAPTER NINETEEN

When Nate and Trent returned to Evolution, the police had cleared out and the gate in the front was pulled down. They silently entered the back of the property on the neighboring lot, and paused by the gate separating it from the patio behind Evolution.

"I'm going in alone," Nate said lowly. "If this goes wrong, there's no sense in us both being there."

"No way, Nate."

"Like you said, if they wanted to kill me, they could have done it already." Nate glanced at the fixed security camera perched just above the door. They were thankfully out of range. "But just in case I need back up . . ."

"How am I supposed to back you up if we're separated?"

"I'll call you. Or if I don't come out in twenty minutes, and you don't hear from me, call the police."

Trent was still shaking his head, but he didn't argue. He likely knew there was no point. Them getting caught up in something together would guarantee neither of them get out of it, and it wasn't like Trent could go in Nate's place to confront Chase or Holden. This was his problem.

"Fifteen minutes," Trent said. "Or I call the cops and then go in myself."

Nate bit his cheek to keep from arguing further. "Be careful."

"No, *you* be careful." Trent jerked him in for a brief kiss. "I love you, Nathaniel Black. You better not get yourself killed before we can go on a real fucking date."

It was so strange to hear the words and feel how much Trent meant them. And it was even stranger to say "I love you" in return before exchanging another fierce kiss and scaling a gate to return to a murder scene.

For the third time since climbing out of the tracks, Nate wondered why he was doing this. Why didn't he just move on and let it go? Going somewhere safe with Trent was the smart choice. Exploring the reality of a long life with a man who wanted him and figuring out how they could possibly make it work with Trent living in California was an even better one. But he couldn't let Theo's murderer go when he was the only one who would dare to investigate why his brother had been pitched into the water, and why other talented psychics were disappearing periodically from this club.

There was no choice but to go on.

Nate slipped into the still unlocked side door and entered Evolution. It looked like an abandoned fairground.

The pool of blood had been sopped up, but the stain still darkened the spot just beyond the stage. Broken glass littered the floor from where people had shoved over tables in their haste to escape, and there were several stray shoes or sandals that had been left behind by their owners. Police tape lay mixed in with the mess.

Skirting the dance floor, Nate crept up the stairs. The discretion was likely pointless since everyone who had reason to remain in the building was a psychic, but charging into something without caution seemed like a worse idea.

With the VIP section even darker than the lower level, Nate hesitated at the top of the staircase. Indecision coursed through him, but the sound of low urgent voices drew him closer.

"—get the fuck out of here."

"No." The second voice was muffled and thick with pain. "I won't just leave Taína and Lia to deal with this. They need me. I'm their—"

"They don't fucking need you, Elijah." Chase's voice rang out louder this time. "It's not safe for you here. Just be smart for once in your life, and *go*."

Nate found the two men huddled in a corner by one of the alcoves. Chase was gripping Elijah's shoulders with both hands.

"I'm not listening to you, Chase!" Elijah shoved Chase away and took a step back. Even in the dim light, his face was damp and swollen from tears. "There's something going on here, and I know you know what it is. I know . . . you're involved somehow."

At that, Chase stiffened, but he didn't confirm or deny the claim. "I'll try to tell you everything if you take your ass back to the apartment, pack up, and wait for me. And if you don't hear from me in the next two hours, get a bus ticket to who cares where and don't tell anyone. I don't give a damn who in the Community you think would help, or that you trust. Or if they exile you for running off. *Don't tell anyone.*"

"But why wouldn't I hear—"

"Go!"

Chase's voice went from urgent to venomous. He shoved Elijah so hard he staggered backwards, but the action seemed to have an effect. Elijah only stared at Chase for a moment longer before turning and fleeing to the other exit stairway. The stricken expression on his face imprinted in Nate's mind.

"Why the fuck would you come back here, Black?"

Nate's gaze snapped from Elijah's retreating back to Chase's rangy form. He was cast mostly in shadow, but his white-blond hair and the glint of his wallet chain and the buckles on his boots gave him away. It was that same glint which caught Nate's eye for a second time, and he remembered the legs of an unknown individual flashing by as he'd fallen onto the tracks. He sucked in a breath.

"It was you."

"I can't tell which 'it' you're referring to, fuck-boy."

Nate took a single step closer. "You were in the subway with me. You . . . You . . ."

Chase turned to face him, nodding encouragingly and wearing a mocking expression. "I . . . I . . . I what, dipshit?"

"You tried to pull me away from the edge of the platform. And you sent me the vision earlier tonight."

"Ding, ding, ding—and he fucking scores." Chase pointed at Nate, his fingers cocked like a gun. "I thought you were smarter than your blowjob of a twin, and expected you to figure it out sooner, but obviously not."

"I was smart enough to know you're the one to confront," Nate said. "And to realize you're involved in what's been going on here, regardless of you sending me that vision tonight."

"Man, you are really an idiot. I sent you the visions all along, asshole. Me. Not Theo communicating from the dead, not the fucking Holy Ghost, not Father Christmas—me. It wasn't my diabolical plot you were cracking with your little boyfriend. I sent them to you."

"How?" Nate challenged. "In some of them, I was Theo. They were his memories."

"No, they were mine." Darkness crossed Chase's face, but he just tilted his head back and narrowed his eyes. "I was in his head when it happened. Watching through his eyes. It's a cool telepath thing."

"Cool," Nate choked out. "To see him drown?"

"Yeah," Chase said flatly. "Pretty wild to be in someone's fucking head when they die, right?"

The pieces were finally clicking together in Nate's mind, but Chase confessing it all out loud struck him silent. There was no relief that he finally knew the truth about the visions. There was only fear that Chase would clam up before saying anything more.

Chase strode closer, boots pounding against the floor. "I didn't want to put my hands in this. I *can't* put my hands in this. I tried my best to warn Theo to stay out of things the first time I realized Jericho was bumping uglies with Ex-Comm, and since he's a useless psychic, he was using your brother to snoop around for him. Little did I know the jerk would take that as a jumping off point to willingly float up shit's creek without a paddle."

Nate couldn't get over the fact of it having been Chase all along. The initial vision, the one of Jericho and Theo talking on the patio . . . "Why didn't he listen?"

"Because he knew about me before he even got here," Chase spat. "He also had an idea about the disappearances, so he wouldn't leave it alone until someone stepped up to put an end to what's been going on." The words lodged like a shuriken in Nate's skull before he had time to respond. "Everyone thought he was all strung out and stressed due to Community popularity contests, but that wasn't half of it. He was strung out and stressed because the dumb fuck *knew*. He'd seen all this shit in his dreams, and he *still got involved*."

"What did he know?" Nate demanded. "What the hell do you mean he knew about you?"

Chase's lip curled. "He had a premonition as a kid. Said that was why he came up here instead of staying down in New Orleans like he'd originally wanted. He'd known all along he would end up here."

A premonition.

lore chase to new york

Lore and Chase—and Theo—going to New York.

How had Nate not made the connection? It was like a punch in his gut, and he felt like he was losing his wind with every new revelation.

"Wh-what do you have to do with my mother?"

"What don't I have to do with *your* mother?"

"What the fuck does that mean?" Nate searched Chase's snarling face for answers, but found none. "Stop playing games and fucking *tell me.*"

"You really are worthless, aren't you?" Chase jerked a thumb at himself. "The clues are right in your face."

And at that, it clicked.

The buzzed platinum hair and silver eyes; the thin, hard-angled frame . . . and the picture in Holden's office. Chase's history—the powerful psychic mother that no one spoke of. The one who'd abandoned him twenty-four years ago. And Theo's premonition. The one that had led him to New York. The connection to their mother.

"Oh my God."

"God has nothing to do with this shit-show, sugar. It's all on *our* fucked-up mother and her fucked-up family."

"But . . . why?" Nate reached out to touch Chase's arm and was surprised when the other man—his half brother—didn't jerk away. "Why would she leave you here with people she was terrified of? Who apparently took her powers?"

"Why? Well, why not?" The thick blanket of nothing eased, and impressions exuded from Chase in a whirlwind of anger and bitterness. "Richard Payne may have knocked her up, but when they shipped her off to the Farm to give birth in what they think is their little sanctuary, she found the nightmare human that is fucking Jasper. And when she pushed out a freakish superhuman baby and Jasper started to get experimental, she panicked. Promised to let him have me, the grand prize, so they'd leave her and the rest of the Blacks alone."

So it'd been Jasper. The same Jasper that Beck had talked about in awed tones, as if he were an enlightened psychic giving his life to the Community. And in reality . . . he was experimenting on the people he was supposed to be rehabilitating. Learning to absorb their powers.

The idea of Chase being left with such a person as a child made Nate sick.

"She didn't want to leave you."

"How the hell would you know?"

"Because I grew up with her." Nate swallowed hard as a lump swelled in his throat. It was too easy to think back on the gray memories of his childhood and see his mother curled into herself with tear-stained cheeks and vacant eyes. "She was always haunted by something, and now I know what."

"Oh ho, is *that so*?" Chase laughed aloud at that—a blunt, ugly sound that filled the entire club. "Your mother knew who she was leaving me with because, from what I remember—and yeah my memories go back that far—he tried it on her first. She just didn't give a fuck that I was basically going to become Jasper's science project. She didn't even care enough to tell my father or the board. She just *ran*."

"Chase—"

"Do you know how long he kept me up on the Farm and poked and prodded me to figure out what made me like me and not a boring fucking empath or telepath like most of the others? And convinced Richard that he was keeping me for *my benefit*? Because all of the power coursing through my veins had *fucked me up*?" His voice continued to rise, damagingly loud in the muted silence of the club. "They believed it, because they trusted him. They still trust him. Would rather take his word for it than mine because as far as they know, I've always been a little *unhinged*. Never mind that I'm this way because he shredded my mind trying to take my talents before realizing my mental shields were too fucking strong."

"He wasn't able to—"

"No," Chase cut in harshly. "I held on, but it hurt. God, it fucking hurt. But I would never let him hear me scream. And he hated me for it."

"Chase." Nate clamped his other hand down on Chase's arm, and dug his fingers in tight. He tried the best he could to push his surprising calm into the clearly deteriorating state of Chase. He was shocked when some of the wildness left Chase's eyes, like clouds clearing after a storm. "I don't doubt what you're saying or what you feel. But right now? I want you to tell me what you meant by him trying to take your talent. My uncle said the same thing, that they took our mother's power, but he couldn't explain how that was possible."

Chase's jaw clenched.

"I may not be multitalented, and I may not have premonitions, but I've spoken to enough people from . . ." Nate hesitated briefly. "From Ex-Comm, to know some people would try to get power and status by any means necessary." When Chase continued to stare down at him through long, pale eyelashes, Nate shook him. "Talk to me, you fucking asshole! You *wanted* me to come here. You *wanted* me to investigate even while you stayed here and did nothing! Don't fucking clam up on me now. I know you care."

"I care more about not ending up on a slab in their compound at the Farm again," Chase said flatly. "And even if I wanted to go up against them, I can't."

"Why?" Nate demanded. "Why couldn't you help your own brother?"

"Because *I can't*. He couldn't get past my shields enough to take my talents, but whatever he did to me up at the Farm has fucked up my head, kiddo. If I even think about leaving the Community, or going against him directly, it's like my brain rebels and shuts down. He made it so I can't leave the Community even if I wanted to."

"But you can tell others to go?" Nate asked, jerking his head in the direction Elijah had gone. "Why?"

"'Cause I can push through the pain for him. But when it comes to me?" Chase shook his head slowly. "My body locks up, and this fucking fear shuts me down. This fear they put into me when I was a kid, and even though I know they're the ones that put it there, I can't escape it. I can't escape the Community. Never will."

"Brainwashing," Nate said. "Actual brainwashing."

"Yeah. It's not like Holden and his preaching about the CW and how he helped runaways like Elijah. The shit Jasper put me through is hardcore mindfucking. Years of it. And there isn't a goddamn thing

I can do about it. Except send my inbred brother my memories and hope he gets a clue."

Nate wanted to shake him again. "Then why did you push me away the whole time?"

Chase threw up his hands. "Are you even listening? I can't escape like you can after this is said and done. I'm stuck here. And if they find out I helped Ex-Comm, I'll end up at the Farm again for *realignment*, because they don't realize Jasper's version of *realignment* is my head being cut open so he can find new ways to make me fucking tick."

Nate shuddered at the very idea. He couldn't imagine how helpless Chase felt to see what was going on around him and not be able to do a thing to stop it. Whether it was a mental block or the promise of being locked away with Jasper . . . he was trapped.

"Because that's what will happen if they find out I ruined their little operation," Chase continued.

"Who's 'they'?"

"I told Theo not to go to the pier," Chase went on. "But he didn't listen, and he got himself dead. They'd already suspected he was on to the truth, but Theo didn't want to accept that she could read him like a picture book."

"She." Nate stared at Chase, unblinking and heart racing. "Beck."

"Yeah. Beck. She's not *just* some spotter like Holden says. She can pick out the location of a psychic in the middle of Times Square."

"So that is the reason she's here," Nate said. "But why? To take the powers for herself? To be stronger? But *how*—"

Chase broke away from Nate's hold, and pressed his own hands to the sides of Nate's face. The words died on his lips as the vision entered his mind. Or maybe it wasn't a vision—it was a memory. Chase's memory.

a cold slab of metal beneath his back, arms twisted and held down by thick leather straps, and IVs everywhere. needles and screens. beeping sounds. people talking. panic. fear. lonely. so lonely. a young voice begging for help. to be let up. to go home. where was home? why did he feel so weak?

and then a face. a shaved head and ink tattooed like a band around bright-green catlike eyes. the slash of a brutal mouth, and two strong hands pressing against the sides of his head. pressure. pain. and then the terrifying sense of his soul being sucked out. growing weaker. his brain screaming as if it was being torn apart. and then a staggering void inside of him. emptiness where there hadn't been before.

Nate stumbled away from Chase, breath ripping out of him in sharp gasps.

"They took something from you. That man—the one with the cat eyes. He absorbed one of your talents."

"Jasper," Chase sneered. "After he failed the first few times, he stopped trying to absorb my talents and focused on controlling me. He was doing too much damage to my head and knew Richard would have his ass if he came back to find me brain damaged or dead."

"So that's . . . that's what my mother saw. Or that's . . . what he did to her when he learned about our family. And when he saw the powerful child she'd given birth to." The words fell from Nate's mouth too fast, jumbling into nonsensical half-statements. "Does Beck know how to do this?" A sick feeling built in Nate's stomach. "Would it have killed you? Did it kill Carrie and Anthony and Oz?"

"It could have if Beck wanted their powers for herself. Or they could be lying strapped down to a metal slab in Jasper's lab on the Farm." Chase shrugged like it didn't matter, even though Nate could feel just how much it did. "Either way, I'm not going down like that again. I was hoping you could figure it out and expose it all, but at this point I'm worried about how much Elijah has been dragged into it. He's associated with the Dreadnoughts, who are associated with Ex-Comm, and now she's taking them out? Fuck that. I think it's time to call it a wrap. You need to go. *Now.*"

"But Holden—"

"I'll take care of Holden," Chase snapped. "Just get the fuck out and take your big, dumb void of a boyfriend with you."

Trent.

He'd forgotten to text Trent.

Nate scrambled to pull his phone out, to see how much time had passed, but froze at a loud clatter from below. He and Chase stared at each other, each rooted to the spot, before spinning to look over the balcony.

Trent stood there with Holden pinned against the wall, his hands locked around Holden's neck.

CHAPTER TWENTY

Nate launched himself at the staircase and nearly collided with Chase. All signs of sarcasm and mockery had fled his expression, and now his stormy eyes were fixed on Trent. More specifically, the position of Trent's hands on Holden's throat.

After sprinting through the corridor, and being outpaced by Chase, Nate skidded to a stop just inside the dance floor. The situation hadn't changed for the better. Holden was clawing frantically at Trent's hands even as their eyes locked. Nate could almost imagine Holden trying to get a hook into Trent's mind to influence him to stop the attack and failing. Panic bounced off him like shockwaves.

"Trent, what the fuck are you doing!"

The shout caught in Nate's throat as Chase took two great leaps forward and slammed himself into Trent's side. The three of them crashed to the floor together.

"Trent!"

Nate rushed forward. He watched in horror as Chase struggled to pin Trent's more muscular form to the floor only to be met with a barrage of punches and knees to the chest. They rolled to the side, and Holden scrambled away.

"He's lost his mind." Holden's voice was a hoarse whisper. He clutched his reddened throat. "Call the police!"

"No." Nate watched the struggle going on a few feet away. He tried to get a read on Trent, but for the first time since they'd crossed paths, there was nothing. It was like Trent, his Trent, wasn't there. There was a mental wall blocking him. "There's something wrong."

"No shit, Nate!"

The strain of Holden's voice was nearly lost in the sounds of the struggle. Chase straddled Trent while forcing his arms down, but was head butted in the process. He fell backward, stunned, and Trent's eyes swung to Holden again. As cold and silent as death itself, Trent grabbed one of the broken beer bottles and dove at Holden. This time, both Nate and Chase jumped for him. Only it was Chase who got there first, and he did so with a pocketknife extended in one hand.

In that moment, a weapon aimed at Trent became more of a concern for Nate than Holden's well-being. When Chase jumped on Trent and once again pinned him to the floor, Nate slid his own arm around Chase's throat. He locked his elbow and squeezed.

"Drop the knife or I'll put you to sleep."

"Tell your fucking boy to drop the bottle," Chase said. "I'll cut his throat if that glass so much as grazes my brother's skin."

For several seconds, the only sounds in the empty club were labored breathing and the squeak of sweaty skin against linoleum with Trent's frequent struggles. He strained against their combined weight and didn't snap out of the fog he was in. His only response was to make a sound of protest when Holden knocked the bottle out of his outstretched hand. Chase immediately dropped his own knife.

With the weapons away and a truce called, Nate eased his hold on Chase. He shoved his half brother to the side and sank to his knees beside Trent. His heart was in his throat as he finally got a good look, and his suspicions were confirmed. Sweat covered Trent's face, but his eyes were frantic and darting. He looked like a cornered animal locked in a cage, except the cage was his own body.

"It's not him doing this." Nate pressed his hands to Trent's cheeks. "Someone's controlling him."

"How do you—"

"I just know!" Nate shouted over Holden. "We need to get out of here. Beck is—"

"Beck is what?"

Nate's head snapped up. He instantly saw her even though he'd been oblivious to her presence at the bar before. A single slight figure with folded arms and no affect whatsoever. There was no glee in her posture or face. She was as calm as ever. Even while mind controlling Trent to commit murder.

"Leave Trent alone," Nate said. "Now."

Beck slid off her barstool. "Or what?"

It was a good question. There was nothing Nate could do while Trent was in her grips. There was very little he could do to her in general.

"The interesting thing about voids is that they're so much easier to control than psychics." She nodded at Trent, and his fighting renewed in an instant. Adrenaline seemed to rush through him, and he practically threw Nate and Chase off him with strength that shouldn't have been possible. They both fell to the floor. "They're also a lot easier to read. His jealousy of your love triangle gives good motive."

"Fuck you," Nate said. "Just tell us what you want."

"Someone needs to tell *me* what the hell is going on." By then, Holden had found his voice again. "Chase, what's happening?"

Even in a life-or-death situation, Chase managed to spear Holden with a look of pure impatience and disgust. "She's been using your place as a honeypot."

"For what?"

Nate staggered to his feet again, edging closer to Trent. With Beck's focus elsewhere, her control over him appeared to be wavering.

"To pick psychics from, you fucking idiot! She's a Community spotter gone haywire. Picks out the good ones and gobbles up their powers for herself." Chase sneered. "I'm pretty sure these new kinetic powers belonged to Carrie."

Holden froze, eyes going wide enough for the whites to appear around his pupil. "My father would never allow this. The Community—"

Beck's lips twisted. Her eyes shone hard and bright. "Sit down, Holden. And stay there until someone kills you."

Holden's eyes bulged. The veins in his head stood out in stark relief against his skin as if he was straining against whatever influence she was exerting over him. At first, it seemed he'd be able to resist. But then he walked backward and slammed into the wall. He sank to the floor as Beck looked on coolly. She turned her attention to Chase.

By then Trent was shaking. Nate could practically smell Trent's fear. It was an overwhelming cloak of horror, but he swallowed his own automatic response to escape the suffocating layers, and pulled Trent into his arms.

"I got you," he whispered. "It's okay. Feel me so you can't feel her."

Trent nodded. He inhaled and exhaled slowly, and clung to Nate. With every fiber, Nate focused on doing exactly what he'd feared for the past couple of weeks—using his own emotions to influence Trent's. Wrapping him in comfort and concern instead of the anger Beck had used to turn him on Holden.

It wasn't until Trent took a deep, shuddering breath and squeezed Nate's arm, did Nate look at the others again.

"—he doesn't know how twisted people like you can become," Chase was snarling at Beck. "How you use the CW's goal of taking in lost psy kids to your advantage because you scout them and find the good ones, right? But I grew up around someone just like you, Beck, so I know how easy it is for you to think it's okay to cannibalize a psy kid if he has no connections or real family. I'm Richard's son, but it didn't even matter since I'm just a bastard who grew up on the Farm. You knew no one would take my word. And you've been doing the same thing here."

As Chase spoke, the pieces of the entire puzzle went from abstract shapes to a concrete big picture.

All the psys who'd disappeared from Evolution *did* have things in common. In fact, they had three.

Their connection to Evolution, their lack of families, and their rare psychic abilities. They were prime targets for someone who wanted to cannibalize their powers. In a way, it had made them perfect victims. And Beck had likely thought Theo was the same. Except, she hadn't taken his powers. She'd killed him in a moment of rage because he'd been too close to her secret. Maybe even because he'd gone against her after they talked and she assumed they'd bonded.

As everything quilted together in his mind, Beck moved closer, unafraid and unhesitating, and pressed her hand to Chase's face. Her eyes turned to slits as his widened into discs. A whisper of a sound escaped his mouth.

"Stop!" Nate leaped to his feet. "Why are you doing this?"

At that, Beck actually laughed—a soft, pleasant sound that didn't fit the horrific picture of Chase's face going slack and his eyes dulling as she attempted to drain him. "Why not? You of all people should know how it feels to have an unappreciated talent. To be surrounded by people stronger than you, and more influential while you're seen as useless. A freak among freaks."

"Not being powerful doesn't make you a freak," Nate said desperately. "Being a psychic vampire and killing people does."

Beck's fingers tightened against Chase's face. He dropped to his knees in front of her. "I was what you said—a psy vampire. I drained anyone I touched until I learned how to control it, and by then I'd gained the ability to be a spotter from one of the first psys I'd ever absorbed. Once I was vetted, the Community decided I was dangerous, but they knew they could also use me as a tool to spot psychics. So I remained as long as Richard agreed to keep a close eye on me."

Her tone changed at the end, spitting the words as if they tasted bad, though it was her own resentment turning them sour. Being picked over and passed over when in reality she had the most powerful talent of them all . . . Nate could see how it had twisted her. And he could see how easy it would be to lash out, especially if she'd already experienced the sensation of draining another psy.

"It doesn't have to be this way, Beck. We can just go. Me and Trent can leave. And Chase—you know he will never leave the Community. Nobody would believe him, anyway."

Beck's posture eased, and Chase gasped. Awareness came back to his features even as he slid to the floor in a limp pile. His eyes flitted between Nate and Holden, and back again, before they closed completely.

"Just tell me why you killed my brother. That's all I want to know."

"Because he fucking betrayed me." Beck's eyes narrowed to slits. "He above anyone should have understood. He was like me. You both are like me. Poor and treated like shit by people like him," she spat, nodding at Holden. "And he still turned his back. The worst part was that he said he was doing it for the Community. Because he really believed it could be something good, but not with someone like me climbing the ranks to get a position of power."

"You're killing people!" Nate shouted. "People just like us."

"No one has ever cared about me in my life, Nathaniel. No one but Jasper. How could you expect me to care?"

Nate opened his mouth to answer, but no words came out. He'd thought he was safe without her hands on him, but pain sliced into his mind. His eyes starred, watering, and he sank to his knees much faster than Chase had. He pitched forward, tears streaming, as the cold violence of the mental assault strengthened. It was like something being ripped from his brain, and he couldn't talk past that pain. He couldn't think. He could do nothing but feel her draining him of the one thing that had simultaneously been a curse and the only thing that had ever made him special.

He saw every moment in his life when he'd cursed his talent, and then very clearly saw all of the moments when it had guided him. Like with Trent. Without feeling Trent's attraction and desire, Nate would never have allowed himself to give in to the temptation of his arms. And without *knowing* his good intentions and kindness, it was entirely possible that Nate would never have gotten in the battered old Nova.

Nate tried to summon the strength to bring down a shield, but he couldn't. His vision dimmed. His fingers and toes went numb.

He was dying.

But as sharply and quickly as the attack had begun, it ended. His brain stopped stretching like a pulled rubber band. Nate was able to look up through his watering eyes and guttering breath, and found himself face-to-face with Beck. She was on the floor beside him, and her eyes were closed.

Nate's eyes slowly tracked upward to see Trent standing above her prone body. He was holding the broken leg of a chair, which he let drop to the floor.

"I guess the void's good for something," he said wearily.

At that point, Nate couldn't help it. Through the fatigue and shock of what had just happened, he laughed. He kept laughing while Trent knelt beside him.

"What did she do to you?"

Nate shook his head. "I'll . . . explain later. It doesn't matter now. I'm fine." He swallowed with difficulty and tried not to gag. Sitting up was dizzying. "How do we handle this? She's so powerful. There's no way she's going to be out for long."

"We need to call the Community."

The voice caused Nate to start. He'd almost forgotten Holden was in the room. He had come out of his own stupor to tend to Chase, who was awake but ghostly pale.

"And by the Community, you mean . . ." Trent trailed off, but his hands tightened on Nate. "Your father?"

"Who else would I call?" Holden demanded. "I almost want to see his face when he realizes it was his own fault this all happened. He put her here."

Nate tensed, and the look Chase was spearing him with gave him pause. Despite his ashen complexion and limp body, Chase had the wherewithal to send a message.

Get the fuck out. You still know too much about everything. They'll want you under their thumb.

"We're leaving," Nate said. "You don't need me for that. Your father and the Community can take it from here."

"But you know more than—"

"I'm tired. She did something to me and . . . I just can't be here anymore." Nate gripped Trent and struggled to stand. "After all of this, I think you owe me a pass on being interrogated, Holden. Just let us go."

Indecision colored Holden, but he nodded. "I'll adjust the cameras and say I hit her, but I can't control what she says after waking."

"Good enough."

For now.

The train rushing through the tunnel was a comforting sound.

Nate had never expected to appreciate the closed-in feeling of riding the subway, or the strange people surrounding him, but the unbearably normal aspects of it all brought him relief.

"You saved us," Nate said when their car of the A train cleared. He looked at Trent. "How does it feel to be the real superhero?"

"Not great since we know the Community is likely going to want to question the hell out of you."

Nate dropped his head back against the pale-blue seat. "I know, but maybe Chase will cover for us. He's the one who told me to leave."

"It feels shitty to walk away knowing he's stuck there against his will. But at least the vampire will be taken care of."

Nate had thought the same thing over and over during the sprint to the subway and the long wait for the train. With a pounding heart and mounting guilt, he'd realized he didn't feel better about finding Theo's killer if it meant leaving Chase behind. Maybe the Community hadn't been behind the disappearances, but Jasper was still up at the Farm performing his experiments and researching multitalented psychics.

It was crushing to realize that he and Trent were small and helpless in the grand scheme of it all.

The train squealed to a stop at Columbus Circle. A few people boarded but sat far enough away from them to be out of earshot.

"This is surreal," Trent said. "Even after all that happened, I still can't believe it happened. I thought I had a handle on the psychic thing, you know? I can logically justify a gene mutation that results in extrasensory abilities, but there is no explanation for psy vampires."

"There's not."

"It's totally fucking supernatural." Trent's brow wrinkled. "And it makes me wonder what else may be out there."

The same thought had crossed Nate's mind, but he preferred to focus on the supernatural insanity at hand. Weariness overcame him. He sunk down on the seat and leaned against Trent.

"What are you thinking, Nate?"

"That I'm tired. And . . ."

"Let me guess. You're sorry for bringing me into this. You regret hitching with me because it put me in danger." Trent nudged him. "Right?"

Nate looked up. "Wrong." When he received one of Trent's epic brow raises, he actually mustered a laugh. "I'm not sorry for dragging you into this because that would mean I'm sorry that we met, and I'm not. I needed you. I still need you. And I love you."

The smile that spread over Trent's face was enough to light up the night. He leaned down to brush a gentle kiss against Nate's lips even as his hands rose to grip Nate's like he never wanted to let go. When they parted, he said, "We needed each other. You protected me too."

Nate snorted. "I didn't do anything."

"Bullshit." Trent's thumb stroked the skin along Nate's neck. "You put the pieces together. Without that, Beck would still be psy sucking and Chase would be watching her do it while terrified to speak against her since the Community has him neutered and microchipped or whatever the hell. He probably thought accusing Community brass was a sure way to wind up back at the Farm for some new conditioning or realignment or whatever."

"Maybe it would have been. Even if they don't know about Jasper, they seem to treat Chase like a dog. Or an experiment." Nate looked down. "I wish I knew what's going to happen."

"What do you mean?"

"Even after finding out why psychics were disappearing and why my brother was killed, I still feel like there's nothing solid beneath my feet. It doesn't feel over. Jasper is still capable of hurting people. And Chase is my brother, and I left him there."

"Yeah," Trent said softly. "I know. But he'll be okay. Like you said, Richard Payne is his father. He won't let Jasper go too far. And it seems like it was mostly Beck who threw a wrench into things recently."

"Yeah. That's true."

They lapsed into silence, Nate's head on Trent's shoulder. After a while, Trent nudged him. "So, what are you going to do now?"

"I have no idea. I've got nowhere to go."

"Nowhere at all?"

Nate forced himself not to look away. Trent couldn't possibly know how that question affected him. Couldn't possibly know what it felt like to belong nowhere and have nothing to return to.

"I don't have a home, Trent."

"Yeah, you do." Trent entwined their fingers. "You can come with me on a real road trip. Cross-country. And then you can live with me in California. We can leave all this behind us."

Hope sparked bright and hot. It was almost unbearable compared to the risk of disappointment. Nate opened himself up to the outpouring of Trent's affection, and the horrors of the night slowly slid to the recesses of his mind.

"Are you sure?" he asked. "You really want to be stuck with some messed-up psy? I bring trouble wherever I go."

"That's okay." Trent brought their intertwined hands up and kissed the back of Nate's hand. "I can handle the trouble as long as we're together."

EPILOGUE

Six Months Later

California was exactly the kind of place Nate had always assumed he'd hate.

Blue skies, palm trees, and sunshine—even on New Year's Eve— so pretty it was almost a guilt trip to not *want* to go outside. Not to mention the people—fit, athletic, and full of pep. It was how he imagined Australia would be like minus the cool accents.

But despite all of that, Nate fucking liked it.

He'd learned to enjoy the sunshine from the safety of the backyard of their tiny bungalow, and he'd started riding his bike to the head shop he worked at in Arcadia. Or more accurately, the head shop where he exploited his talent to do tarot readings for potheads and burnouts who'd initially wandered in to buy pipes, water bongs, and vaporizers. His favorite kind of people.

The type of people Trent befriended at school, brought home, and who listened earnestly while Nate coyly discussed his psychic powers. They seemed to get a kick out of the tarot thing, and they got an even bigger kick out of the fact that he was right on the money about reading their emotions and reactions to things. Word of mouth was how his following at the shop had grown so large.

"So, I don't know if I want to know what that card means." The guy's name was Saint, and he was a model. Another of those word-of-mouth customers.

"It's the lovers reversed." Nate slouched in his papasan under the fan. It blew strands of blond hair everywhere as he peered at the colorful spread of cards. "The lovers can represent choices or a crossroads." Or at least that's what Nate had read on the internet. "But reversed, it implies a lack of harmony. Conflict and an avoidance of responsibility—maybe after . . . a rash or thoughtless decision." Nate hunched over the table, staring into Saint's eyes. He could feel the anxiety rolling off the kid. Rays of worry so thick, Nate could almost see what he was seeing. Flashes of two different men even though Nate could barely see their faces. "For you, I think you're stuck between two guys. One you're in a relationship with and one . . . you recently met. Someone you're not sure about even though the connection is intense."

Saint's eyes bugged out of his head. "Oh fuck. How did you know?"

"It's sort of my thing." Reading emotions while pretending to read tarot cards was awesome. Appearing mysterious was a good excuse for his lack of social and speaking skills. "Do you want to look at the next card?"

"Shit. I don't know." Saint nibbled on his lower lip. He looked between the first two cards, up at Nate, and then down again. "Fuck yeah. Do it."

Nate flipped the card. "Five of swords."

"Is it bad?" Again with the lip gnawing. "It looks bad."

"Not necessarily, but . . ." Nate searched Saint's eyes. He leaned forward enough for their knees to brush. "It can be trouble. A betrayal or a threat by someone you thought you could trust, but who will turn out to be an enemy."

Saint's rosy tan paled, and again the fear was palpable. "What about . . . someone I'm trying to trust, but who I know can be dangerous?"

An image of one of the men flashed again. It was joined by another outpouring of anxiety mixed with the red sharp spikes of fear.

Nate's brows drew down. "Hey, does he— Is the one you're leaving, has he hurt you?"

Saint threw himself against the back of his seat, and Nate knew he'd gone too far. He'd never been so specific before, and it was for precisely this reason. Normal people could be open-minded enough to buy energy reading and pattern predictions, but the fact that Nate had actually plucked a moment out of reality was too far. Especially when, judging by the reaction, it was a secret.

"I have to go," Saint said. "But thank you. This was amazing. And . . . scary."

Nate didn't touch the cards. He sat still and pasted on a placid smile. "I'm sorry. I shouldn't have said that. I just . . ." There was literally no way to explain. "Uh. Y'know. You never know."

God, he sounded stupid. Maybe Saint would think he was stoned.

"It's fine. Don't apologize." A strained smile flashed across the lovely face. Saint dropped three hundred-dollar bills on the table. "Here—call it a huge tip."

"What the hell? Are you actually a model?"

Again, Saint looked astonished. He didn't know that this guess had been due to his cheekbones instead of his vibes. "I'm an Instagram model."

Whatever the hell that meant.

"Cool."

Saint beamed. "Thank you again, Nate. You're amazing. I can't wait to tell my friends about you. Expect to be *booked*."

It was the kind of thing Nate loved to hear, especially from people with rich friends, but his excitement was on pause. He kept thinking about Saint's fear and the flash of a man's face. It was hard to forget when his readings wound up being accurate.

The afternoon trudged along, and Nate closed his setup on the patio for the day. After waving good-bye to the lesbian couple who owned the shop, he drenched himself in layers and scarves to brave the sixty-degree winter day—cold for a Texan—and rode his bike home.

Home.

What a weird concept after several years of moving from crappy apartment to crappy apartment without any belongings to call his own. The same could definitely not be said of the tiny house he and Trent rented. It was insanely overpriced and they were extremely poor, but he loved it. He loved that it was red stucco, he loved the shiny brass knocker on the door, and that the three small rooms had more character than fourteen hundred square feet of white walls in an apartment in Texas. And he *loved* the ability to walk places in the neighborhood.

But the best part was living with Trent. Eating together, laughing, bickering, and having sex almost constantly. Waking up in the secure ring of Trent's arms. Especially after a nightmare. And after all these months, they still plagued him. There were nights when he dreamt of being stuck in someone else's head, of being tormented, and he jerked awake wondering if it had been a vision. But then he remembered he was next to Trent, and he reveled in the feeling of being safe. And being loved.

It was something Nate had only recently realized was not fleeting. Trent wasn't going anywhere. They were a fixed pair.

"Honey, I'm home," he called dryly. "I had a shitty day and I want a drink."

Trent's voice floated from their bedroom. "Beer in the fridge."

Nate grabbed two, kicked off his shoes, and dropped down to the bed beside Trent. He'd been lying on his back and staring up at the ceiling fan.

"You look like how I feel," Nate said, handing over a beer. "What's up?"

"Unless you want to hear about the clusterfuck of people from my quantum physics class arguing over . . . quantum physics at a New Year's Eve get-together, don't ask."

"Heh. I'll pass."

"Good idea."

Nate lay on his back beside Trent. He nearly purred with pleasure when those big, strong arms wound around him, and Trent nuzzled his chest. Cuddling while drinking was a talent they'd perfected early on.

"What about you?"

"I'm probably reading too much into it."

"Reading too much into *what*?" Trent slurped from his bottle. "Something at the shop?"

"Yeah . . . This guy came in. An Instagram model or whatever."

Trent made a face. His irrationally territorial behavior would always be endearing considering how unnecessary it was.

"He asked me about his love life, and when I pulled his cards it was so spot on." Nate frowned as beads of sweat slid down the neck of the bottle. "And I think his boyfriend abuses him?"

"How could you know that?"

Nate shrugged. "I don't know. Sometimes when I get strong enough impressions I also get flashes or images that go along with it, but the weirdest part was that the cards were *so* spot on."

Trent set his beer on the end table and rolled onto his side. "I'm not sure why you're so surprised. Logically speaking, if we live in a world that has psychics of varying types among other things, it's not unreasonable to find out that tarot cards might actually be accurate when read by the right people."

"But I'm not the right person! I'm cheating by using my talent."

Trent shrugged. "I don't know, baby. But is that really what's bothering you?"

"No."

"Are you upset about the situation the dude is in?"

Nate smiled faintly. "Hey, I thought I was the psychic."

"I'd be a fail of a partner if I didn't know you by now."

"True." Nate extended his arm to set his own bottle on the floor before fully curling into Trent. Being surrounded by the warmth and smell of him was always amazing, but that coupled with feeling him inside and out was indescribable. "It drives me nuts when I know someone's in trouble and can't do anything to help. Like . . . what's the point of being able to do this?"

Trent laughed. "You're such a hero, Nate. I've been saying it all along."

"What's that mean?"

"It means that was a total superhero thing to say. The kind of person who would seek a purpose in having a power is the type of person who would put that power to use helping other people if we knew how the fuck to do that."

Nate relaxed against the bed as the words sunk in. "I see what you're saying."

"Good. It's part of why I love you so much."

The words would never cease to make Nate's heart soar. "How are you so good at boyfriending?"

"Just pro at life, basically."

"Oh shut up."

"You can shut me up with a kiss," Trent said. "That's always a good plan."

"Agreed."

Sometimes it was almost impossible to kiss without it quickly escalating to something more. The perk of using his empathy and ability to influence to their advantage when being intimate. The dual sensations hitting both of them at once was a sure fire way to lead almost every touch to a world-rocking round of sex, and Nate was okay with that. In fact, he craved it constantly. Even after six months, Trent was still his addiction. Once they were wrapped up in each other, nothing could interrupt.

Except for Nate getting a call from a number with a New York area code.

They both stopped and stared. It rang once, twice, then several more times as they remained frozen in place, the heat from their lovemaking draining away to leave nothing but icy fear.

The ringing stopped, but a half beat later, Nate's heart jumpstarted when his phone chimed to signal a voice mail.

"I don't want to listen to it," he whispered.

"Maybe it's just Elijah," Trent said, but even he sounded skeptical of the idea. "He might be worried about you."

"I don't think so."

The apprehension in Trent's expression built and built until Nate played the message.

"Nate. It's Holden. Look—I kept my word and left your name out of it, but . . . Chase is gone. He's been missing for a while, and I don't know what to do—"

The call abruptly ended.

They replayed it twice. The last time, Nate put his head in his hands.

"Trent . . . I—"

"You have to go be a hero."

Nate dropped his hands miserably. "He's my brother. And he helped us."

Trent pressed a kiss to his forehead. "I know. And I support that as long as you know that you're not going anywhere without me."

"I wouldn't dream of it."

GET READY FOR BOOK TWO OF THE COMMUNITY:
OVERSIGHT

Holden Payne has it all . . . or so he thinks. As heir to the founder of the Community—an organization that finds, protects, and manages psychics—he's rich, powerful, and treated like royalty. But after a series of disappearances and murders rock the Community, he's branded the fall guy for the scandal and saddled with a babysitter.

Sixtus Rossi is a broad-shouldered, tattooed lumbersexual with a man-bun and a steely gaze. He's also an Invulnerable—supposedly impervious to both psychic abilities and Holden's charms. It's a claim Holden takes as a challenge. Especially if sleeping with Six may help him learn whether the Community had more to do with the disappearances than they claimed.

As Holden uncovers the truth, he also finds himself getting in deep with the man sent to watch him. His plan to seduce Six for information leads to a connection so intense that some of Six's shields come crashing down. And with that comes a frightening realization: Holden has to either stand by the Community that has given him everything, or abandon his old life to protect the people he loves.

Dear Reader,

Thank you for reading Santino Hassell's *Insight*!

We know your time is precious and you have many, many entertainment options, so it means a lot that you've chosen to spend your time reading. We really hope you enjoyed it.

We'd be honored if you'd consider posting a review—good or bad—on sites like **Amazon, Barnes & Noble, Kobo, Goodreads, Twitter, Facebook, Tumblr,** and your blog or website. We'd also be honored if you told your friends and family about this book. Word of mouth is a book's lifeblood!

For more information on upcoming releases, author interviews, blog tours, contests, giveaways, and more, please sign up for our weekly, spam-free newsletter and visit us around the web:

Newsletter: tinyurl.com/RiptideSignup
Twitter: twitter.com/RiptideBooks
Facebook: facebook.com/RiptidePublishing
Goodreads: tinyurl.com/RiptideOnGoodreads
Tumblr: riptidepublishing.tumblr.com

Thank you so much for Reading the Rainbow!

RiptidePublishing.com

ACKNOWLEDGMENTS

This book was a monster to create. I started writing it over six years ago as a YA novel with m/f leads, but that didn't last for long. Once I decided to change it over to an M/M romantic suspense with paranormal elements, the ball started rolling. Slowly.

If it wasn't for Lenore, LenaLena, Kate, and Daniel, I would have never continued writing this novel. And if it wasn't for Sarah Lyons seeing a snippet on Facebook and asking to read more of this five-year-old dusty draft, I would have never published it. So, a big thank-you to her, and to all of my alpha and beta readers (especially Em Anthony, who wrote me the most hilarious feedback) for putting up with my insecurity about this project.

And most of all, thank you to my readers who trust me as I go from subgenre to subgenre. Especially Bay, Sandy, and Vinita on Patreon, my readers in the H2 Facebook group who helped me brainstorm titles, and Natalie Peltier who suggested "Insight"! You guys are everything to me!

ALSO BY
SANTINO HASSELL

After Midnight
Stygian

The Community series
Oversight (coming soon)
Sightlines (coming soon)

Five Boroughs series
Sutphin Boulevard
Sunset Park
First and First
Interborough

Cyberlove series with Megan Erickson
Strong Signal
Fast Connection
Hard Wired

In the Company of Shadows series with Ais Lin
Evenfall
Afterimage
Interludes
Fade
1/27

ABOUT THE AUTHOR

Santino Hassell was raised by a conservative family, but he was anything but traditional. He grew up to be a smart-mouthed, school-cutting grunge kid, then a transient twentysomething, and eventually transformed into an unlikely romance author.

Santino writes queer romance that is heavily influenced by the gritty, urban landscape of New York City, his belief that human relationships are complex and flawed, and his own life experiences.

Website:	santinohassell.com
Facebook:	facebook.com/santinohassellbooks
Facebook Group:	facebook.com/groups/gethasselled
Newsletter:	santinohassell.com/newsletter
Twitter:	twitter.com/SantinoHassell
Instagram:	instagram.com/santinohassell
Amazon:	amazon.com/author/santinohassell

Enjoy more stories like
Insight
at RiptidePublishing.com!